Praise for the Half-Moon Hollow novels

THE SINGLE UNDEAD MOMS CLUB

"*The Single Undead Moms Club* is frequently hilarious yet surprisingly touching."   —*Single Titles*

"Molly Harper once again takes us on a hilarious tour to Half-Moon Hollow to meet the newest vampire on the block."   —*Heroes and Heartbreakers*

THE DANGERS OF DATING A REBOUND VAMPIRE

"Harper can always be depended upon for a page-turning story with a lot of frisky, lighthearted humor, and *The Dangers of Dating a Rebound Vampire* is no exception."   —*RT Book Reviews*

"Molly Harper continues to be my go-to author when I want a story with a solid plot, lots of snark, romance, and a bit of mystery."   —*Harlequin Junkie*

"There is a compelling romance, lots of humor, and even a couple of mysteries in the latest release to keep your full attention at all times."   —*Single Titles*

NICE GIRLS DON'T LIVE FOREVER

RT Reviewers' Choice Award winner!

"Hilariously fun." —*RT Book Reviews* (4½ stars, Top Pick)

"The Jane Jameson books are sheer fun and giggle. No, make that chortling, laugh-out-loud till you gasp for breath fun." —*Night Owl Reviews*

NICE GIRLS DON'T DATE DEAD MEN

"Fast-paced, mysterious, passionate, and hilarious."
—*RT Book Reviews* (4½ stars)

"With its quirky characters and the funny situations they get into, whether they be normal or paranormal, *Nice Girls Don't Date Dead Men* is an amazing novel."
—*Romance Reviews Today*

NICE GIRLS DON'T HAVE FANGS

"Harper's take on vampire lore will intrigue and entertain. . . . Jane's snarky first-person narrative is as charming as it is hilarious."
—*Publishers Weekly* (starred review)

"A chuckle-inducing, southern-fried version of Stephanie Plum." —*Booklist*

Books by Molly Harper

In the World of Half-Moon Hollow

Where the Wild Things Bite
Big Vamp on Campus
Fangs for the Memories
The Single Undead Moms Club
The Dangers of Dating a Rebound Vampire
I'm Dreaming of an Undead Christmas
"Undead Sublet" in *The Undead in My Bed*
A Witch's Handbook of Kisses and Curses
The Care and Feeding of Stray Vampires
Driving Mr. Dead
Nice Girls Don't Bite Their Neighbors
Nice Girls Don't Live Forever
Nice Girls Don't Date Dead Men
Nice Girls Don't Have Fangs

The Naked Werewolf Series

How to Run with a Naked Werewolf
The Art of Seducing a Naked Werewolf
How to Flirt with a Naked Werewolf

The Bluegrass Series

Snow Falling on Bluegrass
Rhythm and Bluegrass
My Bluegrass Baby

Also

Better Homes and Hauntings
And One Last Thing . . .

Available from Pocket Books

Where the Wild Things Bite

MOLLY HARPER

Pocket Books
New York   London   Toronto   Sydney   New Delhi

Pocket Books
An Imprint of Simon & Schuster, Inc.
1230 Avenue of the Americas
New York, NY 10020

This book is a work of fiction. Any references to historical events, real people, or real places are used fictitiously. Other names, characters, places, and events are products of the author's imagination, and any resemblance to actual events or places or persons, living or dead, is entirely coincidental.

First Pocket Books paperback edition August 2016

POCKET and colophon are registered trademarks of Simon & Schuster, Inc.

For information about special discounts for bulk purchases, please contact Simon & Schuster Special Sales at 1-866-506-1949 or business@simonandschuster.com.

The Simon & Schuster Speakers Bureau can bring authors to your live event. For more information or to book an event, contact the Simon & Schuster Speakers Bureau at 1-866-248-3049 or visit our website at www.simonspeakers.com.

Manufactured in the United States of America

10 9 8 7 6 5 4 3 2 1

ISBN 978-1-4767-9440-2
ISBN 978-1-4767-9444-0 (ebook)

For Bobby and Jack

Acknowledgments

By some weird coincidence, I wrote much of this book while traveling. And it is very unnerving to be sitting at an airport gate, writing about a plane crash and the absurd survival tactics that would come afterward. (It was especially unnerving for any fellow travelers who might have been sitting next to me, peeking at my screen.) I would like to thank the staff at airports/airlines in Atlanta, Georgia; Nashville, Tennessee; Chicago, Illinois; Newark, New Jersey; and Paris, France, for keeping me and my fellow travelers safe while I was staring at my computer screen—leading me to have the exact opposite of poor Anna's experience.

As always, I thank my readers, who keep me going and inspired to write tales of the Half-Moon Hollow gang. Thank you to Jeanette Battista, my ever-supportive work wife, for her guidance and patience as I whined my way through another manuscript. Thank you to Abby Zidle, who is always in my corner. Thank you to my family, who were very understanding as I spent so many hours on this book.

Also, I thank the lovely people at the Jardin du Marais Hotel in Paris, who seemed to recognize that I was not a rude American tourist but an author on a deadline who needed coffee and kind words in the courtyard. And my apologies to potted-meat manufacturers for my depictions of their product. I've had bad experiences. That's all I'm going to say.

1

Before you find yourself stranded in the woods with a cranky apex predator, ask yourself: Do I really *want* to go on a camping trip with a vampire? The answer is probably going to be no.

—*Where the Wild Things Bite: A Survival Guide for Camping with the Undead*

An evil transportation-hating monster had devoured my plane. And in its place, the monster had left a little, bite-size plane crumb behind.

I stood on the tarmac of the Louisville airport, staring in horror at the plane crumb as my purse, a brown leather tote bag, dangled from my fingers. This was not a momentous beginning to my trip to Half-Moon Hollow.

Despite the fact that I could see crowds of people milling around the airport through the windows, I felt oddly alone, vulnerable. A handful of planes were parked at nearby gates, but there were no luggage handlers, no flight staff. I'd never boarded from the tarmac before, and the short, rickety mobile staircase being pushed up against the side of the plane like a ladder used for gutter cleaning didn't make me feel more confident in the climb.

When I'd booked my flight to westernmost Kentucky, I knew small planes were the only models capable of flying into Half-Moon Hollow's one-gate airport. But I'd thought the plane would seat at least thirty people. The vessel in front of me would maybe hold a baker's dozen, if someone sat on the pilot's lap. There were only four windows besides the windshield, for God's sake.

"This is the right plane, in case you're wondering," said a gruff voice, which was accompanied by a considerable whiff of wet tobacco.

I turned to find a florid, heavyset man in a pilot's uniform standing behind me. His healthy head of wavy black hair was counterbalanced by a pitted, sallow complexion and undereye bags so heavy they should have been stored on the nearby luggage cart. A lifetime of drinking had thickened his features and left a network of tiny broken capillaries across his broad nose. Given the sweat stains on his uniform, I might have doubted his current sobriety, but I supposed it took considerable motor control to keep that large unlit cigar clamped between his teeth. His name tag read "Ernie."

"That is not a plane," I told Ernie. "That is what happens when planes have babies with go-karts."

Snorting, he pushed past me toward the plane. The olfactory combination of old sweat and wet cigar made me take a step back from him. I was starting to suspect his pilot's license might have been written in crayon.

"Well, if you don't want to fly, there's always a rental car," the pilot snarked, climbing the stairs into the plane. "It's about a four-hour drive, until you hit the gravel roads. You might make it before noon tomorrow."

I frowned at Ernie the pilot's broad back. If there was anything I hated more than flying, it was driving on unfamiliar, treacherous roads alone at night. Besides, there were too many things that could happen to the package between here and the Hollow. I could spill coffee on it while trying to stay awake. It could be stolen while I was stopped at a gas station. A window malfunction could result in the package being sucked out of the car on the highway. I needed to get it back to Jane as soon as humanly (or vampire-ly) possible. So driving was a nonstarter.

I gritted my teeth and breathed deeply through my nose, watching the way the sickly fluorescent outdoor lights played on the dimpled metal of the wings. The tiny, tiny wings.

The pilot stuck his head out of the plane door. "Plane's not gonna get any bigger," he growled at me around the cigar.

"Good point," I muttered as I took the metal stairs. One-in-nine-million chance of dying in a commercial plane crash. One-in-*nine-million* chance. There had to be at least nine million and one other people flying commercial right now. One of them had to have worse luck than me . . . they were probably on a bigger plane, though.

Even though my cargo was completely legal, I still felt the need to look over my shoulder in an extremely obvious manner as I boarded. My superspy skills were supremely lacking. The looks that security gave me as I visibly twitched while sending my bag through the X-ray machine were bad enough. But I'd never hand-delivered an item to a customer before, especially an item of such high value. My bonding and insurance couldn't possibly cover something that was considered priceless to the supernatural community at large. I just wanted to get it out of my hands and into those of my employer, Jane Jameson-Nightengale, as quickly as possible.

Despite my fervent wish that the plane was secretly a TARDIS, it was not, in fact, bigger on the inside. And except for Ernie the pilot, it was completely empty. This was, after all, the last flight from Louisville to the Hollow for the night, which made it a risky proposition, layover-wise. From what Jane had told me, most Hollow residents didn't want to risk being stuck overnight in Louisville, so they planned their connections for earlier in the day. But a client meeting had kept me in Atlanta until the last minute, so I'd booked a late flight. It worked better for me to land late anyway, since Jane, an oddly informal vampire who insisted that our relationship be on a first-name basis, would be meeting me at the airport. Pre-sundown pickup times didn't work for her.

Though minuscule, the interior of the plane was comfortable enough, with its oatmeal-colored plastic walls, the smell of recently applied disinfectant, and its closely arranged seats. Though I clearly had my choice of spots, I took the time to find my assigned berth in the second row. I declined putting my tote bag in the tiny storage compartment at the front of the plane. Despite being the only passenger, I was uncomfortable with the idea of not being able to see my bag at all times. I turned, checking the distance from my seat to the door-slash-emergency exit. Studies showed that passengers were five times more likely to survive a crash if they sat within five rows of the emergency exits.

Unfortunately, this seat also put me directly under a vent for the air system, also known as the "dispenser of aerated bacteria."

Even as I pulled an herbal immune-support chewable out of my bag, I knew I was being silly. The flight would only be an hour long. What were the chances of the plane crashing when it was only in the air for sixty minutes? And surely I wouldn't have enough time to contract anything from Ernie's tobacco-stained germs?

As if he could hear my thoughts, Ernie let loose a phlegmy, rattling cough that seemed to shake the windows. Slowly, I reached up and twisted the vent closed.

Besides, who knew what sort of antibiotic-resistant superbugs previous passengers had sneezed into the ventilation system on earlier flights? I didn't care what the airline said about its amazing HEPA filters, I pulled the neck of my cardigan over my nose and pulled a pack of TSA-approved hand-sanitizing wipes from my bag. I swabbed down my armrests, the window, and—checking to make sure Ernie wasn't watching—the vent cover.

And for some reason, while I was wiping down the safety-procedure card with a fresh towelette, the cruel, ironic bits of my brain were running through the list of famous people who had died in small-plane crashes. Ritchie Valens, John Denver, Aaliyah.

I flopped my head back against the seat, jamming my hair clip into my scalp. I was too tired for this. I'd spent almost two hours in Atlanta traffic just to get to the airport in time for this flight. I'd braved lengthy, draconian security checks. I missed my cozy little re-stored home in Dahlonega. I missed my home office and my thinking couch and my shelves of carefully preserved first-edition books. I promised myself that when I survived this trip, I would reward myself by retreating to my apartment for a week and bingeing on delivered Thai food and Netflix.

I curled forward and rested my head on my hands. My stomach churned, and my head felt all light and swirly. I was too tired to be this nervous. I'd taken my antianxiety meds in the ladies' room in the airport, timing them carefully so I wouldn't climb the walls of the plane from the moment it took off. Why weren't they kicking in?

I heard footsteps on the metal ladder but did not raise my head. Whoever it was moved down the aisle and slide into the seat across from me.

Damn it, did that mean I wasn't the only passenger on this flight? I was going to have to take another immunity booster. I thunked my forehead against the folding tray table. And then I remembered that University of Arizona study that found that up to sixty percent of the tray tables from the major airliners tested positive for MRSA. So I sat up. Surely headrest parasites were a better option than flesh-eating bacteria.

"Hi."

I didn't move. Maybe if I didn't move, he would think I was asleep and leave me alone. Was it beneath me to use possum tactics to avoid politely strained conversation?

"Hello in there?"

Augh. No. The new passenger was a talker, an *insistent* talker.

I was not one of those "we're in this together for the next few hours, so we might as well be polite" passengers. I did not make polite small talk. I didn't talk about what I did for a living or compare my "worst flight ever" experiences with my seatmate. And I definitely didn't "share a cab" to my hotel with a near stranger, no matter how nice he was during beverage service. People who did that ended up on *Dateline*.

"Fear of flying?"

I ceased my forehead abuse long enough to look up at him. The other passenger smiled and quirked his eyebrows, the sort of gesture most people appreciated in a fellow traveler.

Oh, the new passenger was handsome, in that polished, self-aware manner that made women either melt in their seats or shrink into themselves in immediate distrust. Unfortunately for him, I fell into the second category.

I did not dissolve at the sight of his high cheekbones. I didn't coo over his luminous brown eyes or the dark goatee that defined his wide, sensual mouth. The collar of his blue V-necked T-shirt showed a downright lickable collarbone and the beginnings of well-defined pectoral muscles. I did not liquefy. In fact, my initial reaction was to trust him even less than I trusted Ernie.

OK, fine, I did feel these strange little bubbles rise up through my belly, like effervescent butterflies. But most of those butterflies were swatted down by the heavy hand of common sense.

So I might have been a bit more snappish than polite when I responded, "No, fear of awkward conversations before crashing."

But my curt tone only seemed to make him grin, as if my irritation was amusing. It was a sincere grin, without an ounce of condescension, which made him even more handsome. Some tiny nerve inside me twinged, a counterintuitive flicker in my otherwise steady flow of neuroses. That little nerve made me wish, just for once, that I was the kind of woman who could start a conversation with a handsome stranger, approach some new experience—hell, try a new brand of detergent—without analyzing all of the possible ways it could go wrong.

While my mother had made it clear on more than one occasion that I was not "conventionally pretty," I knew I wasn't completely unfortunate-looking. My DNA had provided me with my father's fine-boned features and my mother's wide, full lips, though mine weren't twisted into unhappy lines as often as hers. My eyes were large, the amber color of old whiskey, with an undeserved mischievous tilt. Altogether, my slightly mismatched features made for a pleasant face. And yet men like this, completely at ease with themselves, sent my dented ego into a spiraling tizzy whenever they came near. In other words, my counterintuitive nerve flicker was an idiot and needed to stay quiet.

The handsome new passenger's smooth tones derailed my train of thought yet again. "It's too bad the ride is so short. They don't even have beverage service on this flight. You might have been able to take the edge off."

"I'm not much of a drinker," I told him, giving him a quick, jerky smile that felt like a cheek tremor. I nodded my head toward the back of the plane. "Besides, where would they put the beverage cart?"

"Oh, well, maybe *I'll* be able to distract you," he offered, the corner of his mouth lifting again.

The intimate way he said it, the way he was smiling at me, eyes lingering on my jeans-clad legs, sent a little shiver down my spine, despite the simultaneous warning Klaxons sounding in my head. I pulled my book out of my bag and placed it on the seat next to me, like a shield. It was a tactic I'd used before on the rare occasions when I used public transportation. People were far less likely to ask, "Hey, is that book any good?" when it was intimidating classic literature the size of a brick. And those who did interrupt to ask about the brick-sized book were put off by a prolonged bitch brow.

"And how are you going to do that?" I asked him, holding up the well-worn paperback. "You've got some very serious competition."

Thank you, conversational gods, for not letting the phrase "stiff competition" leave my lips.

"Oh, I'm sure I could come up with a way to entertain you."

And his smile was so full of naughty promise that the only response I could come up with was "Guh."

The conversational gods abandoned me more quickly than I had hoped.

I blushed to the tips of my ears, but he seemed amused by it, so maybe a red face was considered charming on the Planet of the Narrowly Torsoed.

Given that I was from a very different planet—the home of ladies built like lanky twelve-year-old boys—I doubted very much that our definitions of "fun" matched up. Given the flawless delivery of what was a pretty obvious pickup line, he was clearly a practiced flirt. Men generally practiced this sort of skill at parties, clubs. My idea of a good time was a movie marathon with my best friend and assistant, Rachel, featuring at least five different actors playing Sherlock Holmes and then a debate about who did the best job. That's right. Anna Whitfield, one-woman party.

"Do you consider Dante's *Inferno* a little light travel reading?"

"It's an old favorite," I said, without looking up at him.

"Well, you've successfully intimidated me, so congratulations."

I laughed softly, but before I could answer, the door slammed behind us, and the plane started to taxi. A small overhead speaker began to play prerecorded safety instructions, and I relaxed back into the seat. I pulled the safety instruction card from the seat pocket in front of me and began reading along.

"Really?" the stranger asked. I nodded, without looking at him, checking the emergency exit door for opening instructions. It looked like a case of "Pull the big red handle upward and left while trying to contain your terror." Excellent.

I followed along, checking the location of the oxygen masks (there weren't any) and running lights toward the emergency exit (also, no). They really needed to increase the amount of safety equipment required on tiny planes. Or at least make safety cards specific to tiny planes so passengers didn't realize how much safety equipment they weren't getting.

"You have flown before, yes?" the stranger asked.

I ignored him. I would not die in a fiery plane crash because I neglected the (mostly useless) safety card for a pair of beautiful semisweet-chocolate eyes.

The recorded voice ended the safety presentation. I tucked the card away in the seat pouch in front of me, tightened my seatbelt, and clenched my eyes shut while the plane struggled to lift off from the runway. On the third midair dip, I pressed my head back against the seat, as if holding a rigid posture would somehow get the plane in the air safely.

The first three minutes after takeoff and before landing were the most prone to mishaps. For 180 seconds, I prayed the only way I knew how, visualizing the opposite of all of the horrible potential outcomes running through my head. Breathing deeply through my nose, I pictured the plane lifting off, maintaining a nice straight path through the air, and landing in Half-Moon Hollow with my purse and person intact. I was calm. I was safe. The book was in my hands, and I was presenting it to Jane Jameson-Nightengale, intact.

And when I opened my eyes, my purse was open on my lap, and my hands were swimming through the contents, searching for the package. Across the aisle, the stranger's head was bent over a magazine. I felt faint, as if I were falling inside myself, separated from my own body as my arm started to lift. I could see myself yanking the package out of my purse, as if I were watching it happen on a movie screen.

What was I doing? I hadn't pulled the package from my bag since getting through security. Why would I show it to this person I barely knew?

As suddenly as it began, the spell was over, and I practically sagged against my seat. My long, sweater-clad arm was still raised and my hand still stretched as I shook off the strange, dizzy sensation. I'd never felt anything like that before. Was I coming down with something? Had I had some sort of stroke? I didn't feel tingling or numbness in my extremities. I wasn't confused, beyond wondering what the hell had just happened to me. Maybe it was an inner-ear problem? Or maybe the veggie wrap I'd eaten at the airport sandwich shop was contaminated? I should have known better than to trust airport cuisine. I probably had some sort of dirt-borne E. coli from unwashed lettuce.

I glanced across the aisle to the stranger, still poring through his magazine, completely unaware of my inner turmoil. I sighed. I was a very special sort of weird. I turned my attention back to my book. While the takeoff was fairly smooth, the rocking of the plane and the dark, quiet space actually made me a little dizzy again, and I wondered if I really was coming down with some strain of bacteria that affected the inner ear. Stupid airport lettuce.

With the stranger distracted by magazine articles about abdominal workouts that would change his life, I traveled through Dante's rings of hell with the aid of the weak overhead light. After twenty minutes or so, I got tired of the weird, dizzy sensation intermittently flashing through my head and set my book aside.

"Not quite the beach-read romp you were promised?" the stranger asked.

I looked up to find him staring at me again, intently, on the edge of attempted smoldering. And when I didn't respond, he tipped over that edge into full smolder, and I scooted back in my seat. He seemed surprised by this and leaned forward. Maybe he thought I didn't have a close enough view of his cheekbones? Was this the sort of thing that normally got him a response from women? Was he one of those guys who flirted with everything that moved because he was trying to score by the laws of probability?

Forgetting every lesson my mother had ever drilled into my head about good manners and eye contact, I gave him the full-on "disapproving professor" face I'd learned as a teaching assistant.

He was not fazed.

He did, however, get distracted by a child's truck,

a toy left over from a previous flight, rolling down the aisle toward the cockpit. (And, coincidentally, that didn't make me feel much better about the cleanliness of the plane.) Wait, *toward* the cockpit? The plane's nose seemed to be tipping downward. I checked my watch. We were only twenty-five minutes into the flight, which was too early to be starting our descent into the Hollow. I exchanged a glance with my handsome seatmate, who was frowning. Hard.

A metallic crunching noise sounded from the front of the plane, catching our attention. After flipping a few switches and hitting some buttons, Ernie the pilot yanked what looked like an important lever from the control panel and stuck it into his shirt pocket. And then he took a heavy rubber mallet from his laptop bag and began swinging it wildly at the panel. He got up from his seat, snagging what looked like a backpack from the copilot's chair. The stranger and I sat completely still as Ernie eyed him warily.

"What the hell are you doing?" I demanded, as Ernie the Suddenly Destructive Pilot slipped the backpack on and clipped the straps over his thick middle. Some instinct had me reaching for the strap of my tote bag, winding it around my wrist. The plane continued to descend at a smooth, steady pace. "Get back to the controls!"

"I don't want to hurt you. The Kelleys just want the package you're carrying. I know it's not in your suitcase. I checked at the baggage screening," Ernie told me, raising his hands and reaching toward my lap.

I unbuckled my seatbelt and scrambled back in my

seat, jamming my back against the wall. The invasion of space had me grabbing at my bag to feel for the little canister of pepper spray I usually kept clipped to the strap. Of course, that little canister was not currently clipped in place, because that's the sort of chemical agent the TSA frowned on bringing through security. If I lived through this, I was going to write them a long letter.

I clutched the bag to my chest like a newborn. Why was Ernie doing this? How did he know what I had in my bag? Who were the Kelleys? Hell, how did he manage to get into my suitcase? And what sort of person could bribe a pilot to commandeer a (admittedly underpopulated) commercial flight?

Another wave of dizziness hit me, full-force this time, and I had to fight to keep my mind on my mind-numbing terror. This was it. This was the worst-case scenario. The pilot was abandoning the airplane while trying to mug me. I ran through all of the transportation studies I'd read on flight safety and crisis management to try to come up with some sort of solution to this . . . and nothing. I had nothing. None of them covered purse-snatching, plane-abandoning pilots.

Shrugging off the heavy, sleepy weight that dragged at the corners of my brain, I took a deep breath. OK. I would handle this one problem at a time.

Problem one, no one was flying the plane. And Ernie—whom I was absolutely correct in not trusting, yay for me—appeared to have broken off something important from the control panel, which probably rendered the plane unflyable. So, I could draw the conclusion that Ernie was a horrible person and that he had no plans to land the plane. So I seemed to be screwed on that front.

Problem two, Ernie was trying to snatch my bag. All of the personal safety guides I'd read said you should hand your purse over if you're being mugged. It would be easier just to hand him my bag. *It isn't worth dying for. I might as well let him have it*, a soft voice that didn't sound entirely like mine whispered inside my head. *It isn't worth dying for.*

I could feel my arms lift, my hands unwinding the strap from my wrist. Suddenly, a loud, shrill warning beep sounded from the controls. I whipped my head toward it just as the plane dropped suddenly, throwing me against the seat in front of me. I hissed as Ernie bent and tried to yank the bag away, dragging my strap-ringed arm with him

I was going to die. Whether I handed the bag over or not, the plane was going to crash with me on it.

A heretofore unknown spark of anger fired in my belly. I'd been entrusted to take care of Jane Jameson-Nightengale's package. Jane was a high-ranking member of the local World Council for the Equal Treatment of the Undead. She'd trusted me with Council business. She expected me to take care of the package for her, to deliver it safely. She was paying me a handsome sum to do so. And this pilot was trying to take it from me, to kill me for it. He'd put me in a terrifying, no-win situation to intimidate me into handing it over.

This was *bullshit*.

That little spark burned into a full-blown stubborn flame, and I wrapped the leather bag strap around my wrist even tighter.

I wasn't going to give it up. I couldn't do anything about the plane crashing, but I could keep Jane's package from falling into clearly unscrupulous hands. As much as we both loved books, I was sure Jane would rather see it destroyed than dropped into the hands of people willing to kill for it.

Moving with more speed than would be expected in a man of his girth, Ernie yanked at my bag again. But the strap around my wrist wouldn't give. I tugged back on it with all my might, praying that the leather would hold. All the while, the stranger sat completely still, staring at Ernie.

"Are you kidding me?" I yelped as I swung my bag back and smacked Ernie with all my strength. The bag landed broadside against his face, and the impact knocked him back a step. The plane listed, and he lost his balance, rolling into the aisle on his back.

I could not believe that worked.

Ernie pushed to his feet and pulled something from his waistband. A knife, with a strange black blade that looked like one of those expensive ceramic kitchen knives you get at Bed Bath & Beyond. This was definitely the Beyond.

"I didn't want to have to do this," he said, tossing the knife between his hands with the sort of ease that made me think he had some experience with blades. "I just wanted to take the bag without hurting you. But if you're going to be a bitch about it . . ."

Cue more threatening knife gestures. Ernie advanced on me. I glanced down at the tray table and wondered if I could rip it loose and use it as a weapon. Stupid TSA regulations against sharp objects that could be used as weapons. I would kill for a pair of tweezers right now.

"Well, since I'm going down anyway, I guess I'm going to be a bitch about it," I shot back.

Even as Ernie advanced, the stranger stared at us, motionless, that same strange cloudy quality leaching into his eyes.

"Are you going to help me at all here?" I yelled.

When the man didn't move, even as Ernie jabbed the knife forward, I took it as a no. With the blade coming toward my face at an alarming rate, I threw the bag behind me and yanked off the cushion from a nearby seat, shoving it toward him with both hands. The cushion cover split, and the blade sliced through the upholstery between my hands, the tip stopping a scant few inches from my eye.

It worked as a flotation device *and* a shield.

Ernie pulled back, trying to rip the blade from the cushion, but the hilt was stuck in the fabric. I tugged it toward me, careful not to stab myself in the face, and swung the cushion up, striking Ernie's temple with the butt of the knife handle. Clutching at his face, he stumbled back with a yelp, giving me time to wrench the knife free of the cushion.

And still, the stranger didn't move.

"Really?" I barked at him. "You are a useless human being!"

Ernie growled like an angry junkyard dog, hunching over as if he planned to rush me. I held the knife in both hands, the tip shaking as I pointed it at him. Because nothing said "badass prepared to defend herself" like a wobbling knife sandwiched between two sweaty palms.

The plane dove and pitched, making my stomach lurch. Ernie's gaze switched back and forth between the trembling blade and my eyes. And given the smug expression on his face, I didn't think he saw me as a threat. He stepped forward, and I clenched my fingers around the handle.

I gritted my teeth, my voice barely audible as I whimpered. "Please, don't make me do this."

The stranger finally stood, growling, and I shrieked in shock at the flash of vicious-looking fangs, throwing my arms in front of my face, a stupid thing to do when holding a great big blade. I dropped the knife, throwing myself back into the row of seats. The knife skidded down the carpeted aisle, toward Ernie, who scooped it up and pointed it at us.

Damn it.

Also, point of fact, my chatty, cowardly travel companion was a vampire.

With the vampire blocking the aisle, I slid behind him and reached for my bag. Ernie backed away and, as the safety card instructed, moved swiftly toward the emergency exit.

"Get back to the controls!" I cried, as Ernie's hand closed around the red door handle and pulled up. The door burst open, and the pressure in the cabin changed dramatically. It tugged at my ears, making them pop.

"What are you doing?" Ernie yelled, though it sounded less like a challenge and more like . . . whining? I couldn't tell if he was talking to me or the vampire. He glared at us, as if we'd disappointed him somehow. Frankly, I was disappointed that the pilot was not in his seat, flying the fricking plane, so I guessed we were even.

The vampire turned, gave me a long head-to-toe once-over, and angled his body so he was wedged between Ernie and me. He bared his fangs and gave a loud roar that, had he been facing me, probably would have resulted in me crying in the fetal position on the floor. Ernie just rolled his eyes, flipped the vampire the middle finger, and leaped backward out of the plane.

I pushed past the vampire and looked out the side window, watching as a small white parachute opened up beneath us.

"The pilot jumped out of the plane," I said, staring out the window.

"Yes, he did," the vampire observed. Though he sounded more annoyed than paralyzed with fear.

"*Why* did the pilot jump out of the plane?"

"Because the windows don't open?" he suggested.

I whipped my head toward him and gave him a withering glare. He shrugged. The plane continued to descend, and I stepped around the vampire, looking for more parachutes. I found none.

"Damn it!" I grumbled. I scurried to the front of

the plane, where lots of loud noises and flashing colored lights could distract me from the quickly approaching ground. I reached for something that looked like a radio, but I couldn't seem to get a signal or sound from it. I lifted the receiver and saw that the cord leading from the handheld device to the controls had been neatly clipped. And the lever that Ernie had snapped off? It seemed to have been attached to the control marked "Flaps," so I couldn't slow the plane's descent. In fact, there seemed to be a lot of buttons and levers missing. Exactly how many pieces had Ernie broken?

"Damn it!" I yelled again, the sound of the wind whipping through the cabin nearly drowning out my voice. I turned to the vampire, who was standing motionless in the aisle. "I don't suppose you're a pilot or an airplane mechanic?"

Hesitant, he shook his head. "No."

I rolled my eyes and pushed past him to sit in a seat near the open emergency door. I closed the seatbelt around my waist and cinched it as tight as possible, even as my hands shook.

"What are you doing?" the vampire asked, as I kept my tote clutched to my chest. Despite the fact that the NTSB strongly urged against trying to hold on to luggage while trying to escape a wrecked plane, I was going to cling to it like a lifeline. I'd worked to keep that bag. I'd be damned if I'd let it get thrown loose from my corpse now.

"Preparing for the crash. You should strap in, too. Ninety-five percent of people involved in plane crashes survive, but buckling your seatbelt and sitting close to an emergency exit up your chances," I told him, clearly aware that I was babbling. But so far, I'd managed not to break down into hysterical tears, despite pants-wetting terror, so I thought I deserved a bit of a babble. "When we hit the ground, the first ninety seconds are important. Most people end up sustaining injuries in the postcrash fire, which is probably more worrisome to you than to me, since you're . . . uh, highly flammable."

The vampire clearly did not appreciate my advice, giving me what I could only describe as a full-body eye roll.

"I'm trying to help you survive what happens when our plane hits the ground in the next couple of minutes!" I told him.

"We are not going to crash!"

"Tell that to the ground rushing at us!" I yelled, pointing out the window.

The vampire huffed, yanked at my seatbelt buckle, and popped it loose.

"What are you doing!" I screeched, smacking at his hands. He took hold of both of my wrists and dragged me out of my seat.

I could hear a consistent, quiet *slap slap slap* against the belly of the plane and realized that it was tree branches. We were so close to the ground that *tree branches* were smacking against the plane.

"I need to get back into my seat!" I yelled at him.

"Put your arms around my neck," he said, hauling me against him.

Even through the panic, I couldn't help but notice how easily I fit against his solid, muscled frame. That was inconveniently timed.

"Put your arms around my neck, and *hold on*," he repeated, wrapping my arms around said neck.

"What?" I gasped, snapping out of my hands-on ogling. "Why?"

"We're going to jump," he said, leading me toward the open door.

"No!" I yelled. "Are you *crazy*! No!"

I didn't know of any survival statistics for people who leaped out of crashing airplanes without parachutes, but they couldn't be good.

"It will be fine," he grunted, as we inched nearer to the open door, the wind plucking at our clothes and blowing my dark hair over my face.

"Vampires can't fly! I've looked into it!" I insisted, trying to wedge my feet against the seats so he couldn't move me.

"Come on, woman!"

"No!" I yelled, scrambling over his shoulder so I could dig my fingernails into the seats. "This is insane! *You* are insane!"

The vampire grabbed my hips and dragged me down the length of his chest, wrapping my long legs around his waist. He secured me against him with his left hand while he clutched my chin in the other. "It's going to be fine," he promised.

"I don't want to jump out of the plane," I told him.

"OK," he said.

I breathed a sigh of relief. "Really?"

He nodded, tightening his grip around my waist. "I'll do the jumping."

And with that, he took a running start out the door and leaped from the plane.

"You asshooooooOOOOOOOOOOOOOOOOOLE!" I screamed, as we cleared the door and dropped into nothingness. Over the vampire's shoulder, I could see the underbelly of the plane shrink in the distance. The wind tore at my clothes, whipping my hair over my face and around the vampire's.

I squeezed my eyes shut. Time moved at a snail's speed as we plunged through empty space. I heard everything and nothing all at once. My life didn't flash before my eyes, but dozens of questions streamed through my brain. How long would we fall? How much would it hurt to hit the ground? Didn't people black out from fear in situations like this? I would *love* to black out from fear right now. Using some sort of midair rolling maneuver, the vampire turned us so that he was under me. But I was too busy burying my face against his neck to appreciate his chivalrous, impact-absorbing gesture. I squeezed him even tighter, squealing in terror. I heard him wheeze in protest, but if these were my last moments before crashing into the ground, I wanted him to know that I was displeased with his decision to fling me out of a plane without my permission. My bag flapped loose, the leather slapping viciously against my side as we plummeted.

So very, *very* displeased.

I felt him tense under me, and I braced myself for the impact. But instead of splatting against the ground, we landed in cold black water with a tsunami-sized splash. The shock of the impact made me want to gasp, but the vampire clapped his hand over my nose and mouth to keep me from sucking in water. I was able to keep hold of my bag as we sank. I fought, and I clawed, but he clutched me close. For a second, I thought he was going to hold me under, drown me before swimming to the surface himself. But after a few seconds, the bubbles cleared, my eyes adjusted, and I could see him clearly.

He was frowning at me through the water, but it was a concerned frown, as if he was worried about the fact that he was probably drowning me. Between the adrenaline burnout and the cold submersion and the repeated potential for death, my body started to shut down. I was so tired, as if my limbs were made of lead. My lungs burned with the need to draw another breath. I wriggled, trying to get loose from the vampire's grip. He stopped staring at me and blinked rapidly, as if coming out of a fog.

I pushed harder at his chest, kicking toward the surface of the water. He nodded slightly and loosened his grip, his hand sliding over my breasts to grip me under the arms. He dragged me up until my head broke through the water and I was able to draw air. I was not ashamed of the loud, ragged gasps as I sucked in oxygen.

In the distance, I could see flames where the plane had crashed into trees on the far side of the lake. There was no way we would have survived that. The vampire had just saved my life. I shuddered, imagining what I had just escaped, my body smashed against the interior of the plane, possibly burning to death if I survived long enough.

I'd never thought I'd survive a situation like that. Despite my near-constant preparation for the worst possible outcome, I'd always considered myself fate's cannon fodder. I always figured I'd be occupying the first building hit by the world-ending asteroid, among the first wave of people infected by the next great plague. I never considered that I might survive.

What was I going to do now?

Also, this water smelled like dirt and rotting fish. Were there fish? Was Kentucky the sort of place where they had those giant catfish that could drown grown men? What sort of bacterial scum was floating on the surface? Was I going to get a nice case of pinkeye on top of everything el— Ow!

In the process of treading water, the vampire had elbowed me in the eye. The hell?

The vampire turned toward me, grinning, as if he expected me to congratulate him on tossing me out of a plane and giving me a shiner. "Well, that worked out better than I hoped."

"You asshole!" I howled, and swung at him. The motion dragged my purse out of the water and slung it at his face. I couldn't help it. My brain was fried by the constant cycle of terror, and the only response I had left was fury.

"Ow!" he yelped, sinking for a moment as he clutched at the side of his head, while I swam for the nearest shore. "That's a fine thank-you for someone who just saved your life."

"You threw me out of a plane!" I paused my swimming to kick at him, splashing water in his face.

"To *save your life*," he repeated, emphasizing each syllable with a slicing stroke through the water.

"I know. I'm still trying to process my hysterical panic!" I shouted back, grabbing my purse strap when it nearly floated off my shoulder.

"What is it with you?" he demanded. "Why was the pilot trying to take that bag from you? Who the hell are you, woman?"

"I'm nobody!" I swore, as the bag strap dragged at my arm and my stroke faltered. My face dropped into the water, and the vampire slid his hand across my chest, under my bicep, pulling me along with him.

"Pilots don't decide to mug passengers and then abandon their planes for nobodies," the vampire told me. "Now, what's in the bag?"

"He was crazy!" I yelled. "Airline employees get sick of dealing with obnoxious passengers. Combine that with deep vein thrombosis and the long-term effects of pressurized cabins and they lose it. You read about it in the news all the time."

"You really don't," he told me.

I treaded water, working to keep my face in a neutral expression. "We've got to get out of the water. Hypothermia could set in," I said, taking advantage of my overlarge eyes to convey Disney-princess innocence.

He stared at me, his brown eyes reflecting the light of the moon above us as he examined my face for a few awkward moments.

"Come on," he said, sighing, slinging one arm around his chest and pulling me against him while he kicked toward shore. My unusually long legs and arms made me a good swimmer, able to cover long distances in the water with little effort. But he wasn't even letting me try, and frankly, it was pissing me off.

"Would you stop yanking me around like a rag doll?" I grumbled, though I had to admit that we were making much better progress without my aquatic flailings. My arms and legs didn't seem to be getting the right messages from my brain.

"Well, if you would just cooperate, I wouldn't have to yank you around," he growled into my ear. As he bobbed in the water, his mouth inadvertently brushed against the back of my neck, sending a shiver down my spine that had nothing to do with water temperature. "Did you have to dig your claws into me like that?"

"Yeah, I protest when someone tries to drag me out of a plane. What an unreasonable wench I am," I shot back.

"Tell that to the gouge marks in my shoulders."

"They'll heal," I muttered.

"But my shirt won't. It's like you're half-wolverine," he told me, as my feet hit the muddy bottom of the lake. I stumbled, trying to get footing on the slick surface. I'd dressed sensibly for a flight, canvas ballet flats, jeans, a tank top, and a cardigan. I'd wanted shoes I could wear through the security gate without struggling to get them back on. And frankly, it was a miracle they'd stayed on my feet during our impromptu skydive-slash-swim. But they were not much help in the "finding purchase in swamp mud" department.

My feet slipped out from under me, and I dropped under the water again. He pulled me up by my arms as we staggered onto solid ground.

"Is this going to be a thing?" I asked him. "This constant grabbing and dragging? And don't think I didn't notice the underwater breast graze."

"Yeah, I accidentally brushed against your chest while saving your life, taking the impact for you when we jumped out of a plane into a lake. What an unreasonable jerk I am."

I'd just reached knee-deep water when I turned on him and slung my wet hair out of my face. "You lingered."

"You flatter yourself," he told me.

"Look, I am not interested in whatever you're selling. So you can just keep this weird, flirtatious, 'oh, silly female, I'm not really flirting with you, I'm just naturally gregarious and charming' thing that I'm sure works on those girls you neg at the blood bar, and cut it out."

"We just survived a plane crash, and this is the moment you want to tell me that? And I don't bother with girls at the blood bar. At least, not in the last year or so—and you know what, I wasn't even trying to flirt with you!"

"Good. Because it wouldn't work."

"Oh, if I tried, it would work," he insisted, smirking at me.

And for a second, I was sincerely concerned that it *would* work. Because that smirk was chock-full of dangerous, manipulative potential, and I was a mere human who would have to refer to a calendar to remember the last time I'd had sex.

A pregnant silence hung between us for a few seconds before I added, "And it's not like we dropped some huge distance. It was maybe a hundred yards." I stumbled but righted myself before he had to save me from another face-plant. "An airborne skydiving rescue it was not."

"Speaking as the man sandwiched between you and the water, I can tell you it felt like more."

I made an absolutely foul face at him as I unzipped my purse. I'd sealed the package in two airtight plastic bags and closed the outer bag with wax. But there was always the chance that it could leak, or that the bag could have ruptured when we fell out of the freaking plane. I blew out a relieved breath when I saw the bag was intact. The interior of the package was dry and untouched.

"What are you doing?" he asked. "I think your makeup is a loss at this point."

Breathing deeply, I fished my hand through my sodden bag. "My phone is in here," I lied easily. "I was going to try to call 911 or the airline's customer-service complaint line or someone who could maybe fish us out of this godforsaken nowhere."

"I hate to break it to you, sweetheart, but if your phone is still in there, it's a paperweight. The water has probably fried it."

I fished my cell out of the bottom of my purse—which still had several inches of water standing in it—and saw that he was right. My phone was completely soaked, because I'd failed to close the little charger port on my protective phone cover. Damn it. My wallet, paperback, and watch were also soaked through. I supposed the only blessing was that I'd decided to leave my laptop at home instead of bringing it with me. Otherwise, years of research would have been lost.

As I searched through the ruins of my bag, my stomach sank with the realization of exactly how unprepared I was for this situation. If I'd known we were going to be dropping into the wilderness, I would have brought my trusty Swiss Army knife, some waterproof matches, a first-aid kit, water-purifying tablets—most of the emergency supplies I kept handy in my "apocalypse closet."

Unfortunately, airport security frowned on matches and Swiss Army knives almost as much as they did pepper spray, so it was a moot point. The closest thing I had to survival supplies was a granola bar I'd purchased on the flight from Atlanta to Louisville. Thanks to the miracle of modern packaging, it hadn't been smashed when we landed in the lake.

If only I'd thought to put my phone in the sealed plastic bag. It would have made texting more difficult, but my phone might have lived.

"How about yours?" I asked, dumping the excess water out of my purse.

He pulled his phone out of his back pocket and

showed me the waterlogged, fractured screen. "I seem to have landed on it. Along with an unnamed and ungrateful person."

"Pardon me for not being overflowing with gratitude for you tossing me out of a plane! Now, what are your skills?"

He arched an eyebrow. "Beg pardon?"

"Your skills. You vampires all have these deep, dark wells of mysterious capability, with your shadowy origins and the 'oh, I could tell you how I learned to count cards and read Welsh upside down, but I would have to kill you' thing. Plus, most of you have a special vampire talent. So what can you do to help get us out of here? Because I have to tell you, the closest thing I have to outdoorsmanship is carrying a Swiss Army knife, which I couldn't even take through the airport with me. So what are your skills?"

"Do I look like a mountain man?" he asked, gesturing to his well-tailored, though obviously dirty and rumpled, clothes.

"No."

"I am just as out of my element as you are."

"Where the hell are we?" I scanned the shore. Trees. All I could see were trees moving in the gentle summer breeze. No city lights in the distance. No water towers helpfully labeled with the local township's name. Nothing.

I flopped down on my butt on the sandy patch of grass near the muddy shore. I was stranded in the middle of the Kentucky backwoods, with no phone, no transportation, and no idea how to get to civilization. The rest of my anxiety meds were burning in my suitcase on the plane, because I didn't trust myself not to take too many if I packed them in my tote bag. And I was trapped in the bluegrass version of *Deliverance*. With a vampire.

Worst. Case. Scenario.

2

First, establish a food source for the vampire that is not you.

—*Where the Wild Things Bite: A Survival Guide for Camping with the Undead*

Mr. Vampire had no time for me or my need to catch my breath after nearly dying in a horrible air disaster.

"We need to get moving," he said, as I wrapped my arms around my bent knees and tried to rub circulation into my hands. We were fortunate, I supposed, that it was August and relatively warm. I wouldn't court hypothermia on top of my partially medicated emotional trauma.

"What? Why?" I protested. "All of the survival guides say to stay with the wreckage. Rescue crews, the FAA, helpful rednecks with ATVs who see the flames and want to burn an old mattress, they're going to come looking for us. Why would we walk away from the thing they're looking for? Besides, at least with the plane fire, we have some light to see by."

"Because the pilot took the plane off course. We weren't supposed to fly this far south."

"And you know that because your magical vampire power is sensing longitude and latitude?"

"Because while someone was running about the cabin like an insane person, I happened to see our heading on the instrument panel," he told me.

Damn it, I hated it when people out-logicked me. My eyes narrowed at the know-it-all vampire. I'd been more comfortable when I thought he was just a pretty face. "Well, he wasn't supposed to jump out of the plane, either, I'm guessing. Either way, even if we are off course, why wouldn't we want to stay put?"

"Because, unless that pilot just really hated his job, I'm guessing someone paid him to take the flight off course, meaning they probably had some preconceived notion of where the flight would end up. And since they thought the pilot would have your bag, which they are clearly after, for reasons we will discuss eventually, they're probably going to linger in that general area so they could pick up said bag, don't you think?"

I paused, thinking about that. I didn't know this vampire. And under normal circumstances, I wouldn't walk through the woods in the dark with a strange man who *didn't* have fangs. But these weren't normal circumstances, and when it counted, the vampire had stepped between Ernie and me. He could have left me on the plane to die, but he didn't. He could have used me to cushion his fall when we hit the water, but he didn't. If he was going to hurt me, he probably would have done it by now.

Or he was keeping me alive so I would be a convenient source of warm blood when he got peckish on our hike to the nearest highway.

"If that's the case, I think it would be better if we went our separate ways," I told him. "I need to make it to civilization as soon as possible. And I don't think I'm going to be able to do that if I'm only traveling during nighttime hours."

"So you're going to hike out of here alone?" he asked, smirking at me.

"I could . . ." I spluttered, glaring at him. "OK, no, there's actually very little chance of me surviving this scenario on my own. But there's even less chance of me getting out of here alive if my traveling companion eats me."

Given the return of that impish gleam in his eye, I really wished I'd phrased that differently.

"Look, you could maybe do it . . . under the right circumstances . . ." he conceded magnanimously.

"Please, pause less," I snapped at him.

"You're clearly resourceful when cornered, OK? But it would be stupid to try it alone. You know this. Surely you have some sort of mental statistic about the probability of dying while hiking through the woods unprepared and unaccompanied at night."

I didn't have exact figures, but I'd read enough survival guides to know that the probability of surviving "wasn't good." And as much as I hated to admit it, he had a point. And he'd said I was resourceful, which was the first time anyone had ever applied that word to me. "Intelligent" or "thorough" or even "fastidious," sure, but nothing that implied that I was capable outside the research library. It meant a lot, but I wasn't about to tell him so.

"I give you my solemn promise as a vampire, I will not harm a hair on your head," he said, in a tone so serious it sounded like a mockery, while holding up his left hand.

"Most people swear oaths with their right hands," I noted, because I did not, in fact, have a statistic for unprepared solo night-hiking deaths, but I was sure it wasn't optimistic.

"Sassy. You are sassing me now, aren't you?" he said, though he did raise his right hand.

"Yes, I am. And I have one condition," I told him.

He rolled his eyes heavenward and sighed. "What?"

"I do not set one foot into the woods with you until you tell me your name."

"We're wasting time! And we're already in the woods!"

"You got to 'accidental' second base with me earlier— we might as well be on a first-name basis. If nothing else, it's just good manners."

He waved his pale hands at me, flinging water at my face. "This from the woman who could barely be persuaded to have a polite conversation with me when I was being nothing but charming before takeoff?"

"Are you seriously not going to tell me your name?" I exclaimed.

"Not until you tell me yours."

"Anna Whitfield." I slung my hand up to shake his.

He bent over and looked like he was about to kiss my knuckles but instead hauled me to my feet. "Nice to meet you, Anna. My name is Finn Palmeroy."

My lips twitched. He did not look like a Finn. A Slade or a Clint or some other hyper-romantic soap-opera hero name but not Finn. And it seemed that his vampire sight allowed him to see my smirk, even in the moonlight, because he sounded none too amused when he said, "Girls with a name like an angry librarian should not throw stones."

"It's a family name, but fair enough," I said, barely restraining the urge to make a rude gesture. "Let's go."

My ballet flats slipped and slid on my feet while I walked, and I worried about mud sucking them off my feet as the vampire led me into the trees. I shuddered in my sodden clothes. While the air might have been warm, I still felt as if I were getting a full-body hug from a wet sponge. My only comfort was that Finn looked as miserable as I did.

"What about Ernie the pilot?" I asked. "What if we run into him?"

"Trust me, he doesn't want to run into me," he growled, and I could tell by the slight slur to his speech that his fangs had descended.

I dropped back to a safe distance. I'd had very little in-person experience with actual vampires. Not that I had anything against them. We just didn't move in the same circles. I was still in middle school when a recently turned tax consultant named Arnie Frink launched vampires out of the coffin and onto an unsuspecting human public . . . and then humanity had a collective nervous breakdown. Stakes were purchased and used on a grand scale. Curfews were imposed. Halloween was canceled.

It took a few years for human governments and the World Council for the Equal Treatment of the Undead to reach a compromise that both sides could live with. Humans couldn't seem to accept that the monsters they'd always feared didn't want to gnaw on their necks at the first opportunity. Vampires were just looking for a chance to live out in the open without worrying about being staked by their paranoid neighbors.

As a reward for not overthrowing humanity just by virtue of superior upper-body strength, the Council was allowed to establish smaller regional offices in each state in every country. Local Council members policed newly turned vampires for irresponsible feeding behavior, settled quarrels, and generally kept the vampire circles respectable.

My life after the Coming Out, well, it didn't change much. My father the professor was too wrapped up in his work to pay much attention to a total alteration of humanity's view of the world. Other than the possibility of having live (so to speak) subjects to interview about key events in history, he had no interest. My mother thought dealing with the reality of mythical creatures was "too scary" for me, so she kept me from watching the news, reading magazines, or surfing the Internet for vampire news. And when she found out that my school was holding an "Undead American Awareness Week," she threatened to homeschool me. As with the sex-ed lessons, I had to excuse myself from the classroom and do independent study in the library while my classmates learned about vampire culture. Because

Mother didn't sign the permission slip, and her signature was difficult to forge.

A few vampires taught at the college I attended, but strict fraternizing guidelines kept students from forming personal attachments to them. As an adult, working in the history department of a small private university in rural Virginia, I had even less contact with the undead. I spent my hours locked away in the special archives, studying books so old they could crumble into dust at a touch. Those vampires who chose to specialize in history tended toward the more theoretical angles of the field. Objects from their period of origin seemed to make them sad.

Seeing Finn bare his fangs and go into full-on raging undead mode on the plane had been a shock I hadn't quite registered yet. When those fangs came out again now, my hands started to shake, and my legs felt like they would liquefy.

I leaned against an oak tree, the rough bark scratching my waterlogged skin as I struggled to get my breath back. The full impact of what I'd just experienced seemed to land directly on my chest. I focused on breathing in and then out, one breath at a time. I pictured my blood flowing back into my fingertips, my toes, keeping my body warm. It was a technique I'd learned in one of my many, many, *many* therapy sessions, meditating on keeping my body functioning even while my mind spun into chaos.

I burst out laughing, a hysterical half sob that grated on my own nerves. But I couldn't seem to stop, Finn took a step back, and I laughed even harder. All thoughts of the first few minutes after the crash being vital to our survival disappeared from my head, and all I could do was cackle.

I laughed until tears rolled down my already wet cheeks. I seemed to be feeling all of the emotions at once—fear, confusion, anger, fear, joy, relief, fear. It was all I could do to stay upright under the weight of all those feelings. Finn took hold of my elbows, trying to support my weight while pulling me away from the tree.

My feet got tangled up with each other, and I flopped face-first into his chest. I stopped laughing immediately. Finn's arms slipped around my waist to hold me up. My nose seemed to be buried directly between his pecs, which were just as firm and well shaped as I'd suspected them to be on the plane. He smelled like expensive cologne and dryer sheets. How did I end up smelling like lake water and panic sweat, while he smelled like he just rolled out of a fashionable magazine? To my surprise, I didn't fight his hold. I didn't freak out over the invasion—nay, shattering—of my personal space. I wanted to stay right there, where I felt almost safe, with the comforting weight of his arms resting around me. As long as I could suppress the memory of Finn tossing me out of the plane, I could stay there forever.

And because that was one of the strangest thoughts I could remember having in a long time, I started giggling all over again.

"Uh, I don't know what to do here," Finn said, patting my head awkwardly. "We've only taken a few steps. I thought we had a couple of miles to go before one of us collapsed into hysterics."

I snorted into his shirt. I had to pull it together. As much as I deserved to wallow in these crash waves of endorphins, giggling like a loon wasn't going to get me to a warm, safe, dry place.

I pulled away from him, wiping at my damp cheeks. "OK, doll?" he asked, and I shook my head. I also grimaced at the condescending nickname, but chose the better part of "not pissing off a vampire."

"Why didn't you do anything?" I wheezed. "When he was trying to take my bag? When he was jumping out of the plane? Why didn't you stop him?" He hooked his arm through my elbow and tried to budge me along, but I jerked out of his grasp and leaned harder against the tree, bark be damned.

"I was trying, but it didn't work. It's a common problem for me, lately."

"What does that even mean?" I asked.

"Come on," he said, ignoring my question. "We have to keep moving. It will help our clothes dry faster."

"In a place where logic doesn't live," I retorted, though I moved my feet all the same.

We walked deeper into the trees, my limbs seeming all the more heavy. Any energy or adrenaline in my system had been used up, and I was running on fumes. The ground was uneven and smelled strongly of old pennies. My feet snagged on roots that rippled up out of the ground. I deliberately ignored the slap of leaves against my shins, sure that I was wading through a sea of poison ivy. We walked for what felt like forever, with the vampire—Finn, his name was *Finn*—dragging me along half the time, until I could no longer see the glow from the burning plane wreckage.

"Let's stop," he said, helping me lower my butt to a felled log. I wondered why, until twinges of soreness rippled up my legs. My heels and the balls of my feet stung with the beginnings of blisters. And despite the fact that I was soaked to the bone, I was so thirsty I could have wept with it. Where was I going to get water? Would the lake have been safe to drink from? Was it a mistake to leave it? Maybe we should have stayed near the wreckage, even if it meant confronting whoever had downed the plane? Finn could fight them off, couldn't he? I mean, he might need to feed before he did it . . . Wait. I eyed him suspiciously and questioned again whether that was why he was really dragging me along. As a road-trip snack? Was I the human equivalent of Corn Nuts?

I watched as he scrambled up the tree, lithe and graceful as any predator. Well, it seemed he had energy to spare even without turning me into a juice box. He disappeared into the branches above, and I was suddenly sort of jealous. I wanted to be up there with him, moving with so little trouble. I wanted to see the view, to know what it was like to take in the world from such a height. I'd never so much as climbed a rock wall before. I found the number of waivers required by my gym to be off-putting.

"Do you see anything?" I called, and then clamped my lips together. If we were being followed by Ernie or his employers, I probably shouldn't shout. Or if I did, I should just go ahead and shout, "Here we are!" to save some time. At any rate, Finn didn't answer.

A panicked thought hit me. What if he was already gone? What if he was swinging through the trees like some sort of vampire Tarzan? What if he'd left me alone in the woods? I had a head full of information but no survival skills.

Once again, I took several slow, deep breaths. I couldn't respond like this every time Finn got out of my sight, and I couldn't rely on the lovely white rectangular pills to get me through my anxiety.

A few minutes later, I heard the foliage above rustling, and I sighed in relief.

I grinned widely as Finn dropped to the ground in front of me, then quickly schooled my features into a less awestruck expression.

"What?"

"Nothing, that was just impressive," I said, shrugging.

He hauled me up to my feet. "Well, I've got bad news, and I've got worse news."

"Hit me with the worse news first."

He lifted an eyebrow. "Most people ask for the better news first."

"I just want to know what I'm dealing with."

"The worse news is that I don't see lights anywhere. For miles. No signs of civilization. And I can see pretty damn far."

I frowned, thinking of an ad I'd seen at the airport, a big, splashy, colorful poster that had taken up a good portion of the wall near the ladies' room at my gate.

Happy families camping near a lake, fishing, kayaking. It had looked so inviting I actually took a brochure, before remembering that I disliked camping, rough living, and the outdoors in general.

"Maybe we're in the Lakelands Nature Preserve," I told him. "I saw a bunch of posters and stuff at the airport. It's the biggest parcel of untouched land in the state. We're about three hundred miles away from the Hollow, in the middle of what can only be described as 'lake, undeveloped land, more lake, more undeveloped land, more lake.'"

"What about campgrounds? Cabins? Hell, a ranger station?"

"Oh, they have them, ringed all around the outside edge of the woods, because most people are smart enough to stay out of the middle."

Finn groaned.

"Why don't you just run ahead?" I asked. "You can run a lot faster than I can, not to mention see in the dark. You could make it to a road or town much easier without me slowing you down. Send help back for me. I'll stay right here."

He suddenly looked very uncomfortable and glanced down at my bag. "I don't want to leave you alone, especially with the pilot still out there, wandering around."

"You could carry me," I told him, somewhat insulted by the flicker of doubt that crossed his face.

"Well, that's the bad news. We've walked for much longer than I thought. The sun's going to come up in about an hour. And I haven't had any blood in about eight hours. I don't have the strength to carry you without feeding."

I shot him a look that I could only describe as "extreme shade." I wasn't about to let him feed from me. I didn't trust him not to take too much. Maybe he could control his thirst, maybe he couldn't, but I wasn't about to test the theory. We would just have to find some other way.

"I could keep going, try to find help on my own, while you sleep," I offered. He smirked at me, as if he didn't believe I could get five feet on my own. "That facial expression is unnecessary."

"I'm not doubting that *you* could find your way out of here by yourself. I doubt that *anybody* could. You don't know which way to go. You don't have any supplies. And you're dressed for the mall."

I pursed my lips. I was equal parts relieved that his doubts weren't rooted in me personally and annoyed that he was right. My shoes were decidedly mall-friendly. I pointed over the horizon. "Well, the plane was headed in that direction. I'm assuming that if we continued that way, eventually, we would run into other people."

He looked vaguely impressed with my logic and nodded his head. "OK, but you're dead on your feet, kitten. Fatigue sets in, you start making bad decisions, you could get even more lost, hurt, dehydrated."

"I could make it," I insisted, before adding snappishly, "OK, fine, I probably couldn't. And don't call me 'kitten.'"

"Let's just find somewhere to rest for the day. That will be challenge enough, *kitten*."

I grimaced at the nickname but reasoned that he was right. I was tired and sore, and my feet felt like they were on fire. There was no way I was going to make it much farther in what was left of the night.

He tried to slip his arm under mine to tug me along, but I shrugged him off. He raised his hands defensively, as if he was *so scared* of the little human. We staggered on, Finn watching the sky warily, until we found a thicket of pine trees, the branches thick with needles.

Finn started stripping off boughs from the middle of the trunks and stacking them carefully on the lower branches, adding an extra layer of pine needles between him and the sky.

"Really?" I asked, watching him check for thin spots in the coverage.

"You were expecting the Ritz? Trust me, I've had to sleep outside a time or two in my years. This works."

I wondered exactly how many years he was talking about, but I knew that age questions were considered rude in vampire circles.

"I just thought you would know how to find a cave or dig a hole or something."

"Right, all vampires have a sense for the nearest caves, because we're all part bat?"

"The sun is coming up. Is this really the time for undead cultural sensitivity training?" I shot back. "Wait, don't you have some of that mega-SPF 500 sunscreen to protect you in situations like this?"

"Yes," he said. "All vampires carry it on them for emergencies."

"Great."

"It's in my carry-on. On the plane. Which has crashed."

"Sonofabitch." I sighed. "Well, if it makes you feel better, I have an effective, all-natural insect spray, which happens to repel both of the extremely bite-y species of poisonous spiders that live in Kentucky, but it's in my luggage, too."

"My being evaporated by the sun is a bit more of an issue than your getting a couple of bug bites, so no, that doesn't make me feel better. And yes, I can sleep underground, but that wouldn't provide you much protection, now, would it?"

"How much protection are you going to provide me when you're technically dead for the day?"

"Enough that you're sleeping right by my side, kitten."

"Call me 'kitten' one more time, and you're going to 'accidentally' roll over on one of those pointy wooden branches in your sleep."

He hovered way too close, way too fast, his nose nearly touching my forehead. I didn't even have time to stumble back.

"Don't even joke about it," he purred, sliding his hand down my arm and pulling me toward him. My mouth went dry, but other parts were considerably . . . damper. And it had nothing to do with our recent swim. Unlike most people who met me, he hadn't underestimated me on sight. He considered me a threat to his well-being. He didn't treat me like I was made of particularly stupid spun sugar. He didn't assume I would never do him harm while he was sleeping because I was "too nice" or "too calm" or any other number of synonyms for "too weak to do anything but bitch and moan." It was a refreshing change.

It was bad that Finn seeing me as a potential threat was a turn-on, right? That was not something that got well-adjusted grown-up ladies all hot and bothered.

Because I was both hot and bothered when his cheek brushed mine as he whispered, "You need me. I may need you to keep watch during the day, but you need me, too, kitten. For everything else."

What exactly did "everything else" entail?

I was exhausted—mentally, emotionally, physically. Otherwise, I probably would have cowered. A more sensible Anna would have stammered out an apology and possibly passed out. But I'd hit my limit, the wall, I'd been clotheslined by the finish ribbon. And a "one hundred percent done" Anna was an Anna without a sense of self-preservation.

So I poked him. In the chest. Repeatedly.

"Don't. Call. Me. Kitten," I ground out, emphasizing each word with a poke.

Instead of draining me and disposing of my husk-like carcass, Finn grinned at me, with the tiniest edge of madness in his eyes. "Let's get some sleep."

"You are the most confusing man in the world." I sighed, as he gracefully slipped under the lowermost pine boughs.

He poked his head out of the needles. "Well, I'm guessing your experience is limited."

"That's it!" I hissed. "I'm sleeping out here."

I did an about-face to a somewhat clear patch of grass, where I looked for a spot to lay my head.

"Anna."

I ignored him. I knew that he was probably right. It wasn't safe for me to sleep out in the open. It would be better for us to stay closer to each other. I was just so tired and too freaking proud to admit it. I could feel the exhaustion seeping into the marrow of my bones, leaching into my bloodstream.

"Anna."

I whipped my head toward him, prepared to glare for all I was worth. He was half crouched on the ground, head and shoulders emerging from his pine shelter. He seemed totally focused on me, his eyes that same strange, cloudy bluish-white they'd turned on the plane.

I felt like a puppet whose strings had been cut. The energy that kept me in control of my limbs seemed to trickle away, leaving me empty, hollowed out. I was aware that I was standing, but nothing I was doing was keeping me that way. Without any signal from my brain, my feet shuffled toward the trees, where Finn was waiting with his hand outstretched. I slid my fingers into his, and he helped me slide under the canopy of pine. I barely felt the scratch of the needles against my skin as I lay on the ground. Finn took my purse and tucked it under my head. He put a good foot of space between us and laid his head on the ground.

I folded my hands over my stomach and stared up at the branches hanging just a few inches over my face. I was . . . calm. I wasn't upset with Finn anymore. I wasn't angry or scared or worried. I was a blank slate with no concerns at all. And I was shocked at how comfortable I was with this feeling. No medication, no therapy I'd tried could touch its blank, weightless serenity. For the first time in years, I felt free of the anxiety that had fueled so many of my actions and decisions over most of my lifetime. I closed my eyes and went about my nightly ritual of running through all of the things I had to accomplish the next day, reminding myself of big deadlines and problems looming. And while I could feel a sort of tug at the corners of my mind, I found I couldn't think of one single errand or problem beyond two words, bold and red, on the backs of my eyelids: "STAY PUT."

Exhaustion dragged me under, and before my mind dissolved into nothingness, I remembered those two words.

"STAY PUT."

3

The key to survival in any situation involving the undead and hiking: dry socks and not panicking.

—*Where the Wild Things Bite: A Survival Guide*
for Camping with the Undead

There's nothing quite like waking up under a tree and realizing how badly you have to use a ladies' room that is not there.

I rolled over on the dried pine needles, wincing at the occasional sharp poke through my sweater. My mouth felt as if sandpaper and cabbage had had a baby on my tongue, an evil baby. My eyes were sticky, and my lashes felt gummy. My head was pounding, and my feet felt like they were on fire.

In short, everything was awful.

I was on my side, snuggling into Finn's chest, my nose buried in his shirt. His arm was slung around my back, pressing me close. His chin was tucked over the top of my head. It was an intimate, comfortable position—and completely bizarre, considering how little I knew about him and the fact that what I did know I didn't like all that much.

My hands searched for my purse even before I was fully awake, winging above my head in a frantic gesture. I relaxed a bit as I felt the outline of the package and heard the crinkle of plastic. I eased out from under Finn's arms, careful not to wake him.

I couldn't help but admire him as he slept. He looked innocent and young, as if he wasn't scheming six different ways to mock me or throw me out of perfectly good transportation. I stretched my hand up, running my thumb lightly over his bottom lip. From what I'd read, most vampires became more attractive after they were turned. Finn must have started with a pretty high bar. And then I remembered the reason that vampires were attractive. They needed to be able to draw in prey. Carnivorous flowers had bright colors to lure insects. Sneaky sea creatures blended into the sand so little fish would swim right into their open mouths. Vampires had perfect skin, mesmerizing eyes, and teeth so bright and sharp you leaned closer just to get a better look.

Just in case, I pried myself loose from his hold, scooting back. I wasn't sure how quickly vampires needed to feed after waking. If the answer was "immediately," I didn't want to be in grabbing range.

He grumbled as I jostled him, mumbling in his sleep and running his hand over his face. I could see weak light filtering through the upper branches, but Finn's face seemed intact. I would no longer doubt the power of the pine. Though my nose did feel awfully stuffy. Maybe I was allergic to pine pollen? I'd never been exposed to the outdoors all that much. My family weren't exactly the Von Trapps. We did not climb any mountains or ford a single stream.

Also, wasn't western Kentucky home to something called a "pine rattlesnake"? Ignoring the potential for vampire waking, I scrambled out from under the canopy into the weak twilight.

The good news, I supposed, was that I was clearly hydrated enough. The bad news was the lack of toilet tissue. I would not fall into the poison-ivy trap, I promised myself. After a few minutes of careful tree selection and diligent avoiding of "leaves of three," I ambled back to the pines. I wondered if we would finally find something like civilization tonight. Surely we were getting closer to the edge of the preserve.

I blinked into the dim orange-ish light provided by the setting sun. The sky overhead was a dusky orange color, slowly transitioning to the purple in the horizon. But the sun was still very much out. My immediate instinct was to check my cell phone for the time, but as it was now a waterlogged plastic paperweight, I had to guess it was around six thirty. It wouldn't be safe for Finn to come out in the open for at least another ten or twenty minutes, judging by the sun's position. Technically, he could wake up at this hour, but his senses wouldn't be as sharp, and he would move at a much slower pace—basically, me before I've been properly caffeinated.

I stretched, cracking my neck and shaking the pine needles out of my hair. The ache in my feet was like a living thing, creeping up my legs and back and making me despair at the walking I knew I would have to do that night. Fortunately, I had my hunger to distract me. My stomach growled so loudly that I was afraid I might wake up Finn. I'd never been so hungry before, aching and hollow all the way through my middle, as if my stomach were crawling up my throat, demanding attention. My muscles burned with fatigue and poor sleep and just being done with this situation in general. I promised myself that as soon as we hit a town, I would ignore my mostly organic diet entirely and eat the largest, fattiest steak available. And mashed potatoes. And French fries. And a baked potato, swimming in butter. Basically, I would eat *all* of the potatoes.

I reached into my still-damp bag and pulled out the chocolate-chip granola bar. I always carried this sort of thing in my purse, because my metabolism tended to run pretty fast. And I tended to say hurtful things when I was hangry. I was grateful that the wrapper had stayed intact and the bar was dry. I definitely didn't want to eat lake-soaked granola.

Part of me felt guilty for eating the only available food without even offering a bite to Finn. But human food smelled and tasted horrible to vampires anyway, something to do with them lacking the enzymes and functions required to digest it. Their bodies instinctually rejected the solids that could make them very ill. Frankly, it was probably a kindness not to eat it in front of him.

Of course, that didn't solve the problem of what Finn *would* eat when he rose. But if I had to run from him, I would need the calories. I bit into the bar, grimacing at the sudden rush of cheap-chocolate sweetness that coated my tongue and teeth. I forced myself to take small bites, not to wolf it down. All I needed was to make myself sick and lose the granola bar, not to mention what little hydration I had in my system.

I was careful not to touch the granola with my filthy hands, shielding it from my fingertips with the slick foil wrapper. I had never felt so dirty or disheveled in my life. I knew now that I would not have made it as a pioneer woman. This only confirmed the suspicions I'd held since elementary school, when I was usually the first one to die of cholera in *Oregon Trail*.

I accepted that about myself. While I studied the ancient and rare, I was a modern woman. I needed technology and conveniences. Maybe that left me a little unprepared for wilderness treks, but I'd set up my life to avoid this sort of adventure, so I doubted very much that it would happen more than once.

I sat on the ground, far past caring if my jeans got dirty. I felt better with the blood sugar filtering into my system and the emptiness in my stomach fading a little bit. I would get through tonight. I would be able to walk, even if it did kill my feet. I was going to be OK.

All hail the power of chocolate, root of improbable positive thinking.

I glanced under the tree, where I could see a faint impression of his shoes through the branches. Did I really need Finn? I could walk through the woods. I could make it on my own. I mean, I'd made it this far, and I hadn't exactly depended on Finn's services as a guide. Surely Ernie had moved on by now. If I could get to a road, I could send someone back to look for

Finn. Besides, he was a lot more prepared for this trek than I. He was an apex predator.

A somewhat annoying apex predator at that.

I stood, slinging my bag over my shoulder. I wondered if I should leave Finn a note or something, to let him know I was sorry for abandoning him. He might have protested that he'd given up barflies over the last year, but I imagined a guy like him had probably left more than his share of women to wake up alone in his long lifetime. He probably had this coming.

OK, that was classic rationalization, but I was still hungry and tired, and morals were not really high up on my priority list at the moment.

With the sun still glowing, the woods didn't seem so scary. Ignoring every fairy tale that opened with a lone female venturing into the deep, dark forest, I pushed forward. The lush greenery was almost welcoming, slapping gently against my shoulders. My feet sank into the loose earth every other step, and my shoes rubbed against my heels in all the wrong places.

I tried to imagine what was happening in the "real world." What had happened when we didn't land in the Half-Moon Hollow airport? Had Jane been informed of the crash, or had she assumed that I just didn't show up when I was expected to? Had she called Rachel in a panic, demanding to know the whereabouts of her book? Rachel was my emergency contact on all of my airline information, so she definitely would have been informed of the plane crash.

Rachel. She'd promised she'd wait up until she'd gotten my "landed safely" text. We always did that when we traveled separately. But my text hadn't come. Did she think I was dead? In a normal "missing plane" situation, that could be the only believable scenario. Her innermost optimistic brain might tell her that there was some misunderstanding, but her rational mind would tell her that I was gone, that she was in charge of my estate now, such as it was.

I groaned. Had she called my mother yet? I'd told her so much about Mother; I could only imagine that she'd put that particular task off for as long as humanly possible. And if Rachel had called by now, I was sure that Mother had had a full-blown meltdown. Finally, all of her predictions of doom had come true. I hadn't heeded her dire warnings on the dangers of traveling alone, and I wasn't even present to watch her wallow in her triumph. Like all ungrateful children, I had paid the ultimate price for my resistance. She wouldn't know whether to sob hysterically or shout "I told you so" from the rooftops.

Annabelle Whitfield was not a woman who tolerated resistance. Or disobedience. Or separation. Hell, she'd named me after her, hoping I'd want to spend my whole life as "Little Annabelle," like some Southern-fried version of *Grey Gardens*. She'd been such a "devoted" mother, centering her whole life around me from my babyhood. Oh, she kept up a minimal social schedule, for appearance's sake. She was the wife of a respected history professor, after all. She joined the right social clubs, involved me in the right activities, but at home, it was just the two of us. My father, a highly respected Civil War expert working for the University of Virginia, always seemed to be elsewhere. And that was how she liked it, though she always made it sound like such an ordeal to be left behind when he went on his research trips.

How dare he leave Mother alone when our house could catch on fire or a pipe could burst? She just couldn't handle any of that. She wouldn't know what to do. What was she supposed to *do*? I remember being eight years old and thinking that was a silly thing to say. I told her that I would call 911 or a plumber. But that didn't make her happy. How would we pay the plumber? she'd ask me. What if she lost her checkbook? How would we get money for the household expenses? What if she cut her hand while she was making dinner and needed to go to the emergency room? How would we get there? I told her I would call the bank and report the checkbook lost. And if she couldn't drive, I would call a cab, and we'd get to the emergency room. It became this weird game. Mother would make up more and more absolutely absurd worst-case scenarios, and I would come up with ways to fix them. And I didn't even realize that I was taking on all of these adult responsibilities that I had no business doing.

Little by little, she shrank my world down with her anxieties and "what ifs." She needed me too much at home for me to play sports or join school clubs. And I couldn't go out with the few boys who asked. What if he tried to keep me out too late? What if he tried to drive drunk with me in the car? I had to stay home with her, just in case she needed me. We hadn't been

Dr. Phil'ed as a society yet, so I didn't know terms like "enmeshment" and "grooming." I didn't know that she was basically setting me up to never leave home, never get married, never have a life of my own. She wanted me to stay at home forever, taking care of her like the doomed youngest daughter in *Like Water for Chocolate*.

We became a unit, "the Annabelles." My accomplishments were her accomplishments. My struggles her struggles. She referred to us as "we." It was never Anna, it was always "we."

"We" were applying to colleges. And "we" were having trouble with piano lessons. "We" didn't date, because it took too much time away from our studies. Even at a young age, I felt I was losing myself to her, as if she were trying to absorb me, sucking my life away, making it her own.

I knew it was unhealthy, but I'd learned quickly that pulling away from Mother, trying to assert myself as my own individual personality, triggered a total meltdown. An act as simple as asking her to step out of a dressing room while I changed would provoke tears. How could I push her away? How could I be so heartless when she'd done nothing but take care of me? How could I be so cold?

My father was no help. Sometimes I think he only agreed to have a child so my mother would have someone else to talk to. I'd tried to approach him about Mother, but he'd waved me away, told me that I would have to handle it, he was too busy. In a way, Mother seemed as disposable to him as I did. There was no love between them, just civility. They were partners, in the sense that being married got them both what they wanted in life, but that was it.

I learned to work around her. To rebel in my own small ways, starting with insisting that my high school classmates call me Anna and ending with moving to an area outside Atlanta too remote for her to consider visiting. I hadn't seen her face-to-face in more than two years. I'd taken a cue from my father and remained busy with work, too busy to come home for visits or holidays. And while she complained about this in almost every e-mail, voice mail, birthday card, and Christmas present, it was the path of least insanity for both of us.

Would I make it back before she managed to plan a body-less funeral for me? Would she take ashes from the wreckage and put them in some creepy floral urn, with plans to display me on the mantelpiece as evidence of what happens when one doesn't listen to Annabelle Whitfield?

Maybe it would be better if I didn't tell her I was alive after all. I could make a fresh start. A new life, maybe in the Southwest, where no one knew me.

I sighed. That was the fatigue talking. I knew I would eventually have to make contact with Mother. I just wanted to do it on my terms. So much of our relationship had been on her terms, her rules, her refusal to see boundaries. I felt safer at a distance.

Somewhere, in the distance, I heard a branch snap, and not just in a "broke under the weight of a chubby squirrel" way. Someone was moving behind me. Was it

Finn? Would he call out to me, or was he so upset about my abandonment that he was stalking me through the woods like a deer? Or maybe the branch snapper *was* a deer, and I was just overreacting.

I moved faster, lifting my legs in an odd ostrich walk to keep my shoes from sticking. The sounds grew louder, closer to me, and I broke out into a full run, stumbling over fallen logs and dodging branches that whipped at my face.

I clutched my bag to my chest to keep it from dragging on loose limbs. I tried not to panic, but now the noises sounded like they were coming from every direction, and I felt like a trapped animal. I stopped at a small break in the trees, suddenly aware that the only noise I could hear was the ragged sound of my own breathing and my pounding heart. I turned in a slow circle, listening intently and scanning the fading light for predators.

I would not be the girl in the horror movie who called out "Hello?" when she thought she was being followed. That girl always died first.

My hand slipped into my bag and searched for my pills. If ever there was a time for antianxiety meds, this was it. As my fingers fumbled for the empty plastic prescription bottle, I remembered that the ashes of my meds were in a pile of flaming wreckage. I wondered what was going to be worse, my impending bone-shaking, brain-muddling anxiety attack or the dread of its arrival, which was almost as debilitating. Oh, and given that I'd been using those pills for a while now, I might end up suffering from withdrawal symptoms on top of everything else.

What were the chances of death for horror-movie heroines who cried in the fetal position in the dirt?

Suddenly, the smell of burning leather and mud assailed my nose, and I was tackled by a swift, smoldering shape. My yelp was cut short when I hit the dirt, knocking the wind out of me and making my lungs ache. Finn was on top of me, his skin black and flaking like burnt birch bark. I could *hear* him sizzling as the last of the sun's dying rays washed over the areas not covered by his undershirt. His shirt was tied around his brow like a sheik's, shielding his head and neck, but his hands and chest, oh, his poor chest. He was *roasting* alive as we rolled through the underbrush with the momentum of his speed.

Just then, I heard a sharp whooshing noise and saw a long, dark streak fly over us. It struck the tree just over our heads. Someone had fashioned a spear out of a long stick, duct tape, and a black ceramic kitchen knife. And then they'd flung it at us and damn near killed us.

Finn shouted something, but I couldn't make it out over the shock of having a freaking spear thrown at me.

"What?" I barked.

"Move!" Finn yelled, as the white noise of panic cleared my ears.

I heard rustling in the distance, a heavy shape moving through the trees. Finn rolled us, keeping me pinned to his chest as he moved us in the underbrush. The shape stopped, and so did Finn, freezing above me, panting softly as he scanned the tree line. I wriggled out from under him, eased off my sweater, and arranged it around his shoulders to cover more skin.

Finn didn't speak but held a finger to his lips. I nodded frantically. He rolled to his side, letting out a wheezing "uhf" as he landed in the dirt.

I crept closer to the tree and pulled the makeshift spear free from the bark. It was no small task, as the blade had sunk deep. I balanced the stick in my palms, marveling at the weight of the knife, crouching close to Finn's prone form. It had to be Ernie the pilot. How many people could there be roaming the woods with black ceramic knives?

He'd found us. I'd mostly doubted that the pilot had survived. Even with the parachute, I had serious doubts that he'd made it. But he'd been tracking us all day, it seemed, and the idea of him finding us while we were sleeping under the tree made me shudder. Yes, Ernie was chubby and a bit boozy, but he clearly had some survival skills. Maybe he was former military? That would help my pride a little bit, knowing that he was somehow trained to do this sort of thing, and we weren't just terrible at surviving.

If Ernie came near us, would I be able to use the knife? I looked down at Finn, who was suffering because he'd tried to help me.

Yes, I could.

"I've got your knife, Ernie!" I yelled, mustering bravery I didn't have into my voice, praying it didn't quaver as I heard trees moving in the distance. My fingers shook as I tightened my grip around the stick. "And you've pissed off my vampire friend pretty bad! So you probably don't want to come any closer."

After a long moment, I heard something moving toward us. I bared my teeth, though I'm sure it looked more like a terrified grimace than a warrior stare. I moved to stand over Finn, gripping the stick so hard that my knuckles ached. Where was he? Where was he?

Part of me wanted to scream at him to hurry up and attack, anything to end this horrible waiting. And the other part wanted to yell that I gave up, that Ernie could have the book. I was tired of running and hiding when I clearly wasn't very good at it. And I'd never even been in a fistfight before, much less a knife fight. Who was I kidding?

My eyes landed on a distinctive shape in the distance, a darker patch in the irregular pattern of green leaves. The patch came into focus, and I realized it wasn't a patch of leaves. It was a *face*. A rounded, florid face with angry dark eyes and a sneering mouth. Ernie was either unhappy to see me or way too happy to see me. My whole body seemed to seize up. I thought back to nightmares I'd had as a child of looking out a darkened window and seeing some evil face looking back at me, smiling, trying to figure out how to get in my house.

I could see Ernie's face, see the intent in his eyes. This man wanted to hurt me, and there was no hiding from it, no looking away.

Finn groaned, pushing to his feet, drawing my gaze. He wavered, his skin still smoldering as the sun faded over the horizon, but he stayed upright. I glanced back at Ernie's position, but he was gone. Gasping, I gripped the spear tighter.

I heard movement edging slowly away from us, eventually disappearing altogether. I waited for what seemed like an eternity before I felt my shoulders relax. My grip on the spear loosened, and I stumbled away from Finn, bending at the waist and gritting my teeth against the urge to toss up the granola bar. I couldn't spare the calories.

I couldn't believe I'd just done that. My life was in danger *again*. And I'd invited a confrontation with someone whose daily to-do list seemed to include an agenda item labeled "Murder Anna Whitfield." *Again*.

I wasn't built for this sort of thing. I was built for my cozy at-home office, the guest room lined with shelf upon shelf of valuable and obscure old books. Before I'd boarded that stupid plane, a really exciting day for me consisted of finding a new blend of herbal tea at my local Whole Foods. Or maybe that time Rachel tried to make me get a tattoo for my birthday and I had to employ every "urban escape" tip I'd ever read to hail a cab back home before she realized I'd bailed out through the tattoo shop's bathroom window.

How much more was I expected to take? Every time I went through one of these face-offs with Ernie, my probability of survival shrank. So far, I'd slid by on luck and unlikely failures of physics. If I survived, I was never going camping. Not that there was much chance of it before, but those tiny fractions of a chance had definitely been smashed into nothingness in the past twenty-four hours.

All for one stupid job, a job that while important and potentially reputation-building—not to mention remunerative—was just a job. I couldn't spend money or enjoy a good reputation while I was dead.

If I'd expected Finn to be sympathetic or calming when I finally emerged from my one-woman pity party, I would have been sorely disappointed.

"What were you thinking?" he growled, shrugging out of my sweater and his shirt. The raw, ash-covered patches of skin were only half as angry as the sound of his growls as he hunched over me. He looked as if portions of his face were composed of cigarette ash. His lips were red and bleeding, and his eyelids looked so dry they could crack. Mr. Magazine Perfect looked like he'd been ridden hard and hung up disheveled. A flutter of sympathy rippled through my belly. "I told you I would help you. I told you I would get us out of the woods. Why would you try to walk away?" Finn groaned and flopped on the ground. "Kitten, if you're not convinced by now, I don't know what to do for you."

I would let him get away with "kitten," for now. I picked up my sweater and did my best to knock the ashes off of it. (Ew.) "I'm sorry about your skin. Is there anything I can do?"

"Got a pint of blood to spare?" he asked, his eyes closed.

"Nope."

I looked down at the spear in my hand. I could go and hunt . . . something, I supposed. The chances of me actually killing an animal were pretty damned slim, but I could at least try. Come to think of it, I had a much better chance of spearing myself while trying to hunt down an animal, which was part of the reason I didn't own a gun.

"Relax, Anna. I can see how you feel about that, even with my eyes closed." He opened said eyes and squinted into the canopy of leaves over us. His eyes panned as if they were tracking some movement I couldn't sense. He rolled toward the tree and slammed his fist against it. A moment later, a squalling, hissing ball of gray fur tumbled out of the branches above. Finn caught it just before it landed on his face.

"That's a possum," I said, pursing my lips and nodding while he wrestled the marsupial into submission.

"Yes, it is," he rasped. "And as an omnivore, it is nutrient-rich."

"You're going to eat a possum?"

"Technically, I'm going to drink a possum."

"OK." I winced as he considered the best place to sink his teeth. "No judgments, but I'm going to go over there."

"That's probably for the best," he said, nodding. I rounded a larger tree, still clutching the spear. I examined the weird black blade, flicking the surprisingly sharp edge with my finger. I'd read up on ceramic knives when I'd outfitted my kitchen. And while I could see the appeal of blades that never went dull, I found the number of chemicals involved in treating the blades off-putting. I didn't want something with so many "oxides" touching my food. Ceramic blades were nonmagnetic; this wouldn't have shown up when Ernie walked through security at the airport. All he had to do was tape the knife inside his sleeve or pant leg, and he would be golden.

"Ernie, you clever douchebag," I muttered to myself.

From the other side of the tree, I heard a screech and a *crunch-slurp*. I knew Finn was only doing what he had to do to survive, but honestly, that was pretty gross. Once the slurping stopped, I came back around the tree. His skin was healing, the scars seeming to evaporate as he slowly sat up.

"That is freaky."

He blanched, and a shudder ran up his back. "I could say I've had worse, but that would be a lie."

"I am not sorry for you."

"Want a bite?" he asked, offering me the mostly intact carcass. He was already looking better. The burnt patches of his skin were knitting themselves back together, the tendrils of tissue reaching out to recreate the smooth surface. His color, such as it was, was better, returning to the pale pearlescent sheen natural to vampires; though the worst areas hadn't entirely smoothed out, his mouth no longer resembled an open wound. Still, I could resist the lure of possum tartare.

"So how are you?" he asked.

"Sore," I told him. "Like I was thrown out of a plane last night."

"Not going to let go of that anytime soon, are you?"

I shook my head. "No, I am not."

"Are you sure you don't want to try to eat this?" he said, holding up the possum. "We can roast it over a fire or something."

"Not with Ernie still out there. The smoke will lead

him right to us," I muttered, though I wasn't sure if my disdain was really for the possibility of discovery or the idea of eating an overgrown rat.

"Is that really his name?" he asked, wiping at his mouth. I nodded. He sneered in disgust. "Terrible name for an arch-nemesis."

"And no thanks on the possum. I'm a vegetarian," I told him.

"You are?"

"Very recently," I said. "As in within the last five minutes."

He rolled his eyes as he stood. "You're going to need to eat eventually."

"And when that time comes, I will let you know. Besides, the less I eat, the less appealing my blood will be to you."

"Eh, your attitude would make it all sour, anyway," he told me, as we headed away from the last location of Ernie's trampling sounds.

"I don't have an attitude!" I cried, pausing before I added, "I am not making a very good case for myself, am I?"

"No, you are not. And don't do that again, Anna. Please. I can't help you if you run off. I told you, we need each other if we're going to get out of this."

I nodded.

"Good, now that we have that established."

He seemed to have recovered his vampire speed, because he was at my side, snatching my bag from my shoulder and the spear from my hand, before I knew what happened.

"What are you doing?" I cried, lowering my voice so Ernie, wherever he was, wouldn't hear me. "Give that back."

"What is your deal with this bag?" he demanded. "Are you carrying around uncut conflict diamonds? Exotic bird eggs? Mummified organs of former boyfriends? What?"

"Don't!" I cried, trying to grab for the bag, but he held it out of my reach.

"I'm not going to take it. I just want to know what's in your purse. You've been cradling this thing like a baby. I want to know what was worth the pilot trying to mug you as he hijacked our plane."

"Stop it, please," I begged. I cringed as he pulled the package loose from my bag. The plastic bag, battered and cloudy as it was, glistened in the moon's weak early light.

"A book?" he gasped, sounding truly insulted. "All this over a stupid book?"

"Yeah, just a book," I told him, my voice too tremulous to convey the casual tone I was aiming for. "I don't know what all the fuss is, really."

"I mean, I would understand if it was mummy parts or a huge brick of cocaine," he said. "But a *book*? And it looks like it's been beaten all to hell."

Finn examined the worn brown leather cover that I now knew as well as the back of my own hand. The pages were thin as onion skin, delicate, almost translucent vellum, hand-lettered with iron gall ink. It had to be made from metal to have survived for so long.

Friar Thomas, who'd been considerate enough to

write the book in a mix of Latin and Old English despite his Spanish roots, also had a talented hand with illustrations, the heavy woodcut style marks depicting the various stages of transformation for shifters from human to animal.

It had been a shock when Jane sent me the book for verification. Friar Thomas was considered the J. D. Salinger of supernatural researchers, reclusive and not exactly prolific. After being ejected from his order for his heretical ideas that vampires, witches, and other "demonic entities" were not inherently evil and perhaps deserved a conversation or two before being burned at the stake, he didn't have much motivation for writing. Finding one of his books, especially a previously unknown work, was like finding the Hope Diamond at a rummage sale.

Jane had some idea that the book could be useful to the shifter community, but she'd come across so many faked and/or academically flawed volumes in her shop that she didn't want to assume anything. Having never heard of the obscure Franciscan scholar, she'd asked me to determine whether this was authentic or faked by someone who was, as Jane termed it, "banana-balls crazy." It had taken months of calls, e-mails, and burying myself in old dusty church records, but eventually, I determined that *A Contemplation on Shifters from the Old World and the New* was not a "banana-balls crazy" fake but possibly the most definitive work on shapeshifting ever written and a bit of a literary Holy Grail. (Turned out there weren't that many works written on shape-shifting.)

I hadn't come to accept that shapeshifters actually existed yet, because I was a "seeing is believing" type when it came to the supernatural. But honestly, if vampires existed, why not werewolves, zombies, sea serpents, and other monsters? I was rooting against zombies, though, because I *had* come to accept that I would be among the first eaten in the zombie apocalypse.

Having spent years researching supernatural texts, I'd heard stories and rumors, both about Friar Thomas and about the shifters, their odd skill sets and social structures. While were-creatures were supposedly very pack-oriented and communicated freely with other packs, shifters were supposed to keep to themselves. From what I'd read, shifters were supposed to live in small communities, very separated and insular. They didn't talk to one another, and they definitely didn't share their secrets with other shifters. Having this kind of history text could help them understand themselves and overcome the pack separation by tracking down the regional families listed by Friar Thomas. It would also make whoever held the book very powerful. They would have more information about their condition, the best times to shift, the diets that could make their shifts easier, and how far they could stretch their forms—something that apparently could go very wrong if a shifter overreached. And they would obtain the "final chapter"—the element that made the book a scary story shifters told their kids before bedtime.

Friar Thomas had written a "cautionary chapter" to end his magnum opus, detailing his visit with a dying shifter clan in the northern reaches of Siberia. There were only three elderly members left, something they blamed on the use of a home-blended herbal tea that was supposed to make their shifts last longer. While the herbs helped sustain the shifts, long-term users lost their ability to shift or pass on the trait to their children. Friar Thomas posited that the prolonged shifts "burned away" the shifters' magic prematurely. My pet theory was that the herbal concoction was toxic enough that it altered the shifters' DNA and deleted the bits that allowed them to transform. Because most of Russia seemed to be scary, why not its plants?

And if an enterprising shifter could distill those herbs into a highly concentrated serum, Friar Thomas said, he or she could take away another shifter's ability to change in one dose. And he wrote down the best process to produce this serum. So it was basically the shapeshifter version of an A-bomb, and the only copy of the recipe was in the final chapter of this book.

That recipe would give the owner considerable power. The owner could control the other shifter clans with just the threat of using this serum. Frankly, considering how much sway Friar Thomas's work had with supernatural researchers, I was afraid to tell Jane about the final chapter in any communication besides face-to-face conversation. I had pretty decent firewall protection, but you never knew who could break into your e-mail. I didn't want some random hacker guessing my incredibly complicated password and posting that mess on a subreddit somewhere. I'd only told her that there were "issues" with the final chapter that we'd need to discuss in person.

Wait.

"Do I really look like a 'huge brick of cocaine' sort of girl to you?" I demanded in my most offended tone.

He ignored the question. "It must be a pretty valuable book for the pilot to be chasing it down this hard."

"It's not really," I protested, grabbing at the plastic bag. I was tall, but he still loomed over me, holding the bag above my reach, tossing it between his hands at a rate that made me fear for the book's binding. "Sentimental value, that's about it."

"So you won't mind if I break the very carefully sealed wax you've placed around two protective plastic bags?" he said, stepping back and giving me a speculative look while tugging gently at the sides of the bag.

"No big deal," I said with a shrug, making what I hoped was a nonchalant face.

He pulled the lips of the plastic bag just enough for me to hear the wax crackle. I yelped, "No!" and dove for him. He snickered and caught me around the waist, still holding the book out of my reach while he carried me along like a squirmy messenger bag. It was insulting to see the amusement on his face as he walked, as if he did this sort of thing every day. But on the bright side, being carried took the strain off my abused feet, so I enjoyed it while I could. I crossed my arms over my chest, resolved to stay silent while he made this death march just a little easier for me.

OK, fine, I was sort of pouting.

And to be honest, it was a little embarrassing how far he was able to get when I wasn't slowing him down with my clumsy human footsteps. Over sloping hills, through thick trees, on the marshy, wet ground, we traveled at least twice the distance we had the night before, weary and wet and still in plane-related shock. And Finn's hold on my waist was constant and sure, as if he hauled around youngish ectomorphic women under his arm all the time.

What was it like to have that sort of strength? To know that you could snap a tree in half with one good kick. To know that you were capable of running at speeds invisible to the naked eye. Hell, just walking down the street at night without being afraid would be pretty awesome. Then again, Finn's sire had given superpowers to a man with the emotional capacity of a twelve-year-old.

Unable to stand the silence any longer, Finn asked, "So are you going to tell me what the hell is going on with this book? Or can I assume that it contains a tiny brick of cocaine?"

"What is it with you and cocaine?" I asked.

"Mentioning it seems to provoke a response from you."

"Fair enough," I muttered.

He turned me so I had to look up at him while he carried me. "So . . . your name is Anna Whitfield, and you are carrying this book around like it's made of valuable narcotics because . . ."

I sighed. "I'm a bibliographer."

He pulled a face. "One of those people who has sex in libraries?"

"What is *wrong* with you?" I demanded, poking him in the ribs.

"So not someone who has sex in libraries," he said, and while everything about his voice read "disappointment," he was laughing.

"I'm a book expert. In particular, I am an expert on antique books dealing with the supernatural. My client sent me this book for evaluation, and now I'm returning it to her."

"In person, so it *is* a valuable book," he said, flipping the back over so he could read the spine. Again, while carrying me like a bag of potatoes. I think the possum blood had made him cocky.

"Why would I tell you one way or the other?" I sighed.

"*A Contemplation on Shifters from the Old World and the New,*" he read, not even squinting in the dim moonlight.

"I can't comment on that."

He snorted. "A *very* valuable book."

"I didn't say that."

"You didn't need to." He wheezed. Suddenly, his grip around my middle faltered, giving me just enough wiggle room that I had time to put my feet on the ground before he dropped me. He collapsed back against a tree, propping himself up, palms against his knees. I grabbed for the bag, but he still swept it aside to where I couldn't reach it.

The rough patches of skin looked as if they'd opened back up, returning to their previous burned state. Carrying me around like people-luggage seemed to have exhausted what little energy and restoration he'd collected from the possum blood. Clearly, I was hoofing it for the rest of the evening.

"I might have overestimated the nutritional content of possum," he said. "This has never happened to me before."

"I hear it happens to a lot of guys," I said sweetly, earning myself a glare. I managed to suppress my smile. "And hey, you're still able to keep the book away from me, so you have a little strength left."

"Well, I do that just to irritate you," he said.

"And why would you do that?"

"Because it's funny. You're like a little kitten, all spitting and claws and making a big show of putting up a fight. You're adorable."

Well, now I knew where the irritating nickname came from. "I don't put on a show," I insisted. "That's how I fight . . . as far as I know. Believe it or not, that fight on the plane was my first real physical altercation with someone. Also, I fought off a knife-wielding attacker with a seat cushion. I am proud of that."

"Eh, there's a big difference between fighting and managing to survive with dumb luck. Here." He swung the book haphazardly, without looking up, nearly smacking me in the face with the plastic covering.

I grunted, glaring as I took it from his hand and shoved the book back into my purse. "A bibliographer studies and appraises antique books. I specialize in books dealing with the supernatural. And this book happens to be an old text on the origins of shapeshifters."

"Shapeshifters? Is that a thing?" he asked, screwing up his face into an expression of disbelief.

"You would know better than I, Mr. Vampire."

He scrubbed a hand over his face, his beautiful, ir-ritated face. "I still can't believe I'm on the hiking trek from hell because of a stupid book."

"It's of interest to collectors," I said, struggling to keep my tone casual.

"So how do you know it's not written by some crackpot?"

I thought about justifying the book as the work of Friar Thomas but didn't want to add any shine to it in Finn's eyes. "It's pretty straightforward for crack-pot material. It doesn't run to flights of fancy or wild tales. It reads like a genealogy, tracing the spread of shifter populations from every corner of the globe, which is, I suppose, how the book got here in the first place."

"So maybe you should try to find shifters, wherever they are, and give it to them, if they need it so much."

"Oh, no. I am going to return it to Jane, the rightful owner, and then I never want to lay eyes on it again," I said.

Finn's hands seemed to slip off his knees, and he pitched forward, almost face-planting in the dirt. He righted himself, overcorrecting and standing so quickly that he knocked his head against the tree. He hissed, rubbing his hand against his scalp. "Jane? You're going to the Hollow to meet a woman named *Jane*?"

I nodded. "Jane Jameson-Nightengale. She's a vam-pire client in Half-Moon Hollow. The book belongs to her."

If he hadn't already been paper-pale, I would swear he turned even whiter. He cleared his throat and stepped away from the tree. He didn't even bother dragging me along as he walked. "Yeah, I know Jane."

"Oh, you're a friend of hers?" I asked, snagging the spear from the ground.

"No, I said I know her."

I paused. That was disconcerting. I'd found Jane to be absolutely charming in the phone and e-mail conversations we'd had over the last month or two. Part of the reason I'd been so eager to hand-deliver the book to her—other than wanting it out of my possession and off my liability insurance—was that I wanted to meet her in person. She was funny in a sharp, quirky way cultivated by people who spent a lot of time in their own heads. She seemed like a kindred spirit, someone who would understand a life lived between the pages.

If Finn didn't like her, what did that say about Jane's true personality? Or, rather, what did it say about Finn's? But he didn't say anything more, and I didn't want to press the issue.

Finn stayed silent for another few minutes, then stopped, sagging against a nearby oak. He looked winded and miserable, like someone who'd just run a marathon through a minefield. Oh, the woes of vampire bravado.

I carefully cupped his chin in my hand and tilted his face toward the moonlight. "Is that normal, as far as sun exposure goes?"

"The burns are pretty typical." He nodded. "It would be different if I'd had human blood. I'd recover more quickly." I dropped my hand back to my waist. "I know, I know, you're not volunteering."

And for once, it was *me* pulling *him* away from the tree and dragging him in my wake. I handed the spear off to him, thinking he could use it as a walking stick. He examined it, yanking the tape loose and freeing the blade, which he handed to me. I raised my brow at this unprecedented sign of trust. If I were in his position, I would not give the closest available weapon to someone I hardly knew. What sort of vampire just handed a ten-inch blade to . . . someone he found completely nonthreatening. There was no way Finn thought I was going to come after him with the knife. This wasn't a show of trust. He was probably hoping I would trip and impale myself so he could have a guilt-free midnight snack.

"I didn't even say anything." I tucked the blade into my bag and hoped I could prevent impalement. His feet weren't exactly sluggish, but he wasn't quite as nimble as he'd been a few minutes before. He wrenched his arm loose from my grip, his tone gruff as he followed behind me.

"Yeah, but you were thinking it."

4

If there's a lesson you can take from vampires, it's "take what resources you can, when you can, even if it's in a less than ethical manner." We call this "survival of the sneakiest."

—*Where the Wild Things Bite: A Survival Guide for Camping with the Undead*

Trudging was what happened when you were too miserable and tired to want to walk but too scared to stay in one place. We knew we had to keep moving. We didn't know where Ernie was, and Finn swore that he couldn't hear or smell him following us. But as hard as Finn was working just to stay upright, I wasn't sure his senses were up to par.

I could feel my body shutting down, every movement making me ache and creak like an old woman. And to add a cherry to that particularly awful sundae, I didn't know if those symptoms were genuine exhaustion or based on not having my medications. I'd never been off them long enough to have withdrawal symptoms.

How much longer could I go without water before I did damage to my kidneys? That granola bar seemed so long ago. How much body fat did I have before I started burning off muscle?

Still, it was Finn who had become the burden between the two of us. There were times when I had to sling his arms over my shoulders to help move him along. We took too many breaks and made too little progress. The only advantage was that we were too exhausted to talk and therefore harder to track.

The silence gave me time to think. I tended to shrink in on myself when stressed, retreating into my own mind, where it was safe. I could control all of the moving pieces in my head. And while I was still watching for uneven ground and low-hanging branches, I could mull over that nagging worry in my mind. Something about this situation had bothered me since the moment Ernie abandoned the controls of the plane—something beyond the whole "life in peril" element that had become almost passé in the last twenty-four hours. How did anyone but Jane know that I had the book in the first place?

Jane had sent it to me by the usual courier service, unaware of the treasure she was shipping, but the package hadn't been tampered with when it arrived. I'd been very discreet while researching the book, as I was with any project. Surely Jane knew better than to tell people who was doing her research for her or the subject I was researching. Jane ran an occult bookstore. She knew how competitive the market could be for potentially valuable paranormal-themed texts. And

she was a Council member, so she knew how dangerous and ruthless the supernatural community could be
in general. "Cutthroat" wasn't just a metaphor to vampires. They would actually cut throats, and bellies and
any number of other parts, when they didn't get what
they wanted from vendors like me. It was the reason I
worked-slash-lived in a secure building and performed
most of my customer service online.

In my head, I catalogued all of the contacts I'd
made while researching Friar Thomas and his work. I'd
barely dropped a hint of what I was working on while
searching the online forums for academic paranormal
researchers. I'd called a historical society in Madrid for
information about Friar Thomas and his monastery of
origin, but I hadn't even mentioned his writing. Heck,
all I'd gotten out of the not entirely helpful transla-
tor was that Thomas was "encouraged to leave" his
order when his superiors found that he was "prone to
fantastical beliefs verging on lunacy." And I'd already
known that before I made the call. Friar Thomas was
considered the Matt Drudge of supernatural scholars.

I'd consulted a library in Washington, D.C., but . . .
sonofabitch. I knew that skinny, pinched-mouth clerk
was just a little too "hover-y" while I was doing my
cross-referencing. Obviously, she'd seen the book and
gotten some idea of how valuable it was and done
her own internet searching. Honestly, if you couldn't
trust librarians anymore, who could you trust? I was
so going to file a complaint on the library's customer
service page . . . if I lived long enough.

A shift in Finn's weight dragged me out of my mental composition of a scathing complaint letter. He was practically sagging to his knees, he was so tired, his head lolling to the side. I couldn't keep this up for much longer. I couldn't carry his weight and mine, and I didn't know how to hunt for something to feed him. If we could just stop for a while and rest long enough for Finn to recover fully from his burns, maybe he'd gain enough strength to hunt something more nutritionally fulfilling than possum.

I squinted, taking in our surroundings for the first time in several hours. I'd been so focused on the next rise, the next rock, the next tree root, that I literally hadn't seen the landscape for the trees. We were skirting around a sort of ravine separating two huge limestone outcroppings. The chasm was deep, and I couldn't make out the bottom, but that wasn't saying much, considering the darkness. But there were trees growing tall enough that I could see the top branches waving in the breeze like black-green lace fans, so I assumed there *was* a bottom. The outcropping on our side seemed to go on forever, and I couldn't see us getting around it anytime soon. Trying would just exhaust us even further.

But just a few yards away, I saw a dark spot in the very bottom of the rock. I gently lowered Finn to the ground and let him rest against a tree while I investigated. The dark spot was a hole, a sort of mini-cave, just deep enough for both of us to crawl in and be sheltered from the sun but not so large that it could shelter a bear or something. It wouldn't solve the hunger or thirst issues or the fact that I would probably emerge from the mini-cave covered in ten different kinds of exotic fungus. But we would be able to rest for a while without threat of Finn's impending immolation.

He crawled into the opening and collapsed on the ground. I would have to drag him farther into the recess to shield him from the sun, but this was enough for now. And I could make out his features in the dim light and monitor how he was doing. I wasn't ashamed of curling into him. He didn't have body heat, but he seemed to absorb and retain mine, making him a sort of tepid water bottle. And it was reassuring, knowing that he was there in the darkness of the trees, that he hadn't left me.

Through the night, I kept expecting to wake up and find him gone, the book gone. I had reason not to trust Finn, but I wanted to believe that his promises were genuine. He'd had several chances to take the book already. I wanted to believe that if he was going to take it, he would have done it by now. Instead, he'd slowed down on the mockery. He'd taken my needs into account. Hell, he'd offered me his exsanguinated possum. Either we were trauma bonding, or Finn wasn't the selfish flirt I'd thought him on the plane.

Finn stirred. His lips were curled back from his teeth, and his fangs had eased out of his gumline. I'd never seen fangs up close. They were sort of beautiful in an odd, animalistic way, white and sharp and inherently threatening. I touched my fingertip to them, like Sleeping Beauty unable to resist pressing her fingertip to the spindle. I felt the sharp press against my skin, splitting the tissue open cell by cell. His lips moved ever so slightly, and I jerked my hand back as if burned.

This was crazy. He could kill me, easily. He could decide that it wasn't worth dragging me along when I was a ready source of blood. He could decide to take the book, now that I'd told him what it was—like an *idiot*. (I could only blame low blood sugar for that decision. Honestly.) He could just lose his grip on his instincts and sink his teeth into my neck. And I didn't have any disinfectant handy. I'd probably end up with vampire-bite gangrene.

A tiny drop of blood formed on my skin, like a ruby glistening in the moonlight. I squeezed my finger, and the droplet grew. I watched it run along the skin of my finger and drop onto the ground and immediately regretted the waste. Finn could have used that.

I glanced down at my travel companion. I couldn't do much for myself. I couldn't magically produce water. I couldn't eat my purse or the precious book inside. (Pretty sure the binding was poisonous.) Hell, I couldn't even come up with more comfortable shoes. But I could do something to make Finn's life a little easier.

I just hoped it didn't get me killed.

Grimacing, I pressed my injured finger against his fang and pushed harder, opening the wound ever so slightly. I pulled it back again, just in case the presence of blood woke him up and made him lunge for me. I held my hand inches over his face and let the blood drip over his lips. Nothing. No lunging. His tongue edged out, licking at the tiny bits of sustenance. It felt like I was teasing him, taunting a predator with hints of food without actually giving him something he could survive on.

I squeezed again, easing my fingertip against his lips, ringing the soft skin lightly. His mouth closed over my flesh, drawing weakly against the wound and pulling a bit of blood into his mouth. He groaned in a desperate relief that made my knees feel odd and jellied.

I sat back on my heels, waiting for his eyes to pop open and for him to pounce on me like a raging lion. But he didn't lunge. He didn't bite down on my hand. I didn't know if that was because he was unconscious or just so weak he couldn't move.

His tongue ran up and down the pad of my finger, coaxing more blood from me. The cool suction, combined with the contented purring noises he was making, made a peculiar warmth gather in my belly. He took long pulls from the digit, increasing in strength. Those sensations echoed through my middle, thrumming between my thighs as he drank me down.

I watched as his body relaxed, as the rough patches of skin went smooth and whole. All of that from just a few drops of my blood? Was human blood really that much more nutritious to vampires than animal blood?

I eased my finger out of his mouth ever so slightly, and his head followed, rising from the ground to continue feeding. That throbbing pull swelled, and I had to rub my thighs together to ease the ache. And despite the fact that I hadn't had one in a while, I realized I was on the verge of having an orgasm. In a cave. With a vampire. Sucking on my finger.

Nope. Nope. Nope.

Wincing, I tugged my hand free of his mouth. Finn released it with a wet, slightly obscene *pop*, and I tucked it against my chest. I watched him warily as I scooted as far away as possible. He didn't move. But he looked better than he had when he'd flopped down on the rocky soil. He looked more relaxed and peaceful, though, technically, he was still dead.

I laid my head down, using my purse as a pillow. I wasn't sure if I'd done a smart thing, making him stronger. But it seemed wrong to let him suffer, when he'd ignored his instincts and left my neck alone.

Of course, I was still miserable. Still hungry, still thirsty, still sore. Also sort of weirded out that I'd basically gotten off on finger-feeding an unconscious man. That was a new one for me. I wasn't even sure what part was more disturbing, the feeding or the fact that my nipples were still achy and stiff.

I closed my eyes. I just wanted to drift off into a dark, soft place where I wasn't thirsty or hungry or in pain. I would dream of sandwiches thick with turkey and avocado and bacon on grilled sourdough. I would dream of a coconut cake the size of a manhole cover and swimming in a lake made of melted chocolate. I would dream of Finn's long, piano player's fingers dragging great swipes of raspberry coulis up my neck and dribbling it into my mouth.

I wouldn't think about that now. I was going full-on Scarlett O'Hara. I would think about it tomorrow.

I dozed, fitful, waiting to hear the crunch of footsteps approaching the cave, for Finn to launch himself across the space and finish his meal. Or, at least, it felt like dozing. But I must have slept for some time, because it was very dark when I woke up to find Finn gone.

Just gone.

Gasping, I snaked my hands up over my head to feel for my bag. It was there. I could even feel the rectangular shape of the book inside the leather, along with the solid weight of the knife. I jerked up, nearly whacking my head against the rock ceiling. The little cave was empty, and the silence—whether from the shock of waking up alone or the lack of Finn's mocking chatter—was deafening. My hands shook as I pulled the bag around my shoulder, giving me something to cling to.

He'd left me, just walked away and left me alone in the woods with an angry pilot lurking nearby. And even more shocking, I wasn't angry. I was hurt, truly and deeply, in a way I hadn't expected. I knew we weren't exactly bosom companions, but I thought we'd built some sort of tentative trust. I'd half carried his ass through the woods. Hell, I'd let the man drink from my finger! I'd let Finn beyond boundaries I kept up to protect myself from this sort of hurt. And he'd hurt me anyway.

Maybe this was the low blood sugar doing the thinking for me, but I thought I actually felt my heart crack a bit.

I flopped down on the ground and gave myself permission to lie there and be crushed and miserable about this unexpected betrayal for thirty seconds. Thirty seconds of abject self-pity, and then I would haul myself to my feet and get moving. I closed my eyes and pictured all of the horrible things that could happen to me wandering through the woods alone.

Ernie could catch up with me. I could wander off a cliff in the dark. I could be attacked by a wolf. They had wolves in Kentucky, right? Starvation, dehydration, poison ivy, broken limbs, attacks from an undiscovered tribe of mutated backwoods mole people. I let every potentially deadly outcome flit through my brain until some perverse impulse made me picture them happening to Finn instead. I imagined Finn in the gullet of a wolf. I imagined Finn wandering off the cliff because he was just so busy thinking about how awesome and clever he was. I pictured Finn crawling through the woods, knowing the sun was about to rise and he had no shelter, whispering, "I never should have left Anna alone. I regret so much."

Apparently, I had a vicious streak when I was hangry.

And that was thirty seconds done. I pressed the heels of my hands into my eyes and took a deep breath. Should I just stay put and wait until morning to start moving? The obvious advantage was that I would be able to see where the hell I was going and avoid the poison ivy and angry forest creatures. The disadvantage was that it would also make it that much easier for Ernie to see me. And it would put me out in the woods for that much longer, meaning I would get that much more dehydrated and hungry.

My feet, which burned and ached all at once, were going to hurt either way. And abrasions were probably going to get infected, which would make them hurt even worse, but honestly, dying of starvation would be decidedly worse than foot owies.

"OK," I told myself. "You've had a really rough start to your evening. But you're going to slide out of this cave, and you're going to walk through this stupid fricking forest, and you're going to deliver this fricking book. You're going to buy a brick of Xanax the size of a cinder block. You're going to sue that airline for everything it's worth for hiring a psychopath for its night shift flights. And then you're going to file a complaint with the Council and report that one of their undead citizens is a coward who abandons perfectly nice ladies in the woods. And *then* you're going to eat an enormous steak the size of your head. Right. Good plan."

I felt a hand on my shoulder. I yelped and swatted the fingers away. Finn was hovering over me, his face inches from my own. I thought I would hit him. (Or I would try really hard.) I thought I'd yell or cry or try to poke him in the eye. But I didn't. Because he hadn't left. He hadn't abandoned me to wander off a cliff or end up in a wolf's digestive tract. He'd come back for me. And I knew that didn't mean he was a good person. I knew that didn't mean I could trust him entirely. But that didn't matter right now, because he'd come back.

Finn snorted, sounding much more like himself. "Don't worry, kitten. I'm not going to bite."

"Sorry," I croaked, rolling my shoulders and wincing against the throb of pain radiating through my head. Was it dehydration, exhaustion from switching to a nocturnal schedule, or a plain old stress migraine?

Dealer's choice. "It's not a vampire thing. It's a being barely awake and finding someone just a few inches from my face thing."

"No offense taken. You snore, by the way."

"I do not!" I huffed, sitting up as much as the rock would allow. "I am a delicate flower."

Finn snickered. "Oh, yes. Delicate flowers are known for dirty cheeks and third-day clothes."

"Hey, when I have access to water and grooming supplies, I am a solid seven," I grumbled. Before Finn could offer me false protests and assurances, I asked, "How are you feeling?"

"Better," he said, sounding surprised as he smacked his lips. He eyed me speculatively. "Less like the walking dead. Not so hungry."

"Maybe you just needed some rest," I replied, with as little guile as possible.

"Maybe."

I rubbed my eyes and tried to ignore the horrible taste of grit and thirst on my tongue. I could only imagine how bad my breath was right now. My kingdom for a Tic Tac. "What time is it?"

"Not sure. The sun set a while ago, gave me a chance to scout around. And I found this in an old deer stand about a mile away. Here, come out into the moonlight."

We scooted out from under the rock, and I saw that he was holding something in his hands, a bag. He reached into it and held an object to my lips before I recognized it as a water bottle. I gasped, taking a huge gulp.

It was amazing how excited and grateful I felt at the mere thought of a drink of water. I didn't care what brand it was, how it had been filtered, or how it had been stored. I just wanted it inside my body. This was how mismatched people ended up trauma-bonded after disasters, I thought. If Finn had brought me something with bubbles, I probably would have performed explicit favors for him involving feathers and chocolate pudding.

Despite being lukewarm, the water was ambrosial against my parched throat, clean and wet and heavenly. I wanted to weep in relief, but that would only waste the hydration I was taking in. It took some serious mental effort to pull the bottle away from my mouth.

"You take some," I said, pressing the bottle into his hand.

"I'm all right," he said. "Water isn't as important for me as blood. And I can get that again at some point tonight. Drink up."

I nodded, drinking a few more sips before giving him the bottle. "Take it before I drink it all. I need to make it last."

He grinned and held it to my lips again. "I don't think that will be a problem."

I dutifully drained the entire contents of the bottle, so full now that I felt like I was sloshing. "My night just got infinitely better. Thank you, Finn."

"So giving you these would be an embarrassment of riches, huh?" he asked, presenting a pair of old brown canvas work boots.

"Oh, my God!" I cried. I threw my arms around him

and buried my face in his neck and squeezed him tight, deodorant be damned. "Thank you! Thank you! Thank you! I have never been so excited to get such an ugly pair of shoes!"

And through ugly-shoe denial, I could just pretend the whole finger-sucking incident had never happened.

"Oh, all right, then," Finn said, slowing wrapping his arms around my shoulders. "Do we hug now?"

"Yes," I whimpered into his neck, my voice muffled against his skin.

"Are you OK?" he asked, patting my back.

I nodded. "Uh-huh."

A long, awkward moment of silence passed, and my face was still buried against his neck.

Finn chuckled into my hair. "If I had known I would have gotten this sort of response, I would have given you cast-off hunter's boots much sooner."

I snatched them from his hands. They were too big, even for my long, narrow feet, but they were still better suited to the terrain than my ballet flats. And they would protect me all the way up to my shins, which was definitely a plus.

"I don't want to think about who might have worn these before me," I said, shuddering as I laced up the left boot. "I can only hope they don't have toe fungus."

"I wouldn't worry about fungus," he said, shrugging. "Spiders. Spiders I would worry about."

"Why? Why would you say that?" I cried, tossing the right boot (and its potential arachnid inhabitants) behind us, against the rock ledge. It bounced off the limestone with a *thunk*. He chuckled and took the left boot from my foot. "Have something else to drink, kitten. I'll check your boots for spiders."

And it seemed we were back to "kitten." I think I preferred "doll." There was a certain prewar charm to "doll." He produced another bottle from his magical bag, something yellow called Ale-8-One.

"I don't think I need to drink beer right now," I told him, shaking my head as he smacked my boots repeatedly against the rocks, beating any potential spider squatters senseless. It was possibly the most romantic thing a man had ever done for me. And that was just freaking sad. "That's what gets people into trouble when they're hypothermic. They drink, thinking the alcohol will warm them up, but it just thins their blood and dehydrates them."

"First of all, it's sort of horrifying that you can remember that when you're practically keeling over from dehydration, you stubborn woman. And second, this isn't a beer. It's a soda. Some regional favorite they only produce around here. And yes, I checked the label. It's not expired. You need the blood sugar, doll, come on."

Yay, I was "doll" again. Also, if he managed to find pudding and feathers, I was probably in big trouble.

I squinted at the label and saw that it indeed stated that the beverage was a soft drink. I shrugged and took a sip, wincing at the odd gingery-lemon taste, which was exacerbated by the warmth of the bottle. I smacked my lips around the mouthful, sighing and drinking more when Finn tipped the bottle toward my mouth. It wasn't so bad, I supposed, when you drank it fast. And I could already feel the surge of sugar flowing through my system.

Finn knelt in front of me, removed a little first-aid kit from the bag, and dabbed at the worst of my blisters with an antiseptic wipe. And while my inner germophobe appreciated the gesture, damn, that burned. He carefully bandaged my damaged feet and eased them into the boots, lacing them tight around my ankles. His hands lingered on my shins as he took stock of my face.

"Better?" he asked.

I nodded. "What about you? Aren't you thirsty?"

"I'll take care of it later. Now, can you walk?"

I glanced down at my feet, wondering if the boots would make the blister situation better or worse. But the blood sugar from the soda did indeed make me feel like Popeye after a round of canned spinach. I nodded. "I think so."

I hopped to my feet and did a few test steps. Even without socks, the boots were still more comfortable than the flats. Finn held my hand, spinning me as I did a little turn.

"You go first," he said, jerking his head toward the . . . well, butt-load of trees.

"Don't look at my butt," I grumbled.

"But how will I ensure your safety if I don't keep a close watch on you?" he asked, his tone saccharine and innocent.

"You could enjoy this less, you know." I snorted, my eyes adjusting to the darkness as we walked.

"But why would I want to?"

"So you found a deer blind, all the way out here? Is it even legal to have a hunting blind out here? This is state land."

"I'm not sure about the legalities of sniping deer on taxpayer property, but if it makes you feel better, I did liberate the poacher's supplies," he said, handing me the bag. "So let that be a lesson to them."

I opened the bag and angled it toward the moon so I could make out a few more bottles of Ale-8, a half-empty bottle of Wild Turkey, plus several bottles of water, saltine crackers, and some dusty cans of dubious origin.

"What exactly is potted meat?" he asked, picking up one of the cans and examining the label.

"You don't want to know." I shuddered, remembering my dad's recipes for convenient field meals.

"There are enough preservatives in this can to keep this 'fresh' until kingdom come," I said, checking the expiration date on the can, which was still three years away. I couldn't use my health anxieties as an excuse to avoid the meat, because, technically, it was edible. By the strictest definitions of human food. "Because who would want to lose the opportunity to eat a nummy treasure like this?"

"I have a feeling I want to be in the next county when you open that can."

"Wait until you read the list of ingredients," I told him, breaking open the package of crackers. I stuffed several in my mouth as we walked. The sensation of food hitting my tongue seemed odd and foreign, and the crackers stuck to my dry tongue. But I diligently filled my cheeks and then drank enough water to wash them down.

"Feel better?" he asked, as I nodded, chipmunk cheeks be damned.

"Maybe later on the potted meat," I said, sticking the cans in the bag.

"Probably the right choice," he said. "It couldn't be worse than the possum, though."

"I accept my position as the slower, weaker, and less-willing-to-eat-mystery-meat person on this hike from hell."

"You're human. It's not a fair comparison. You're never going to be as fast as I am, unless I turn you."

Around another cracker, my voice was garbled. "Was that a ham-handed shortcut to asking whether I want to become a vampire?"

"Well, considering the peril we've experienced over the last day or so, it's not a completely absurd question. Consider it a precautionary gesture. Obviously, you're into that sort of thing. Having all of the information, so you know what to do."

I could appreciate that he had figured out that bit of my personality. But I'd barely figured out how I felt about Ale-8. I wasn't able to make a huge decision like "Eternal Life: Pro or Con?" at the moment.

"No. For right now, that is not something I am interested in. It's not that I think vampires are horrible or anything," I insisted. "I just don't know enough about you or your lifestyle to make a decision one way or another. I don't think I'd make a very good vampire."

"I think you'd make an excellent vampire," he told

me, grinning broadly as he tapped the Ale-8, reminding me to keep drinking. "You're tenacious and relatively sneaky."

"Thank you."

"And vicious when you have to be."

I protested, "I'm not vicious!"

"Says the girl who has repeatedly threatened someone with a knife right in front of me."

I poked my finger into his face, which he did not
seem to appreciate, given the way he sneered at it.
"OK, for the record, it was the same someone on each
of those occasions. And I was defending myself, and
you, I might add, because you weren't doing anything
to help."

"On the second occasion, I was too busy curled up
on the ground in the fetal position, smoking and slowly
dissolving into ash," he told me. "Because you wan-
dered away, during daylight hours. After I asked you
not to."

"Those pauses are unnecessary," I told him.

"Not when dealing with your level of righteous in-
dignation."

Stuffing more delicious, salty carbs into my mouth,
I opened my bag and checked on the book. It was
safe. And I was eating for the first time since that my
granola bar. For the moment, life was good.

"We should keep moving," I told him. "I'm hydrated,
and I have food in my belly. We should take advantage
of that while we can. It's not like we were going to
do some *Swiss Family Robinson* thing and stay here
long-term."

"You are one big ray of sunshine, aren't you, kitten?"

"I'm just saying, we shouldn't waste our time building a giant water wheel and pirate traps," I told him.

"I just wanted a little rest before we started trekking," he grumbled.

"Oh, poor darling," I cooed, patting his shoulder.

"Don't patronize me," he chided me in a strident tone that was clearly meant to be some sort of impersonation.

"That sounds nothing like me," I told him. "And I wasn't going to patronize you. I was going to tell you to suck it up."

"I think I like it better when you patronize me."

"Trust me, you wouldn't."

5

~~

Much like in space, in the woods, no one can hear your embarrassing confessions that will ultimately bond you together with your vampire companion.

—Where the Wild Things Bite: A Survival Guide for Camping with the Undead

It turns out that there was a profound level of hunger I had to reach before I could eat potted meat, and I had not hit it yet. I already felt bloated and sloshy from consuming a dozen saltines and two bottles of liquid. I felt bloated and sloshy but absolutely at peace.

Unfortunately, that peace was short-lived. My body processed those drinks pretty quickly, and almost as soon as I'd finished the second bottle, my bladder protested mightily.

I made a sudden break for the trees, startling Finn, who was still staring out into the distance, trying to pick up on lights or signs or Ernie's white pilot's shirt. He caught my wrist, and the strength of his grip made me wince. He loosened his hold immediately, his expression softening. "Where are you going?"

"Uh, all of that nature is calling me." I realized that in my urgency to leave, I'd shoved my bag and the hunter's supplies into his hands. The fact that I could part with my bag, even mentally, after all I'd been through to keep it, bothered me.

Had I really let my guard down around Finn that much? I mean, yes, I knew that I trusted him a little more than I had the moment he'd thrown me out of the plane. The fact that he hadn't abandoned me when he had the chance spoke well for him, but there was so much I didn't know about him, so much he'd avoided telling me. And deep down, even after the plane crash and the starvation and the blisters, I was still the same girl from the real world who hadn't been on a date in almost a year because she had trouble trusting strange men without a background check.

"Well, you're not going alone."

"I wasn't expecting to," I told him. My need overran my concern about tripping, and I made for the nearest tree.

"Stay over there!" I whispered, unbuttoning my jeans.

"Wouldn't dream of violating your space right now," he swore.

"And hum or something," I told him. "Stupid vampire superhearing."

I addressed the problem with as much dignity as possible and returned to where Finn was waiting.

"Don't say a word," I told him, taking my bag back and dropping to the ground beside him.

He shook his head. "Wasn't going to. You've seen me eat a possum. I am now aware that you have functioning internal organs. Moments like this are going to come up when two people are stuck out here with no barriers or filters . . . except the enormous walls that you throw up around yourself like a force field."

"What?"

"I'm just saying that after surviving a plane crash and sleeping in various weird outdoor locations with you, I know absolutely nothing concrete about you, other than that your name is Anna and you don't have sex in libraries."

"You are not going to let that one go, are you?"

"Oh, come on, not even once, during your wild college days?"

I yawned and plopped my head back down on the ground. "You have listened to me while I've spoken, right?"

"You'd be surprised what I hear when you speak," he muttered. "Come on, this will go easier if we get to know each other a little bit better. Where are you from?"

"Where are *you* from?" I countered.

"Where-are-you-from? That's a strange-sounding place. Is it in Canada?"

"I live near Atlanta," I told him, rolling my eyes.

"You don't sound like you're from Georgia," he noted. "I thought Georgia accents were supposed to be all peaches and custard. You are decidedly peach-less."

"I'm from Virginia originally. And you?"

"Cleveland."

I snorted. Of all of the exotic origin stories I'd expected, the dashing vampire from Cleveland had not even entered my mind. Somehow a childhood in Cleveland just didn't live up to the "lonely soul trekking through history" hype, even if he'd been born in colonial Cleveland. "And *when* are you from?"

"I was born in the early forties."

I snorted again, closing my eyes.

"What's with the horse noises?" he asked, shaking my foot.

"I don't know. It's kind of disappointing. You know, you think vampires, and you think of a lone figure standing in front of an ancient Romanian castle, his cape blowing in the wind. Not pulling a little Radio Flyer wagon around Cleveland."

"I lived through a world war!" he protested.

"When you were a toddler."

"You get cranky when you're faced with starvation."

"Right back at you," I told him. "So what do you do for a living?"

He didn't answer. I supposed I'd touched a nerve, mocking his Cleveland roots. So I asked, a bit more gently, "Do you do anything for a living? Vampires do have to earn a living, right?"

"Let's talk about something else."

"No. I think I want to know," I said, gasping suddenly, as if seized by a brilliant discovery. "Are you a stripper?"

He burst out laughing, and I felt a little better about pressing him into this conversational corner. "No."

Under my breath, I said, "You've got the body."

I wanted to clap my hand over my mouth, but that would have tipped Finn off to exactly how embarrassed I was to have let that little gem spill from my lips. But honestly, who could blame me?

A man who looked like Finn knew how good-looking he was, even in our current frazzled state. A man didn't walk around like he did, with the flirty smirk and the deep V-necks, without some idea of how he affected the women in his path. But he didn't need to know that *I* was (profoundly, pathetically) aware of how good-looking he was. He certainly didn't need to know that I'd almost come apart just letting him slide my finger in and out of his mouth. So I clenched my arms, forcing them to stay at my sides in what I hoped looked like a relaxed pose, and pretended I'd just made some smartass joke.

"But to my everlasting shame, I don't have the musicality." Smirking all the while, he pressed his hands over his silent heart, as if to mourn his lost potential in pole work. I laughed, and he asked, "Can we talk about you for a minute?"

"You already know what I do for a living, which is not having sex in libraries."

"It's a deep personal disappointment to me. Plus, you make funny faces when I mention it."

"What else do you want to know?"

"Why did you move to Atlanta?"

"It was close enough to the contacts I'd developed but far enough away that . . ." I trailed off. The stupid fatigue and hunger had my mouth running off at all kinds of inconvenient speeds. I would much rather wax poetic about Finn and his lickable collarbone than disgorge my parental issues to someone who would have little to no interest. Because if I had to bet on

Finn's level of "giving a damn," I was coming down hard on the side of "no interest."

"Your mother, huh?"

I glared at him. "I thought you said you couldn't read minds."

He shrugged. "I can't. I just figured someone who is as organized and neurotic as you has to have problems with one parent. And your responses aren't quite right for a girl with daddy issues."

I rolled toward him, eyes narrowed. He was right, I supposed. It was difficult to develop daddy issues when your mother's personality was so overwhelming. "Are you saying you've been *trying* to poke my 'daddy issue' buttons?"

He could have at least feigned guilt as he pursed his lips, letting his eyes slide down my frame as if he was searching for those buttons at this very moment. But sadly, he didn't bother. "Occasionally."

"You, sir, are a horrible individual."

He scoffed. "Come on, I needed to know what sort of girl I was doing the forest death march with, didn't I? I needed to know how to motivate you properly if you started to slow down."

"So now that you know, why do you even care about the rest of my background?"

"Is it so hard to believe I'm just curious about you?"

I paused for a second before throwing my hands up. "Yes!"

"Well, the fact that you won't tell me just makes me more curious. But on a less defensive topic, how did you get into the not-having-sex-in-libraries business?"

"How is that supposed to make me *less* defensive?" I asked him.

He slung an arm around my shoulders. "Come on, tell me something about yourself. Something important to you."

I was lost. He was so close, and it felt good to be near someone who could possibly understand how scared and uncertain and uncomfortable I was. I closed my eyes, and he ran his hand along my arm, making it relax underneath his touch.

I sighed. "I studied library science and classic literature in college. I got a student position at the college library, something my mother only allowed because work hours in the library were required for my major. And it was definitely expected that I finish my degree. I wasn't very good at working with the public, as you can imagine—too many people making too many demands, and the books were always so filthy when they came back in the return. I went through a bottle of hand sanitizer a week, and my sinuses . . ." I let loose a small shudder, which made Finn smile. "Because my father was a faculty member, they let me work in the special collections, where the public rarely visited because the books were so rare we didn't loan them out. There was this big box of battered old books in the storage closet that no one had bothered to catalogue because they were in such bad condition. The library had just accepted the donation from an alumna's family and forgotten about them. My boss told me to throw them out, without telling anyone, but as I was breaking down the box, I noticed a name scrawled on the inside front page of one of the journals. U.S. Army Lieutenant Randall Tenney. I recognized it, because my father had spent quite a bit of time researching Tenney, who served as an aide-de-camp to Robert E. Lee, right up until Gettysburg, where he'd disappeared off the battlefield, never to be heard from or seen again. My father spent years trying to track down what happened to him, going through eyewitness accounts and field-hospital records. It was frustrating to him, not being able to prove what happened to someone who should have been safe, back at the administrative camp, someone who was well known among the men and should have been noticed when he went missing. But he never found anything."

"That's not all that unusual," Finn told me. "Vampires are always attracted to battlegrounds, particularly epic battles. The noise, the chaos, the bloodshed. Who's going to notice that a few soldiers among thousands go missing?"

"Well, what was unusual was the dates scrawled across the front page of this book. August 1863, a month after Gettysburg, to May 1883, twenty years after Gettysburg. I stopped what I was doing and started reading through the book, which was no small feat, I tell you, trying to read that spidery, cramped handwriting on pages so delicate I thought they'd crumble in my hands. And you're right, vampires were attracted to the Battle of Gettysburg. The diary entries were all written by Tenney, who stated that vampires were picking soldiers from both armies off the field as soon as the sun set. He tried to help a wounded man back to camp and was bitten for his troubles. He woke up three days later, feeling as if he'd failed Lee, failed the South, and deserted, however accidentally. And he couldn't go back to the Confederacy as a vampire, so he gave up and moved out west. I approached the World Council's local office, near my college, and asked them to contact Tenney for me, to let him know that I'd found his diary and ask if he wanted it back, and he did. He even traveled to Richmond to reclaim it from the Council office. I didn't go to meet him, of course, I was too intimidated, but he wrote me a lovely thank-you note and sent my father a full accounting of what happened to him on the battlefield."

"What did your father think of that?"

"He looked at me differently afterward," I told him. "It was like he saw me as a person for the first time, not as his child or some problem that my mother needed to deal with, but a person who had potential, someone he could treat like an equal. He talked to me, took an interest in my studies. I don't know if he was thrilled with the subject matter I had become interested in, but the fact that I'd solved a puzzle he couldn't? It made a big difference to him. And I couldn't get enough of the special collections after that. It was like everything we knew in the history books was, well, not wrong but just sort of a top layer of icing on a deeper, richer cake." At the mere mention of cake, my stomach growled, and I groaned. Finn chuckled and commenced rubbing his hand along my arm again to distract me.

"There was this whole second layer of history that

happened in the shadows that humans weren't even aware existed. And if I was learning about that history, I wasn't just building on the work of other students and teachers who had tumbled over those events ad nauseam, but I was discovering something new, something unknown. It was fascinating and exciting, and I loved it. I got my master's degree in historical literature and wrote my thesis on the movements of vampires throughout Europe to avoid the dangers of the Inquisition, using diaries and Council records to verify my theories. I learned to deal politely with the undead, using e-mail and the Internet as a protective filter. And then I went to work on my doctoral thesis."

I closed my eyes and stilled my hands. I hadn't even realized I was wringing them, cracking and twisting my fingers just so I had something to do with all of the nervous energy gathering in my body. This was the hard part. The years of my life I didn't like to talk about, not even with my therapist, when I could effectively deflect. The final ugly break from my mother. My father's death, so soon after I'd finally started building some sort of relationship with him. Michael's betrayal and the loss of my work, my reputation in academia. The years that had—however temporarily—derailed my life.

"So I should be calling you Dr. Kitten?" Finn prodded me. "Somehow I like that even more."

"No, I ended up not completing the program," I said, pulling away from Finn's touch, tucking my chin against my chest, and wrapping my arms around myself to fight off the chill that crept up my spine.

"Really?"

I tried to sound nonchalant about it, like the loss of my PhD didn't bother me in the slightest, like it wasn't something my mother held over my head as proof that I couldn't make it all by myself after all. "Mm-hmmm."

"What stopped you?"

"Nothing, I just didn't finish," I told him. "Now, can we talk about you for a while? I think I've earned a couple of answers from you now, Finn."

He eyed me for a long time and nodded. I pulled out my bottle of water. Sipping with one hand, I did a sort of "you may proceed" gesture. He cleared his throat. "I was born in the forties. I had a relatively normal childhood. Grew up in the suburbs of Cleveland. I had a good buddy, Max, who I stuck with through thick and thin. Postwar America was the land of opportunity, lots of cash flowing around for people smart enough to grab a hold of it."

"What does that mean, exactly?"

"Not important," he said, shaking his head.

"Seems important."

"Our undefined system worked pretty well until the seventies. We contracted with a vampire who did not have a sense of humor about us not being able to deliver some product he'd 'ordered' from another vampire's warehouse. The vampire wanted us to have enough time to pay him off, so Max and I got turned."

"Just like that?" I asked. Now that I had some insight into Finn's background, his obnoxious kitten-based nicknames, the relatively chivalrous manners, hell, his insistence that he was right simply by nature of possessing fangs *and* a penis, made a lot more sense. I was dealing with 1950s *Ozzie and Harriet* sensibilities.

"Well, I'm sparing you some pretty terrifying details, but yeah, I wasn't going to let my friend wander through eternity alone. But it worked out OK for him. He ended up having a daughter before he was turned. Because we were still in the coffin, he missed a lot of her growing up, but he, uh, reconnected with her recently. He's getting to know her and her son, his grandson, something I tease *Grandpa* Max about mercilessly whenever I get the chance."

"And what did his daughter think of her dad just showing up after all those years?"

"It was complicated," he admitted, frowning. "But Libby's a very sweet girl. Forgiving. And she wants to have a relationship with Max, so that's a good sign, I think."

"Who was your sire?"

"Not a nice person, and let's just leave it at that."

"And have you ever turned anyone?" I asked. He didn't respond. "I am going to interpret your pregnant silence as a yes."

The silence went way past its due date before he spoke. "It's complicated. I liked her, quite a bit."

"And to thank you for giving her eternal life without wrinkle cream, she gave you the 'let's just be friends' talk?"

"Something like that." Finn's lips quirked, and I could tell that he was holding in a laugh. "I thought we were headed in the non–'just friends' direction, and for once, I wanted that. I wanted something long-term, maybe even permanent, for the first time in a long while. But she couldn't take the way I edited the information I gave her. She didn't accept my . . ." He trailed off, miles away for a moment.

"Your pauses are becoming suspicious."

"You find everything suspicious."

"True enough," I admitted.

"Have you ever loved anyone?"

"Definitely not."

"Spoken like someone who has been hurt in that fashion humans find so dramatic and humiliating," he said, making me gasp. "Is that why you find me so objectionable? Because I remind you of the idiot who clearly wounded your psyche for life?"

"I-I don't find you—I didn't—objectionable," I stuttered. "And you don't remind me of the idiot—who was not actually an idiot but a very intelligent doctoral student. So intelligent, in fact, that he figured out how to earn that doctorate without doing any original work."

"So now I'm objectionable *and* stupid," he said, rolling his eyes.

"You're not stupid, not at all. You're just—you—"

"Come on, kitten, spit it out, you haven't had any problems insulting me before."

I blew a frustrated breath through clenched teeth. "You're charming in a way I find completely offensive. You don't think a girl like me knows what it means when you smile and turn on the charm? It means you're five seconds away from asking for money or trying to sell me something."

"What do you mean, a girl like you?" he asked. When I made a skeptical face, he added, "You have to know you're gorgeous, right?"

I snorted derisively, because no, I did not "know" that. "I'm just saying, I'm sure I'm not your type."

"How about you let me decide what my type is, thanks very much, and I don't appreciate the insinuation that I'm some shameless, shallow dick," he retorted.

I bit my lip to keep from snickering, making him add, "OK, fine, but I'm not shameless or shallow."

I lifted an eyebrow. He jostled my arm, and I lost my grip on a full-on guffaw.

"OK, I'm not shallow," he said, and before I could respond, he added, "Don't lift your eyebrow again, woman."

Still giggling, I pillowed my head against my arm, blinking against the growing weight of my eyelids. "I'm sorry. I'm rude to you."

"Consistently," he noted. "You are *consistently* rude to me."

"I tend to react that way to strong personalities," I told him. "To people I think might try too hard to influence me or flatter me. I get . . ."

"Cranky? Snappish? Defensive to the point of pathology?"

"True enough again." I sighed.

"And—as the target of said pathology—can I ask why?"

"I mentioned before," I said, stopping to yawn. He shifted me toward his body, letting me rest against his side. "My father was a highly respected academic. He taught Civil War history and strategy, even consulted at West Point a few times. He traveled . . . a lot, to different Civil War battle sites to do research, give lectures, that sort of thing. Which left me alone with my mother. She was, well, polite Southern people call it 'high strung.' Everything was a trial. Everything was high drama. I didn't know that it was unusual. I didn't spend enough time in other kids' houses to see how their moms behaved."

"Other kids? Not 'friends'?"

"I didn't have time for friends, too much 'helping' at home," I said.

"What about your father?"

"I don't really think he cared as long as he could continue his work without being bothered. He wasn't really what you would call a hands-on parent, other than making sure that I had all of the right paperwork filled out when it came time to apply for college."

"How did your mom handle that?"

"Oh, sure, she was all for me attending college, but I had to attend the school where my father taught, and I had to live at home. It was to save money, she told me. But, honestly, she didn't want me to leave. She wanted me to get my little useless degree so she could at least claim that I was a college graduate when people asked—I mean, we were a family of *academics*. We did have standards to maintain—but then she wanted me to stay home.

"And I almost let her do it, that's what scares me the most. I totally bought into the idea that the world was out to get me. I was terrified of everything. Shopping at night, because it meant crossing a parking lot alone in the dark. Ordering something over the Internet, because I was handing my address and credit card information over to a stranger. Learning to drive long distances alone, which was a constant exercise in my mother calling me every five minutes to make sure I wasn't dead in a ditch somewhere. I read every survival book and worst-case-scenario guide I could get, so when my mother started asking me what if, I had an answer for her. I told myself if I knew what to do, it couldn't be that bad. It became a habit."

"I was wondering how you knew all of the plane-crash information."

I closed my eyes, shrugging. "Habit."

"Do you see her often?"

"Not in . . . three years, maybe? My father's funeral. I was traveling, trying to make it home in time, but she didn't tell me the service plans until the very last minute, and I missed it. Which made me look like a horrible, uninvolved daughter when I wasn't able to travel in time to make the visitation. Now she's living in a retirement community in Florida with a bunch of other widows who also complain about their absent adult children. She's very happy there, or as happy as she's capable of being. I'd like to have a relationship with her, but for her, that means living my life for me, through me. I can't be an extension of another person."

He ran his fingers lightly over my hair but said nothing. And I appreciated that. So many people over the years had responded to any discussion of my family estrangement with "But she's your *mother.* You can't just ignore your *mother.*" Or "I'm sure that's just her way of showing how much she loves you." They didn't know what it was like to grow up with her, but somehow thought they knew what was best for me. Or at least they knew that the way I was living my life was offensive to their view of the world, and I must change that right away. So I stopped talking about it with most people. The fact that Finn hadn't reacted with advice or platitudes made me think that I'd been right to trust him with the information.

Even if he did try to smolder at me.

Obscure soda-based blood sugar only carried me so far.

It was Finn's turn to be the strong one, supporting my arms and helping me over obstacles as we took a wide circle around the ravine.

We trekked through one long thicket of trees after another, my feet dragging behind us. The glucose and pep I'd picked up from that Ale-8 had abandoned me hours before, and I was crashing hard. The ground seemed to sneak up on me, rising and falling, tripping me up as I struggled to control where I put my feet. I refused to let him stop for breaks. I refused to slow us down. I had to get out of the woods.

"Why haven't we seen helicopters or search lights or something?" I huffed as he helped me over a massive fallen log. "They can't just assume that we're dead because the plane was reduced to a charcoal briquette. That's rude."

"Well, I'm sure . . . they've got to be . . ." Finn was struggling to find something cheerful to say. I could tell by the strained expression on his face. It was the same face my mother made when I did something different with my hair, though she always gave up and told me what she really thought. "Maybe the rescue crews are looking in the wrong place. Maybe they don't believe there could be survivors."

I found that terribly depressing, that Finn would try to sugarcoat our situation after being so openly and irritatingly frank for so long. And I was angry that he thought he needed to protect me from reality when it was so clear that our situation was growing more hopeless. And then there was the even more confusing undercurrent of gratitude that he would try. Clearly, the lack of fluids was shutting down the more rational bits of my brain.

The hem of my jeans caught on the log's branch, and I stumbled, landing hard on my butt. I groaned, wincing at the resounding pain of the impact. Hissing, I threw my other leg over the log and buried my face in my hands. "I hate this. I hate how lousy I feel now that the Ale-8 superstrength has evaporated. I hate bugs and the humidity and the mud. I hate how much it hurts to walk, and I hate feeling weak. I hate that we're in a place called 'the lakelands' and we haven't come across *one freaking lake* except for the one we crashed into! 'Lakelands' implies more than one lake! I hate how one place can be so fricking hot and fricking cold all in one day. Pick a fricking temperature and stick with it!" I flopped back on the ground, not giving a single damn about getting my clothes any dirtier.

"You done now?" Finn looked vaguely amused by my tantrum, perhaps because it was directed at circumstances in general and not at him.

"Sort of." I sighed, standing and brushing the bark chunks off my jeans.

"Drink some more."

I drank again, while he scanned the horizon for danger.

"Come on." Before I could ask what he meant, he picked me up, carrying me bridal-style for a few steps before slinging me around his back.

"No, we've talked about this," I muttered into the skin of his neck. "You'll tire yourself out, and I'll have to carry your heavy vampire butt through the woods again. I don't have it in me until I get my steak."

"Your steak?"

I nodded, rubbing my cheek against the lovely cool of his neck. "I'm going to eat all of the steak when I get out of this. I mean, *all* of the steak. As in 'all of the steak in the world.' You can come and watch."

"That's a tempting offer. And what will you have for dessert?"

"I was thinking about something involving chocolate pudding and raspberry coulis."

Finn stopped. "Really? I think I would like to hear more about that."

"Later. If I talk about it now, I'll tell you too much."

"But I want to hear your thoughts about chocolate pudding and raspberry coulis. Desperately."

"Nope."

"Spoilsport." He was moving again, and I was reveling guiltily in not having to walk, promising myself that I would make him put me down in just a few steps. As soon as I got my wind back, I would make him conserve his strength. But for right now, I was comfortable for the first time in a while, so I was going to enjoy it. I raised my head with a start. "What is it?"

"Can you stand for a second?" he asked, gently unfolding my legs from his waist so my feet touched the ground. He walked toward a large tree, the trunk the thickness of a smart car, while staring up into the branches.

"Finn?"

His hands shoved through the thick kudzu growing up the trunk. He grinned and yanked the kudzu vines hard, bringing a good chunk of them rippling down the tree and revealing a rusty metal ladder. The bark had grown over portions of the metal, permanently securing it as part of the tree.

"What is it?" I asked. "Another deer stand? Check and see if there's a shower or a freezer stocked with Ben and Jerry's."

"I'll be right back." He climbed up the ladder gracefully, his dust-covered butt disappearing through the low-hanging branches.

"Or maybe some lights in the distance. Water towers. Helpful signs stating, 'You are this far from civilization.'"

Finn did not respond to my requests. I wondered if he was going to just launch himself from tree to tree Tarzan-style and disappear.

"Finn?"

With Finn out of sight, I folded to the ground. I was exhausted and sore and hungry—not potted-meat hungry but hungry. And even with the hand-me-down boots, my feet were killing me.

I leaned against the tree, tucking my head between my knees. Without Finn there, I let a few miserable tears seep through my eyelids. I indulged for a few seconds before I wiped my cheeks and commanded myself to stop. My body couldn't spare the water needed to cry.

I heard a rustling overhead and swiped my filthy hands across my cheeks one last time. I didn't even care about the grime and potential bacteria. I had enough spine to want to avoid Finn's pity at all costs. It was bad enough he had taken to hauling me around the woods like a child.

I pushed to my feet, wincing at the pain in my knees as I did so. "What is it?"

He grinned broadly. "There's a lake!"

I exclaimed, "Finally, the lakelands' reputation comes through!"

6

Take advantage of creature comforts where you can. Physical discomfort leads to resentment. You don't want that resentment to fester should you find yourself in a Peruvian soccer team situation.

—*Where the Wild Things Bite: A Survival Guide for Camping with the Undead*

Even with my weak human senses, I could smell the water before we saw it. It had that same slightly fishy, coppery odor as our "landing site." I wondered whether that smell reminded Finn of blood. We heard the gentle sound of water moving against the shore. Given the unrelenting landscape of "trees, rocks, more trees, trees, trees," it was lovely to see a wide expanse of sparkling water, rippling in the pale light. Now we just had to get around it.

"We are sure this isn't the same lake we landed in, right?" I asked, hands on hips as we stood, admiring the view.

"Based on the lack of smoldering wreckage, I'm going to say yes," Finn said, nodding.

"I'm just saying, 'walk in a straight line if possible' hasn't been the greatest navigation plan."

"Everything can't be planned," he said. "Sometimes you just have to act on instinct."

"My main instinct is flight."

"Having flown with you, I disagree."

I struck out at him, smacking his shoulder. "That's not funny."

He caught my wrist and wrapped his arm around me, squeezing me to his side. His voice was almost fond as he chuckled into my hair. "You have strong instincts, kitten, you just need to hush all of the noise in your head long enough to listen to them." I stopped, putting a few steps between us as he continued. "It's written all over your face. You're always arguing with yourself, always trying to figure out the consequences ten steps ahead of time. Sometimes you just have to let life happen to you."

"*You* let life happen to you, and now you drink blood and can't go out during the day," I countered.

"You're not wrong," he said, stripping off his shirt. I watched him tug the stained material over his head, revealing a physique that was just as muscled and well wrought as I'd suspected it to be—even if I had underestimated the inherent lickability of his collarbone.

And I had officially reached "just can't even" levels of sexual frustration.

All of the noise in my head reduced itself to white noise and the whimpers of my overstimulated libido. When he reached for the button of his pants, time seemed to catch up with me, my brain started working again, and I had enough sense to whip around so my back was facing him.

"What are you doing?" I yelped.

"I'm going to go for a swim, wash off in the lake," he suggested, nodding toward the glittering water. "Join me?"

"Oh, sure. I'll just go pluck the fruit of a shampoo tree in yonder meadow," I scoffed, throwing an arm toward the woods. Unfortunately, that brought the unpleasant odor of . . . me wafting up from under my sweater. That was not helping me with the whole "argument against bathing" thing. I was grossing myself out, and I didn't even have supersenses.

He dropped his shirt on a relatively dry-looking, flat rock. "Come on, how can you see water like that and not want to wash up?"

"Would you like me to alphabetize my reasons or organize them by importance?"

He grinned broadly, teeth gleaming in the bluish glow of the moon, as he wriggled his hips and let his pants fall around his ankles. "I figured you would have them. Hit me."

I stared up at the host of gloriously visible stars above us, to avoid the spectacle of Finn standing there in very little besides a naughty smile. I'd guessed he was fit just from the highly unlikely triangular hip-to-shoulder ratio. But good Lord. His abdominals had abdominals. He looked like a nocturnal commercial for boxer briefs.

While my rational brain knew the name for those abdominal muscles that formed a distinct V shape over his hip bones, the rest of my brain was concentrated on keeping me from making "grabby paws" at said hip bones and keeping up conversation.

"That's a very dangerous offer to make to a woman you've thrown out of a plane."

"You keep saying 'thrown.' What do you mean, 'thrown'?" he exclaimed, throwing his arms wide, which did some interesting things in terms of moving parts of his anatomy. "I jumped, cradling you carefully in my arms and using *my body* to shield you from harm."

"It's very difficult to make that distinction when you're paralyzed with fear."

"Fine, but why don't you want to swim in the lake? Despite the fact that we're dirty, sticky, and somewhat smelly and deserve to do something nice for ourselves?"

"I've seen a horror movie? I've seen wacky camp movies? The minute I take my clothes off and leave them on the shore, either I will be hacked up by a psycho in a hockey mask, or some smartass kids from the rival camp will steal them so I have to streak."

"Rest assured that if any delinquents or serial killers try to get you, I will use my vampire speed to defend you or your clothes. What else have you got?"

"It's dark and unchlorinated, and I can't see the bottom. I don't know what kind of gross fish and possible lake monsters are living in that water."

"The lake monster thing seems unlikely, but even if there was some ancient predator lurking in central Kentucky, wouldn't I be able to take it?"

"I don't know. I've never seen you fistfight Nessie."

"All right, I give you my solemn vow to protect you from all prehistoric lake monsters. What else?"

"We don't know what people have been doing in that water. The bottom could be littered with fishhooks and broken bottles and used hypodermic needles that we could step on."

He knelt in front of me and laid his palms on my fully clothed thighs. "You think there's a big population of hard-drinking fishermen with intravenous drug problems in this particular state nature preserve?"

"I don't know. I wouldn't have guessed we would find a fully stocked deer-sniping bunker in the trees, but we did."

Finn rolled his eyes and kicked off his shoes, then tugged off my carefully tied boots in record time. My bag disappeared from my shoulder and landed safely next to his clothes on the rock. And somehow my clothes, save for my sensible white cotton underwear and bra, seemed to evaporate off as a blur of white moved around me.

And then the bra and panties disappeared, too, appearing in a perfectly folded pile next to his clothes.

"What are you doing! That is a misuse of vampire speed!" I cried, clapping my hands over my important bits. The blur stopped, and a half-naked Finn stood before me. Grinning, he dropped his underwear, and I averted my eyes from sheer embarrassment.

Caught between mortification and shock, I ended up giggling hysterically instead of screaming, my laughter echoing off the surface of the water and bouncing into the trees. "What is *wrong* with you? And is there a medication for it?"

Well, in terms of responses to panic, frantic laughter was a new one.

Ignoring my attempts to cover myself, Finn scooped me up bridal-style and carried me out into the water. Even through my squirming and laughing, I noted that his hands stayed in "respectable" locations—behind my knees, under my arms. "We're going to wash off. I will protect you from ax murderers and sea monsters and hypodermic needles."

"Lake monsters," I corrected.

"Those, too."

I squealed, sealing my face against the crook of Finn's neck, accepting that no matter what I did, he was going to take me out into this lake. I'd never been skinny-dipping before, a fact I was sure would shock Finn not at all. I'd never even swum in a lake, beyond our postcrash aqua-dash. And I wasn't sure how I felt about doing it now. Part of me welcomed the respite, the chance to be even partially clean, but the idea of leaving the book on the shore, unprotected, when Ernie the pilot or some overcurious bear could wander by and—

"Holy hell, that's cold!" I exclaimed, as the water slapped against my ass like an unforgiving palm. I was practically climbing Finn, clamping my arms around his neck and scrambling up his chest to try to get away from the uncomfortably chilly water. And I was basically smashing his face into my naked cleavage in the process.

"Sorry," I muttered, hissing as I loosened my grip and dropped back into the freezing-freaking-cold water.

He smirked. "I wasn't complaining."

"You are to immediately delete my naked breasts from your memory!" I told him, shivering at the cool water flowing over my skin. I could practically feel the layers of sweat and grime dissolving.

"Nope. I never forget a beautiful pair of breasts," he said solemnly. He dropped my legs into the water so he could tap his temple with his fingers. "They are forever stored in the 'beautiful breast storage' vault. Also, if you keep shivering against me like that, we're going to have some other issues to resolve."

I slapped at the surface of the water, splashing his smug face. He gasped, dropping me into the lake full-on. I sprang to the surface, wheezing with shock. He splashed me, and I smacked the water back at him. Soon we were diving and rough-housing like a pair of kids. I would never admit it, but it eventually felt rather nice.

"See?" he said. "This isn't so bad."

"The water still smells a little weird," I complained lightly.

Scoffing, he ducked my head under the surface, plunging me into the cool, quiet wet. I bobbed up and flopped onto my back, letting my long, wet hair smack him in the face. He laughed, diving out of the way.

With him splashing contentedly out of my range, I floated on my back, staring at the stars above us. With so little light pollution out here in the sticks, the bits of stardust stood out, bold and clear. They looked so close it felt like I could reach out and touch them. The little specks of light were reflecting perfectly against the surface of the water, making it seem as though we were swimming among them.

I felt very small and insignificant in comparison to this vast expanse of sky, which I supposed was the whole point of people staring up at the stars. And still, I felt more relaxed than I had in days. It could have been the clean hair and the distinct lack of someone trying to kill me, but my "ordeal" suddenly didn't seem so bad, especially with that sky spreading over my head.

When was the last time I had done something like this? I obviously wasn't a camper. I didn't go stargazing. I rarely left my apartment unless it was for research. When was the last time I had contemplated something outside my little sphere? I'd become so focused on controlling my health, my environment, my career, that I couldn't see anything beyond it. I'd become completely self-involved, the center of my own universe. The only other person to achieve this anti-Copernican feat was my mother . . . Great. I'd become my freaking mother.

Competent or not, my therapist was getting fired when I got home.

Quietly, I heard Finn paddle up to my side, nudging my shoulder so I spun in a wide circle. He balanced his chin on my shoulder, and I felt his feet bump against my knees under the water, as if he was cradling my body with his under the surface.

I curled my hand around his head, securing us together as we spun. I didn't want to live my life like that anymore, trapped in a fishbowl of my own making. I didn't know if Finn would be the right person for me to try to expand that sphere with, but for now, I appreciated his company and damned if I didn't enjoy his attention. He made me feel . . . Well, he made me want to curl into a tiny shrimp-shaped ball of insecurity when he took his shirt off. But he made me try new things and challenge myself, and he made me laugh. He made me angry, and I wasn't afraid to let him know when he did it; a minor miracle, considering I'd spent years burying my negative emotions under layers of guilt and compliance. He was not my ideal man, by any definition I'd ever used for myself. But he might be what I needed.

"Admit that I was right." His voice was a smug tickle against the shell of my ear.

"OK, OK, we needed a bath," I confessed. "We *were* getting a little gamey."

"You know, a lesser vampire would take advantage of the situation," he said, ghosting his hand over my bare belly under the water. "Moonlight, nudity, your tender gratitude."

I rolled, treading so close to him my feet bumped against his shins. "I think you're overestimating the tenderness of my gratitude."

He squinted at me for a long moment. "Am I?"

A teasing grin quirked my lips. "I don't know if you've noticed this, but I don't like you that much."

"You know, you're right about a lot of things," he told me. "But not that. You like me plenty."

The sly smile slipped from his lips, and for once, he looked earnest. He slowly ducked his head and kissed me. Actually, "kissed" wasn't an adequate word for what he did to my mouth. It was like he was speaking some language all his own and was trying to teach me with lips and teeth and tongue.

His hands slipped along my body under the cool water, pinning me against him, letting me appreciate the firm smoothness of his skin. My knees rose, bracing against his hips to anchor me to him. He turned us, round and round, as he spanned his hand across my collarbone. I twisted my fingers into his hair and pulled him close.

His fingers explored, teasing and petting me until I was gasping against his mouth. I didn't think. The noise in my head receded. I didn't think about the book or the danger or the miles and miles of woods between us and civilization. There was only Finn and his lips and the sensation of the water against my skin.

And that's when the trouble started.

Maybe it was the sense memory, revived from being submerged in the cold water again. Or maybe it was that at the touch of Finn's lips, my brain basically shut down all nonessential functions, such as worrying or second-guessing myself, giving it time to reboot like an overworked hard drive. Or it could have been the scent of Finn and the coppery water that brought forth a question that had been nagging at the far reaches of my brain.

Why hadn't Finn done anything when Ernie was attacking me on the plane?

In my head, the mid-flight knife fight with Ernie played out. I could see the shiny black edge bursting through the cushion, barely missing my face. I could feel the tilt of the plane under my feet, the sick sensation of dropping from the sky on the mad whim of the wind. Finn was sitting in his seat, frozen, while I knocked the knife out of the pilot's grasp. His face was impassive, and his eyes were blank.

And this was the part that my mind just couldn't process: Ernie looked at Finn with disgust and asked, "What are you doing?"

At the time, I'd been confused about whom he was talking to. And then the fear and the adrenaline clouded my brain, keeping me from recalling some of the finer points of our earliest moments of misadventure. But now, I realized, Ernie had been talking to Finn. He was asking, "Aren't you going to do anything?" as if Finn was somehow falling down on the job. There was something Finn was supposed to be doing that he wasn't.

Because Finn was supposed to be helping Ernie take the book from me.

He was supposed to be helping Ernie, not sitting there like a handsome statue, watching it play out. And Ernie wasn't pleased to be carrying all of the weight in my robbery and/or murder.

Finn was working with Ernie, or at the very least, he knew something he wasn't letting on. Maybe the only reason he was keeping me safe from the psycho pilot was to keep the book for himself? Maybe he wanted to deliver the book to whoever had hired Ernie, along with someone who could help interpret its value? Or maybe he was just pissed off that whoever had hired him had hired someone else to crash the plane and take Finn down with it, so he was throwing any road-blocks he could into his employers' path. Maybe my brain was running off on some paranoid track. But something was wrong. Something had been wrong since the moment I'd stepped onto that damn plane.

Why would Finn kiss me? Why would he keep me safe? Why would he work so hard to get water and food for me? Because he was trying to get me to trust him. Because it would make me easier to manage if I was healthy and grateful to him. It would make me easier to handle, the way he was handling me—quite literally—now.

I pulled away from Finn, and he followed, his mouth making hungry motions against the air. "What?"

Right. Not the time to panic. I was just naked, in a dirty body of water, with an apex predator who'd lied to me and strung me along for his own amusement and/or possible profit. Also, his hands were on my bare breasts.

I would panic later, after I got away from him. I would give myself a stern talking to about my pattern of trusting handsome faces and letting myself get distracted from my goals. But for right now, I needed to get out of a situation where Finn could very easily drown me if he suspected I'd figured him out.

Betrayal bloomed hot and sharp in my chest, like acid being poured over a long-scarred wound. How could I have trusted Finn, even a little bit? How could

I have not guessed what he was after all along? Had I really thought he liked me? Was I really that pathetic? Had he been laughing at me this whole time? Was I ever going to learn?

I stroked backward, away from him, a vacant smile pasted on my lips. His hands stretched out toward me, as if to follow, but he hung back, staring at me. His head cocked to the side as he studied me, most likely because I was the first person to voluntarily break off a kiss with him since the 1960s.

"We should get going," I told him, fighting hard to keep my voice steady. I prayed that Finn couldn't hear the pounding of my thoroughly cracked heart. "We don't want to waste too much time."

It was all details, keeping my face neutral, making my limbs move smoothly as I swam steadily back to shore. He treaded along beside me, frowning all the while. "You all right, kitten?"

I bit back a sob that threatened to make my whole body convulse. He was really playing up the whole "smitten vampire" angle to perfection, with the cute nicknames and the feigned concern. It was a lie. Every time he smiled at me. Every time he touched me with gentleness. Every time he called me "kitten." All lies. Unless, of course, in World War II–era Cleveland, "kitten" had originally meant "you hormone-addled moron."

I could taste bile rising in my throat, and I prayed I wouldn't throw up my crackers. And Finn was still talking in this halting, worried manner that made it even harder not to scream.

"I shouldn't have stripped you like that, without your permission. I'm sorry. I know you're not used to that sort of thing."

I gritted my teeth against my nausea and the bite of cool evening air against my wet face and hair. Of course, I wouldn't be used to being naked with a man, skinny-dipping and kissing and being generally naughty. But it was the way he said it, the pity, like I was some invalid, that grated across my nerves.

I rose out of the water, thankful that the bandages protected my injured feet from the bottom muck. I crossed my arms over my chest and scrambled as gracefully as I could to my clothes. Sliding into the jeans and sweater felt blissful against my skin, even if the clothes were dirty. They were warm and dry, and I was chilled to the bone, soaked through with regret and anger.

I should have known, I told myself sternly. Hadn't I learned anything from Michael? The loss of my doctorate wasn't enough to warn me off pretty men and their empty promises? When the hell was I going to grow up?

It was my mother's voice inside my head, demanding these things of me, making me feel like that stupid, slow, small girl who was never quite enough. I closed my eyes against it and focused on Finn's voice. He was still talking, asking me to say something, anything, but I ignored him as I reached the shore. I wrung the water out of my hair, resigned to dreadlocks by the time I left this place, and tied it up with an elastic. I slid into my boots and tied them tight. I slung the bag over my shoulder.

Finn, of course, was already dressed, because of his dirty, cheating vampire superpowers. But he hadn't put his shoes on yet, and that was something I hoped would work to my advantage. He put a cool hand around my shoulder, attempting to turn me. "Kitten, please talk to me."

I'd warned him not to call me "kitten."

My hand wrapped around the strap of the purse, gathering it into the tightest, densest parcel I could manage. Finn was faster than me, and stronger; that wasn't going to change. But he expected me to be his timid little kitty cat. He would *not* expect me to smack him in the face with my purse.

"You sonofabitch!" I yelled, swinging the bag directly at his face. As I smacked him over and over, I let loose a string of profanity that would have sent my mother into an early stroke. "How could you?" I demanded. "I trusted you!"

He swept my feet out from under me, sending me pitching into the damp grass. He straddled my hips, but I still had hold of my bag. I grabbed the ceramic knife and swept it forward, pressing it against his throat. I forced him to sit up, rolling us so that he was sprawled on the ground and I straddled him.

Sure, the knife wouldn't kill him, but it would hurt like a bitch.

"Look, if you don't want me touching you, all you have to say is no!" Finn insisted, his eyes glittering angrily.

Apologetic Finn was gone, replaced by angry, unpredictable Finn. Dangerous Finn, who'd reminded me just after our jump that he'd done me a favor, helping me to survive, and not to test him, not to threaten him even as a joke. Dangerous Finn did not appreciate me holding a knife to his throat. Dangerous Finn looked like he was calculating exactly how far I could push down the knife before he tossed me into the trees.

"This has nothing to do with you touching me, or kissing me, which is going to stop, too, by the way."

"Then what is this about?" he asked, twitching his hips as if he was going to reverse our positions again.

I pressed the blade tighter against his throat, drawing just the tiniest drop of blood. Finn's head dropped away from the blade, and his body stilled. I watched the small ruby drop well against his skin and fought the urge to throw the knife away and apologize, even as the wound closed. "You were helping Ernie! You're after the book, too. This whole thing, from the very beginning, was a scam."

There was a moment in which I could practically see the explanation forming in his eyes, the beginnings of a reassuring smile forming on his mouth. And I wanted that. I'd held on to some scrap of hope that I was wrong, that this was a misunderstanding and I'd overreacted. I wanted him to offer completely acceptable explanations about how I'd misinterpreted the situation. I would have gladly accepted whatever embarrassment was due to me. But instead, he shook his head and said, "I can explain, Anna."

"I don't want to hear it," I spat at him.

That was a lie. I totally wanted to hear it.

"Why put up the act? Why 'rescue' me and drag me all over creation when you could have just killed me?"

"I wouldn't do that!" He reached for my arms, and I gave him a look that could only be described as "murder eyes." He backed away, hands in the "surrender" pose. "I wouldn't hurt you. I didn't know they were going to crash the plane. And afterward, I helped you because I wanted you to trust me. And I wasn't sure if I was really going to take it or not. I figured, why worry you?"

I barely restrained the urge to cover my face with my hands, making me vulnerable to losing the knife. It was humiliating, the lengths he'd gone to in order to make me think that he had no clue about my package. I'd thought I was so sneaky, so clever. I'd been so proud of my subterfuge. I'd believed, for just one minute, that I was capable of something that didn't center on being stuck in my own head.

Clearly, I was wrong.

"That first time the pilot came after us in the woods. It seems awfully convenient that you showed up just as he threw the spear. And then he just ran away, leaving you to 'protect' me. Have you been working together this whole time, or did you have some sort of bad-guy break-up on the plane?"

"No, it's not like that, Anna."

"You were going to just, what, keep me here in the woods until you figured out how to get me to your bosses?"

"No, I was supposed to get the book from you. I owe a debt to a family of shifters—which are a real thing, by the way. They sent me after you when they heard that you had the book. They've been looking for a complete copy of Friar Thomas's manuscript for years."

"So what, you were supposed to take the book and toss me out of the plane?"

He shook his head. "No, nothing that violent."

"Pardon me for nitpicking, but Ernie trying to stab me felt pretty damned violent."

"It was supposed to be left to me. I was supposed to use my talent against you. I can get into other people's heads. It's not quite mind-reading. I'm more like a passenger who gets handed the controls. I can see what that person thinks; I can see a little of their history. But the point is that I can control them. I can make them move, make them do what I want. I was supposed to make you hand over the book in the middle of the flight and then nod off into a nap. Easy-peasy, no harm done."

"Except for the part where I get off the plane without the book I'm supposed to deliver to a vampire and face a possible draining."

"Oh, Jane wouldn't hurt you. She's too much of a goody-goody," Finn grumbled.

"What?"

"Never mind. Look, I'm sorry. It was my job. It was nothing personal. I didn't know the pilot was going to hijack the flight. He must have been a backup plan, in case I failed. The shifters have good reason not to trust me. And when we were halfway through the flight and I hadn't taken it from you, Ernie followed plan B."

"*I* have good reason not to trust you!" I shouted.

"Just put the knife down, and I'll explain. I don't want to hurt you. I've never wanted to hurt you."

I rolled my shoulders, gripping the knife handle and pressing it down against his throat. He hissed, squirming away from the pressure of the blade. "Well, that's too bad, because I don't particularly care if I hurt you."

In that moment, he looked oddly relieved, like he was happy I was resisting him. The tension drained out of his body, and he sank into the ground. I really hoped this wasn't a sex thing.

"So when you were just sitting there on the plane, staring at me, while Ernie was trying to *stab me in the face*, were you trying to get me to give up and let him kill me?"

"No!" he exclaimed. "I was in your head but could barely get control because of the sheer amount of noise in there. The anxiety, the fear. Is that what it's like all the time?"

I didn't respond. I couldn't let him think that sympathetic, almost piteous tone affected me in the least. I merely stared at him, giving him the deadest expression I could manage. Of course it was like that inside my head all the time, but damned if I was going to tell him that.

"Well, it was the saddest thing I'd ever felt," he said. "I couldn't get around it, so I turned my attentions to Ernie. I tried to get him to sit down at the controls, take over the plane again, but I was a little distracted by the knife fight and the impending plane crash. I couldn't get Ernie under control, either, so I had to step in between you. And you know the rest."

I stared at him for a long, long time, and a sudden thought bubbled up to the surface of my brain. "So that first night, when you kept trying to persuade me to climb under the tree and go to sleep and then I basically lost control of all my motor function and don't remember how I ended up under that pine canopy, was that you?"

"Yes," he said, wincing. "You were so tired and shocked, it was like all of your defenses were down. It was a lot easier to persuade you. But I haven't done it to you since."

I wasn't sure whether it was the way my eyes narrowed or the vicious snarl I let loose, but Finn suddenly rolled out from under me, smacking my knife hand aside before I could swing it toward him.

"How could you do that?" I yelled at him, punching him in the sides. My blows had no effect on him as he pinned me to the ground. "How could you do that to me? How could you?"

"I'm sorry, Anna."

"Save it," I growled, baring my teeth at him. "Find a way out of here on your own."

"I have just as much reason to want to get the book to Jane as you do. Frankly, I take it a little personally when my employers try to kill me. I mean, cheating me out of money, that I've come to expect, but there's such a thing as professional standards."

"I can't trust you, Finn! Is that even your real name?"

"Look, I've told you everything. What do I have to

lose at this point?" he demanded. "If I was going to take the book, if I was going to hurt you, don't you think I would have done it by now? You don't put the energy into a long con without a payoff, Anna."

"So what's your payoff? What are you conning me for? I'd really like to know so I can give it to you and you can leave me the hell alone."

"That was a bad way to phrase it. There is no con, I just want to help you!" he protested. "I like you. I like the way you make me feel. I like the way you talk to me, the fact that you don't fall for a good portion of my bullshit. I can be me instead of the person I think you want me to be. And maybe it's selfish to want to keep feeling that way, damn the consequences. I'm a selfish person, Anna. For a long time, I've thought that was the smart way to be: look out for yourself, and only yourself, because no one's going to do it for you. But there are times with you when you make me want to be more."

I pushed him, and to my surprise, he eased his body off mine. "Don't. Don't say that to me when you don't mean it. Stop trying to find my angles," I said, shaking my head.

"I'm not."

"I don't think you can help it. Lying is so easy for you, you don't even realize you're doing it." I pushed to my feet, backing away from him. "Just stay away from me, Finn."

He sighed. "I can't do that. You won't make it out of here by yourself."

"We'll see," I growled. I scooped his shoes off the

ground and threw them into the lake. Slipping the knife back into the bag so I wouldn't trip directly on it, I took off running toward the trees. From the looks of the sky, I had a few hours until the sun rose and it was safe for me to move around without worrying about Finn. He could be right behind me for all I knew. I stopped, listening for the sound of him moving nearby. But when I didn't hear so much as a leaf rustling, I took off running again, taking a strange serpentine pattern through the trees that I hoped would be harder to follow. I touched as many objects as possible, crisscrossing my own path, and tried to make it as difficult as possible to keep track of me. I was amazed at how fast I was able to move now that I had some calories and water in my system and some decent shoes on my feet.

But I was keenly aware that if Finn really wanted to catch me, he would have caught me by now. Something was keeping him from running me down like one of the possums he enjoyed so much. Maybe it was embarrassment that I'd figured him out? Or maybe he just didn't like running in waterlogged shoes.

Maybe he was toying with me again.

I ran as far as I could before my side started to ache and my breathing sounded like something from an obscene phone call. With all of my attempts at misdirection, I wasn't sure how far I'd actually gone, but I couldn't hear or smell the lake anymore, so that had to count for something.

I came to an oak with a particularly low-growing branch and used it to throw my leg up over the next branch in a none-too-graceful fashion. And then I did it again, and again, silently thanking Rachel for those stupid Pilates she made us do on weekday mornings. Before long, I was a good twenty feet off the ground, settled in a sort of cradle formed in the crux of four branches, surrounded by nice, concealing foliage. I pulled a bottle of water from my bag and sipped it until my mouth didn't feel so dry. And wished for the hundredth time that I hadn't packed my meds in my checked suitcase.

I fought to keep my breathing under control and catalogued myself from head to toe. *Boots: intact. Feet: still aching like hell. Lungs: dear God, no. Hands: bark, you evil skin-scraping bitch. Heart: equally scraped up. Head: never mind.*

I buried my face in my abraded hands. I couldn't believe I'd fallen for this again. I was ashamed that I'd thought for one second that Finn could actually want someone like me. Sad, socially awkward Anna with her near-agoraphobia and survival statistics. Oh, yeah, I was just the sort of girl to attract the attention of a handsome man with eternal life and killer cheekbones.

Michael had taught me that lesson and I was too quick to forget it. I took a longer drink from the water bottle and threw my arms around my head, as if to block those thoughts out of my brain.

Michael Malone had been a charming classmate in my graduate school's fairly small history department. We'd met at a doctoral-student mixer, and he'd actually sought me out, asking my adviser to introduce us. I suspected that it was because of my father's reputation, but he was just so handsome and charming in that "sensitive, shy academic type who has life all figured out" sort of way that I didn't care.

He'd become a fixture in my peer review groups, my class schedule, the very small social circle I developed. He was so sweet, giving me silly little presents and taking me to parties and calling me his "girl." He'd fulfilled all of the stupid, teen-rom-com-fueled dreams of a girl who hadn't been allowed to date in high school. Even though we were hundreds of miles away from my father and his home campus, Michael kept pressing me. Couldn't I introduce him to the renowned Daniel R. Whitfield, PhD? Couldn't I discuss Michael's research area of interest with my father or maybe even show him some pages from Michael's doctoral thesis to get some feedback? Didn't I want my father to get to know my boyfriend better?

But I'd only just established some connection with my father, a relationship that my mother couldn't control. I didn't want to complicate it by asking for favors my father rarely granted for his colleagues, much less a grad student he didn't know. Michael had been so disappointed that I scrambled to try to make it up to him, "helping him" with his coursework and taking him to faculty events where I hadn't even been invited, so I could parlay my father's reputation into introducing Michael to important people.

I wished that he'd been a typical guy, pressuring me into irresponsible use of tequila and a physical relationship I wasn't ready for. But to be honest, he'd rarely pushed for much outside of our academic lives. I'd worked so hard to try to turn whatever it was that we had into a real relationship, something that would make me normal, something I could bring back to my mother and show her, "Look, see, there are good people in the world and one of them likes me," that I didn't register how one-sided it was. He kept pressing me. Couldn't I just devote an hour or two to grading papers for the class he TA'd, so he could research? Couldn't I just let him pick my father's brain about this or that topic? Couldn't I just let him peek at my doctoral project so he'd know if his work was comparable? Couldn't I just? He always made it sound so reasonable and trifling to ask, like I was some unreasonable person for not immediately agreeing. It was "just" and "only."

Michael's demands and the weight carried by my father's reputation meant that I had to work twice as hard as the other students just to come off as somewhat competent. There were times when I hid at the library archives just to get some peace and quiet, searching through the occult selections only recently deemed "possibly not insane ravings" since the vampires' Coming Out. I'd felt drawn to supernatural texts, not just because of the "new" depths to plumb, a rarity in historical circles, but because I felt a certain kinship with creatures of the night—odd, disenfranchised, and only able to leave their homes during certain hours.

For my PhD, I'd used the contacts I'd built at the Council to politely request information, and they'd sent a crate of books that a woman named Ophelia Lambert had deemed "too tiresome to catalogue."

I'd pored over them. Some turned out to be nothing, the ancient equivalent of dime-store novels. Others were invaluable in helping me understand the secret history of the undead, how vampires had helped shape the new American government with their financial and underground cultural influence on players such as Washington, Franklin, and Jefferson. In the end, I learned a lot more about ancient books and their management than what my professors deemed acceptable history. But I'd loved every minute of it, and I shared my joy with Michael. He'd told me it was adorable that I was researching something so obscure, but he wondered if it wouldn't be better to focus on something like his treatise on underappreciated Civil War generals of neutral states.

He'd never shown a moment's interest in my work, in my interests, right until the moment he submitted his own take on vampire movements throughout early Colonial America to the thesis committee, along with original research documents and materials he'd taken from my apartment. His own thesis, the one I'd put hours into helping him research and type and proof, had been a feint. All along, he'd been taking the notes and research I'd shared with him and shaped them into his own convoluted theory about vampires' influence on the colonies, showing it to his advisers and asking them to keep the "revolutionary material" quiet.

In general, innocent people don't worry about having an alibi. And people who would never think of stealing someone else's research don't think to build a case that they were the authors of their own work.

Michael copied all of my notes in his own dated journals. He could show e-mailed discussions with his adviser about the material. He'd taken his own photos of the documents—stored in my room, thank you very much. He even followed up on the phone interviews I'd done with members of the Council, so if asked, they could verify his claims that he'd spoken to them. By the time he was done, I looked like the sad, psycho girlfriend who was copying *his* work word-for-word while he was devoting his life to the pursuit of knowledge. He'd routed me so thoroughly I didn't stand a chance in front of an academic review board. The review board had been so impressed by his "groundbreaking" research that they'd fast-tracked him for a faculty position. Hell, he'd gotten an interview with *Smithsonian Magazine* out of it.

And when I'd confronted Michael about his lies, his response was to placidly fold his wire-rim glasses on his desk and tell me, "Prove it."

To put it lightly, I was devastated. That thesis represented years of my life, and it was all gone. No one at the university believed me, not even my own adviser, who had supervised me for two years. Michael had managed to convince *her* that I'd spent all that time simply reporting to her on what I'd watched *him* learn. I supposed I didn't help myself, running to the dean with my frantic, hysterical claims that Michael had stolen my research, while he remained cool as a cucumber. A cucumber with a degree and a job offer. And I had no original research, no paper, and nothing to show for my years of work.

I basically had a mental breakdown. Those scenes in the BBC movies where a young noblewoman is sent home from polite society in disgrace and locked in her family's attic until she comes to her senses? Well, my parents didn't have an attic. My father was humiliated beyond description to have his daughter leave her problem without a degree. The progress we'd built toward a healthy relationship evaporated. He left for another research trip, leaving me to my mother's tender care.

My mother told me not to worry, not to let my failure bother me. I mean, clearly, it was entirely my fault that I'd brought this level of shame to the family doorstep, but it didn't matter in the long run. After all, I would have been coming home soon enough to take care of Mother anyway, so why would I need a silly old doctorate? It was as if Michael had proven my mother right. Every bad thing she'd ever said about men or work or the outside world was confirmed. I saw my life stretching out before me like a long hallway, and every door was labeled "exhaustion and unhappiness." I would never have a life of my own, a home of my own, a family. My life was supposed to be taking care of her. So I told her no. For the first time in my life, I told my mother no and meant it.

To say she was shocked was an understatement. Hell, I was shocked.

I took off in the middle of the night. I found an apartment and stayed in it. I found a doctor well versed in balancing antianxiety medications. I lived off savings bonds for almost a year, hiding in my apartment, reading, researching supernatural topics that would never lead to publication but that I found interesting. Rachel, a library science major who had been assigned as my research intern before I was labeled "academic poison," was the one who finally got me off my ass and working again. Recently graduated, she'd lost her interest in academia after seeing how I was treated and was now interested in helping me make "cold, hard cash."

Also, she may have had too many glasses of chardonnay at a campus wine-and-cheese mixer and told one of Michael's chief supporters that he would always work at a second-tier school unless he removed his head from his own ass. Which may have ruined her chances for a good letter of recommendation . . . considering that said chief supporter was her adviser.

With Rachel's urging, I finally worked up the nerve to use those vampire contacts, the few friends I had left in academic circles for references. It was ridiculously difficult at first, but I had some family money to survive on until my clients figured out that "freelance" didn't mean "free." Eventually, I developed a reputation for being the go-to gal when you had a supernaturally themed book but no information about it.

Mother refused to speak to me until I apologized, a condition that evaporated when I failed to do so for more than a year. My massive, spectacular failure was not only a public embarrassment for her—intolerable— but the first time I wouldn't allow my mother to step in and make it all better—inconceivable.

I didn't want to be doted on. And she didn't know how to handle that. It broke our relationship, because

I wouldn't fall into line with what she needed from me. The only thing I could say I was proud of from that time in my life was that I didn't go crawling back to my mother, no matter how much she pressured me to. I had enough stiff-necked pride not to do that.

I still smarted over not having my PhD, though. I'd wanted that, to show to my father. And Michael's actions had taken that away. I wasn't sure I would ever be able to start another program. I would be too intimidated, too wary of other students. For now, my life was enough.

Or at least it was until I got dropped into this hell-hole.

I hated Kentucky. So very much.

I leaned back carefully against the tree trunk. I just had to wait until sunrise. Just until Finn was no longer able to get around. And then I could get far, far away from him. And if Ernie got in my way? God help him.

7

You're going to need to keep a pocket knife handy. Don't think about why, just do it.

—*Where the Wild Things Bite: A Survival Guide for Camping with the Undead*

If scientists ever figured out how to convert anger into energy, scorned, pissed-off women would be a renewable resource. We could power the world with our bitter, burning light.

The moment the sun rose over the trees, I hopped down from my oak cradle and set off for the horizon. I was far more prepared for the trek than I'd been the night after the plane crash. I had solid, non-blister-making shoes, a belly full of crackers, and enough anger to fuel me up steep forest embankments I was sure would eventually turn into sidewalks and streets.

Now that I didn't have Finn tagging along, distracting and deviling me, I recalled a good portion of the survival guides I'd read. I remembered that the white powder on the outside of an aspen tree could be rubbed on my skin for a natural sunscreen, protecting my nose from the worst of my "reintroduction" to sunshine. I used the knife to sharpen my walking stick for more threatening-to-Finn's-chest purposes. I even spotted a few wild mushrooms and little edible white-flowered plants called trout lilies. But I didn't partake, because I wasn't hungry enough to add misidentified poisons and/or hallucinogens to my daily routine. Also, trout lilies sounded sort of disgusting.

And in even further good news, I was making what felt like good progress now that I could see where I was going. I'd almost forgotten what it was like to feel the sun on my cheeks, to see my path through the woods without worrying about tripping.

I missed Finn. It was weird, but I felt so alone walking through the trees. I'd liked knowing that there was someone in the world who knew I was alive. I missed the assurance of Finn's steps beside me. I missed his voice, his teasing.

Nope, I told myself. That way lay madness. Finn was a bad person who had played around with my brain and tricked me into a weird Stockholm/survivor syndrome seminaked relationship. The fact that he was planning to continue to do so, and most likely drop me into the hands of his employers when I was no longer useful to him, hurt the most. I'd shared things with Finn that I'd never shared with any man. Hell, it had taken me years to talk to Rachel about my messed-up family dynamic, and she was my best friend. He'd taken the trust I'd given him and thrown it back in my face. He'd taken any hope I'd had of—

Nope. Nope. Again with the nope. I had to stop

thinking about Finn. I had to think of something that didn't threaten to drive me nuts. I would think of Rachel, who I knew would be happy to see me when I finally got home. I would think of the Jai Courtney movies I had lined up on my Netflix queue, which Rachel had promised she wouldn't watch without me. And I would dream of the enormous steak I was going to eat, which I now pictured with a side of warm Krispy Kreme doughnuts.

My stomach growled at the thought of food. The sun was far past noon, and it had been a long time since the last of my crackers. I searched through my bag, touching the plastic book covering to assure myself, once again, that it was OK. I still had two bottles of water, a few bottles of Ale-8, and the tins of mystery meat among my supplies.

Grimacing, I read the potted-meat label as I sat on a log in the shade. If nothing else, this long woodsy nightmare taught me how comfortable I had it at home. I wouldn't take for granted sunshine or being able to get food or water whenever I wanted it ever again. And I would give Rachel a raise, because she'd had to deal with my mother this whole time, and she would probably need the extra money to pay for counseling.

Just as my butt brushed the ground, I heard a threatening buzz rising above my head. I glanced up just in time to see a small, dark shape flinging itself toward my eyes. Shrieking, I threw my weight forward as a dozen wasps dive-bombed my scalp.

I landed knees-first on the hardened dirt and crab-walked as fast as my limbs would carry me. All the while, the wasps were circling over my head, buzzing angrily in my ears. One of them caught its creepy little wings in my hair and stung my palm when I batted at it to smack it loose.

Cradling my injured hand, I tried to figure out what the hell just happened.

Just above eye level, a wasp's nest the size of a beer keg was hanging by a very thin connection to a low-hanging branch. These wasps did not appear to be master builders, considering that the weight of the nest was bowing the whip-thin branch to its limit. And the wasps seemed to know their eviction was imminent, given the way they swarmed out of the imperiled hive at the merest threat . . . like my daring to sit under it to have my dinner.

I shuddered as the little bastards erupted over the gray papery surface, like Satan's birthday piñata. And now that I was no longer panicking, I could feel the burning pain radiating from the left side of the nape of my neck and my left hand. Using the cleanest nails on my right hand, I scraped the stinger loose from the back of my hand and rinsed the wound with bottled water. My neck stings were a lost cause, since I couldn't even see them to treat them. I was just going to have to suffer through it.

I didn't want to sound paranoid, but I was pretty sure the woods were trying to kill me.

"I'm just going to have to find another picnic spot," I grumbled, very slowly crawling back until the wasps lost interest in flying at my face. I pushed to my feet and hitched my bag over my shoulder, shoving the potted-meat can back inside.

Turning on my heel, I held up both hands and flipped the wasps the bird, which, when you thought about it, was sort of a zoologically funny concept. In response, a lone kamikaze insect flew at the right side of my nape and gave me a matching sting. "Ouch!" I yelped. "I'm going, I'm going! Little winged pricks."

I got as far as the adrenaline and wasp-venom madness could carry me and then flopped petulantly onto my butt in a little clearing with no branches overhead. Waspy jerks. I took a soda bottle out of my bag and held it to the back of my neck, hoping to find some relief from the cool container against the wounds.

Wait, wouldn't that just grind the stingers deeper into my skin? I pulled the soda bottle away and set it on the ground.

I tried not to find it suspicious that the potted-meat label failed to list exactly what the ingredients were, only "miscellaneous cow and pig parts, water, spice mix, and other things." If I was going to choose a portion of that explanation that bothered me the most, I was going to choose "miscellaneous parts." What didn't the manufacturer want me to know was going into the meat? Even hot dog manufacturers were more honest about their recipes.

My stomach growled again, and despite my doubts, my mouth was watering at the very prospect of *food*. I sighed, opened the can with its brittle aluminum pull-ring, and popped the top open. I was pretty sure that the contents only met the loosest possible definition of the word "meat."

Several odd little brown lumps swam in a congealed gravy-like sauce. The smell was enough to make me consider permanent vegetarianism. It wasn't spoiled, just very . . . very vinegary, like old dress shoes worn without socks.

"Thank you, brain, for that super-appetizing thought." I wiped my hands as best I could on my sweater and reached into the can. I pinched my nose and slid a chunk of meat into my mouth.

It was as gross as predicted, clammy and cold and overseasoned in an effort to hide the parts of the animal that were compressed into the jiggly cubes. I winced as I moved my teeth through it, but I couldn't help reveling in the chance to finally *chew* something that took effort.

The woman who, just days ago, had used a sanitizing wipe to clean off an airplane vent was now using her filthy fingers to dig potted meat out of a can. It was safe to say I had gotten over my germophobia.

I swallowed the next bite and the next, lecturing myself to slow down, not to make myself sick. But I just couldn't stop. For the first time since I'd left the airport, there was a possibility that I might not end a meal as hungry as I started it. I was so distracted by a potentially full belly that I didn't even hear the monster coming up behind me.

I'd never been a big fan of movies where the feckless heroine screams her head off when confronted by a monster in the woods. But now I retracted all of my scoffing at the B-list actresses and their over-the-top theatrics. Screaming was precisely the type of reaction you should have when confronted with an eight-foot Greek mythological nightmare.

How had something so big, with so many horrifying parts, moved so quickly and quietly? It walked on goat's legs, bent at awkward angles over cloven hooves. Its lion's torso led to two huge humanoid arms ending in massive, sharply clawed paws. And while I was concerned about all of those features, it was the giant hooded cobra head atop the muscled shoulders that really had me worried. The creature hissed so loudly it could have been heard as a roar, opening its mouth to reveal fangs dripping with poison.

You know, on any other trip, it would be weird to be attacked by a goat-lion-snake-monster in broad daylight.

I leaped to my feet. Was this real? Had I finally gone insane? Was this some sort of fever dream, or was I maybe already dead? Or maybe this was a normal side effect of eating potted meat of indeterminate age?

None of this self-examination was helpful, considering the monster was still standing over me, panting and snarling. This had to be a shifter. Also, shifters were clearly a thing. A big, scary thing. Chimeras wandering around western Kentucky would have made the news, right?

Despite the overwhelming weight of *fight* over my natural *flight* response, I felt weirdly reluctant to use the knife or the stick. For one thing, instead of holding either, I had an open can of potted meat in my hand. Second, I'd swung the blade at Ernie because he was actively trying to kill me. What if this shifter was just trying to scare me? Still, given the height, this person also had to be a pretty big shifter. From what I'd read, no matter what their type, they couldn't shift into anything significantly larger than their human body mass. Given the difference in our sizes, I was pretty sure whoever was behind all of those creature features would be able to wrestle me to the ground in seconds.

The fight instinct lost out to more sensible doubts about my bicep strength. I rolled my shoulder, preparing to bolt, and gritted my teeth against the pain that throbbed in my neck. In my head, I doubled my planned donation to a wasp-killing charity.

Wait.

Friar Thomas's book. A significant shock, whether from pain or emotional trauma, was supposed to be enough to jolt the shifter back to his human shape. Friar Thomas had once startled a resistant Russian shifter out of his bear shape by slapping him in the face with a hymnal. Sure, the former bear-man was offended, but at least he and Friar Thomas could have a friendly conversation. I cringed back from the monster, even though I knew that underneath the scary mask, he was probably an office-supply salesman named Marv.

At the very least, I figured he would be a lot less intimidating if he had a human face. So I reared back and poked the creature in its big golden snake eye with my thumb and forefinger.

I yanked my hand back, wiping it against my shirt. I

hadn't felt scales, just warm human skin and a wet eye. By the way, *yech*.

It seemed that the snake creature was a "skin magic" shifter, more common to the Southeastern tribes. Beneath the illusion of fur, scales, and so on, they remained human and vulnerable. They couldn't even use the claws and fangs they projected for defense, because those things weren't real. Other tribes were able to change physical form, something Friar Thomas referred to as "true shifting," labeling those tribes as more dangerous and unstable. But the skin magic shifters depended on intimidation.

And while all of this was very interesting, it was still shocking when the chimera let out a distinctly *feminine* howl and dropped to its knees, collapsing on its face in the grass.

A blue light shimmered across its skin and revealed an unusually tall, broad-shouldered woman in her late thirties with a no-nonsense cap of white-blond hair. She wore camo cargo pants, a black T-shirt, and an extremely irritated expression half covered by the hand she had clamped over her shiny-clean, raw-boned face.

"Whoops," I muttered, taking a step back.

"Why would you do that?" she growled in a gruff Midwestern accent.

"Why wouldn't you block my swing?" I yelled back.

"Who pokes a giant snake-lion-goat in the eye?"

"Well, I didn't take a lot of self-defense classes, but I think you'll find that no matter the species, a person has a hard time bullying you if you've poked them in the eye."

"I don't want to bully you! I just want to talk to you!"

"Yes, please excuse me for misreading the intent of your hissing cobra fangs." I took a step back.

"I just want the book," she panted. "Give it to me, and we'll stop chasing you."

"So I'm assuming that *you* crashed my plane?" She nodded, and my free hand curled forward in a threatening gesture. She scrambled back across the grass.

"Don't try to poke me in the eye again," she warned me.

"Don't crash any more of my planes," I told her, brandishing the can with my other hand in a way I hoped was threatening.

"My family crashed the plane. If it makes you feel better, I voted against it."

Actually, that did make me feel better. I liked knowing that while she might be turning into a six-and-a-half-foot cobra, I wasn't dealing with a total psychopath.

"Why do you need it so badly? Why are you so willing to hurt me over this thing? Can't you just negotiate with Jane to buy it from her? I'll give you her contact information."

The woman ran a hand through her hair, and it fell in disarray around her face, reminding me of a fluffy baby chick. Why couldn't she turn into a giant baby chick? That would have been a much-appreciated change of pace. "You've told her how valuable that book is. She'll never sell it to us. We thought it would be better that she thought it was lost in the crash."

"You had enough money to crash a plane," I noted. "Murder-by-pilot has to be a pretty expensive proposition. Plus, I can't help but notice that you left out the part where *I* would also be lost in the crash."

"Actually, that wasn't as expensive as you would think. Ernie really hated his job." She jerked her shoulders. "We bought out the rest of the seats so no one else would get hurt. You were collateral damage."

I blew out an irritated breath. "That creates very little hope for me regarding the airline industry. Also, screw you and your whole family. *Collateral damage.*"

The woman put her hands to the ground, as if to push up to a standing position.

I held the potted meat can in what I hoped was a threatening manner. "Ah, ah, ah. Not so fast. Stay on the ground."

The woman sank back down, glaring at me with eyes the color of a bottomless Scottish lake. "You wouldn't understand. We're not like werewolves. We're not like witches. No one has ever bothered to study us in any sort of serious way. Hell, most people don't even know we exist. There's still so much we don't know about ourselves. We're obsessive about our shifting, to the point where we can't function. We don't know why we're this way or how it started. We don't know why some families turn out generation upon generation of talented shifters, while the trait is fading out of other families so fast they don't even consider themselves shifters. Some of us can't control the shifts, so we have to live in hiding for fear we'll suddenly turn into a giant rabbit in front of our human neighbors. Others are driven mad trying to find the right form, that perfect form that will make us feel whole. We're so spread out and we're not exactly known for being organized. We each keep to our own little group, and we don't talk to each other. You know, some of us actually think we're cursed to be this way, can you believe that? Of all the backward-ass things? We've been hearing for years that Friar Thomas wrote a book that would give us the answers we need. We've been searching for a copy for years, and *nothing*. Until some pain-in-the-ass librarian friend of my cousin Ensel spotted you with it at the library. What are the odds?"

"I've wondered the same myself," I muttered.

"Having that book will help us understand ourselves in a way we never have before. It's like a how-to guide on handling your gift without driving yourself insane. Isn't that a better use for it than giving it to some rich old vampire and letting it mold in her library?"

I noted that she didn't mention the final chapter's "shifter A-bomb." Was it because she didn't know about it? Or because she didn't think I knew about it and didn't want to tip me off? Well, I certainly wasn't about to bring it into the conversation.

"But it's not up to me to make that decision. I've been hired to do a job. I'm taking it rather personally that you keep trying to kill me in the process, so I'm going to stick with it," I told her.

The fluffy chick sighed, brushing her hands off on her pants and rolling to her knees. "Well, I'm telling you now, I'm not letting you out of these woods with it."

I believed her. And that didn't exactly endear me to her. I felt for the knife, wondering if I could pull it out of the bag before she pushed up from the ground and tackled me. After the eye poke, she knew to watch me for sudden movements, so probably not.

I tried to think of something else from Friar Thomas's work that I could use, like an acute sensitivity to poison ivy or a particularly thin spot in the skull that I could exploit with a rock, but mostly it was genealogical information and details about the act of shifting itself.

I had to stop thinking like myself. I had to stop being so analytical. What would Finn do in a situation like this, once attempts to charm this woman had failed and he was forced to use his wits instead of his wiles? I didn't have strength on my side. I didn't have a weapon. But I did have something that the shifter woman didn't.

Potted meat.

I whipped my hand toward her, splashing the foul, vinegary sauce into her face. She screamed, though I couldn't tell if that was rage or disgust, as she wiped her eyes with the tail of her shirt. "Why my eyes again, you hateful bitch?!"

"Because you keep leaving them unprotected!" I yelled. I jogged back toward the wasps, careful that she was able to see me, even with the potted-meat sauce stinging her eyes. The shifter roared as she stumbled after me. I scanned the branches overhead, listening for the sound of buzzing. After a few minutes of steady, careful running, I spotted my wasp assailants, circling lazily around the top of the hive. I cut a wide circle around the opposite side of the tree, avoiding the insects' attention, and waited behind the trunk. When I heard the shifter's heavy footsteps approaching, I slowly pulled the overworked, springy branch back as far as it would go.

The movement roused a few wasps, which meandered out of the hive but didn't come closer to me. The shifter woman barreled through the trees, and I let go of the branch. It snapped forward, and the already tenuous connection between the nest and the wood snapped from the momentum. The hive launched toward the shifter, sailing in a beautiful arc and landing at her feet. It exploded on impact, and a red cloud of wasps burst around her.

The terrified animal noise that came out of the shifter's mouth made me want to clap my hands over my ears. Instead, self-preservation had me running, doubling around so I was back on course. The shifter screamed and screamed as the wasps attacked her.

I pumped my legs, eager to get as far away from the noise as possible. I eventually slowed, but I kept moving at a steady pace, the shifter's howls echoing in my ears. I'd hurt her, seriously. And while her screams were deeply unpleasant, I couldn't find it in me to be sorry. While I appreciated that she had voted against crashing my plane, her family clearly had plans to kill me. She got off easy.

Eventually, the woman's screams faded into nothing, and the light around me turned purple. I didn't want to stop. It was irrational, but I just kept holding on to the hope that the next hill I climbed would make way for a city block. At this point, I would settle for a cabin and a helpful forest ranger.

I was much more careful, scanning my immediate surroundings for additional insect Death Stars as I moved. Without that deliberate, constant scan, I might not have spotted the conical orange flowers in the underbrush. I knew I should recognize them from somewhere, but I couldn't remember why.

They reminded me a little of snapdragons, with their rumpled petals, but I knew that was the wrong name. It was a pretty name. Gah, why couldn't I remember it? It was jimsonwe—no, that was something else. Gemweed? No, jewelweed. Jewelweed grew in profusion in Kentucky and was an excellent natural treatment for poison ivy and insect stings. I stooped to pick as many of the blooms as I could. I rubbed them gently between my palms, trying to express the plant oils into the sting on my hand. Eventually, the throbbing eased, and I breathed a sigh of relief. I pressed more flowers between my hands and rubbed the oil into my neck.

"Thank you, obsessive-compulsive reading tendencies. You have served me well, once again." I hummed happily, though I still wanted to burn that hive like Darth Vader wanted to crush the Rebel Forces.

It was beyond dark, and I wasn't able to see the trees in front of me. It was probably time for me to stop for the day. But I didn't want to make a fire, for fear of catching some other shifter's attention. Also, I didn't know how. I didn't want to try to find a place to sleep for the night, because I now knew that covert wasp death traps were a possibility. Basically, I was trying to deny the fact that nighttime existed.

Sound plan, really.

I stopped to open a soda, hoping that a little glucose would lift my mood, but before I could bring the bottle to my lips, a hand slipped around my mouth and pulled me back into a stand of pine trees. Struggling against the hard body tucked against my back, I sank my teeth into the hand, breaking the skin. I heard a pained hiss in my ear, and the hand yanked away. I whipped my head around to find Finn standing behind me, a finger (uninjured) pressed to his lips. And when I saw that it was Finn, I fought even harder. He shook his head back and forth violently but didn't make a sound.

Behind us, I heard the murmur of voices, feet shuffling through the grass. I could see flashlights bobbing as a group of at least six men walked past us.

People! I struggled against Finn's grasp. This could be a search party or a rescue squad. Why was he trying to keep us from being found by people who might want to help us? People who might have supplies or cell phones or even a spare Tic Tac?

I inhaled sharply, but Finn cupped his fingers, recently healed, against my lips and whispered, "Shhh." I sneered and stomped the heel of my boot on his toes, grinding it into the dirt. His eyes narrowed, and he clenched his teeth against the pain, but he still didn't make a sound.

We stayed locked like that, staring each other down, even while I heard the voices outside our shelter. And then I heard the voices say, "Earl found her half-dead about three miles from here. Said the librarian bitch threw a hornet's nest at her!"

I froze.

Another deeper voice added, "I'm telling ya, this book better be worth the trouble, John. Crashing a plane, Susannah half-dead from wasp stings. Wandering in the damn woods, up to our asses in deer ticks."

"It will be," the first shifter promised. "It will all be worth it, once we find the book."

My breath caught. The shifters! And they did not sound happy with me. They sounded gruff, with some odd, discordant Midwestern accent that drew out their vowel sounds and roughened their voices. I squinted at the shadows cast through their flashlight beams. Very large, very wide shadows. These were not petite shapeshifters. I shrank back, unintentionally curling my body against Finn's. His hand skimmed down my side in what I was sure was supposed to be a comforting gesture.

A little bit of the weight dragging on my conscience let loose, now that I knew I hadn't killed the shifter woman (all the way, at least) with an insect bomb. I might have said that proved my pacifist leanings, but I was still crushing a man's foot under my heel, knowing full well he couldn't make a sound without risking exposure.

I was coming to understand that I was a complicated person.

As the voices faded, I bit down on Finn's fingers again. He yanked them out of my mouth and gave me a light shove so he could pull his foot from under my heel.

"Get away from me," I growled quietly. "I told you to leave me alone."

"I just saved your life," he rumbled. He swept his hand toward the retreating voices. "Those were my employers. They're looking for you. I can't fight them off, because I've been living on possum. If I really wanted to hurt you, if I was still trying to get them the book, I would have turned you over to them. Also, as a side note, you smell really nice."

"And isn't it convenient that you just happened by when they did?" I whispered, pushing my way out of the trees and into the open air, away from Finn and his welcome, familiar, spicy amber smell and his stupid, handsome face. I watched the flashlight beams move farther away and marched swiftly in the opposite direction. "And I smell like flowers because I was stung by half a wasp's nest. It was not an effort to smell pretty for you."

"Are you kidding?" Finn threw up his arms as he kept pace with me. "You still don't trust me?"

"Let me pronounce this very slowly so you understand me, Mr. Puppet Master Manipulator. I'll even make hand gestures." I held up both of my middle fingers while shaking my head slowly. "Noooo."

"Hey, if you're referring to my talent, I could have used it against you after you figured me out!" he shot back. "I could have forced you to stay with me, to toddle along quietly while I handed the book over to my bosses and got the debt taken off my name, but I didn't."

"Most people don't want credit for not being a supervillain, Finn. Most people leave 'control an innocent bystander like a puppet' off their day planner in general. And before you get too excited about your new-found virtue, let's just remember that you *have* used your superpower against me."

"Just that once," he confessed.

"It's amazing how 'just that once' doesn't make me feel better," I grumbled. I shoved my way out of the pines, sure to make the branches whip back and smack him in the face.

He yelped as softly as he could and followed me out, rubbing his hand over his injured cheeks. "That first night we were together, I was afraid you were going to leave me while I was sleeping for the day. Which you did anyway, which proves my influence over you wasn't that strong in the first place."

"So I'm supposed to be happy that I have too much 'noise in my head' for you to be able to hypnotize me properly?"

"No, you should be happy that I've been trying so hard to treat you differently from every other mark I've targeted over the years. My heart just wasn't in it. I didn't want inside your head, so I couldn't get inside your head. That's why the pilot was so annoyed with me."

"Again, I am not seeing any reason for me to swoon in gratitude."

Tugging at my arm gently, he asked, "Would you just sit down for a second?"

And when I didn't comply, Finn forced me to sit and put my open, intact soda in my hand. "Drink."

When I tried to stand, he pulled me down to the ground, into his lap, wrapping his arm around my waist. He forced me to stay put, putting the bottle to my lips.

"You have some serious issues with personal boundaries," I sniped at him, my voice making the aluminum vibrate. I wanted to fight. I wanted him to know I could give him pain beyond a crushed toe and branches to the cheekbones. But it was so comfortable being cradled in his lap, leaning back against him, with my head tilted against the curve of his neck, with his familiar scent filling my head. I relaxed against him and appreciated that I wasn't alone and terrified for a few minutes.

Wait.

"Are you doing it right now?" I asked him. "Controlling my brain?"

"No!" he insisted. "You can tell when I'm in someone else's head. I don't talk. I don't move. My eyes go sort of cloudy, according to what I've heard. It's like I go into a sort of trance-y dream state."

"Well, that's something." I sighed.

"If I was not in control of my talent, kitten, I wouldn't sleep next to you," he said.

"And that's something random."

"I lost control of my talent a while back. It was like a power surge, which was great. Better range, more complete influence over the target. When I slept through the days, my mind would literally wander, and I would end up inside the head of some soccer mom two blocks away. I would sink so deep into her brain that I would end up walking around my apartment and mirroring her actions."

"So you're a sleepwalker," I said, not quite understanding his urgency. Or why he kept trying to force-feed me soda.

Finn nodded. "A sleepwalker with the ability to rip off doorknobs if they kept me from leaving a room and walking out into the daylight, if that's what the soccer mom did. I had some pretty serious burns. And I developed a phobia of going to sleep. Every time I did, I thought, is this it? If I drift off, is this going to be the day I don't wake up? It was terrifying and draining. And it made me make some not so great decisions."

"This is where I repeat my thesis that most of your decisions are bad decisions."

"I have a handle on it now," he promised me. "I worked with a friend on some meditation techniques. He had the same problem to an extent, except his control was taken from him by a curse."

Finn tipped the bottle, and I let the soda pass my lips while he spoke. It was warm and a little too sweet, but my mouth was so dry I didn't care. "I've been living my life like this for a very long time, before I was a vampire. I don't know any other way to be. The charm, the little conversational tricks, picking up on people's tells, I learned it from my father. And he learned it from his. We started out as carnival folk, fortune-tellers gouging Dust Bowl farmers, but Jimmy Palmeroy stepped it up. He always knew how to put on the right airs, to rub the right elbows. He thought big. He took my friend Max in when we were kids and told me that from that day on, we were going to earn our keep. We pulled all the classics. Salting the mine. Pig in the poke. Max was particularly good at the badger game."

I didn't want to know what any of those things were, particularly if a real badger was involved.

"Like I said, there was plenty of cash up for grabs back then, for people who knew how to grab it. Max and I just figured out how to do that without start-up capital."

"So . . . you were con men?"

"I like to think of it as more like Robin Hood–style bandits who took riches and distributed them to the needy. But in this case, we were the needy. We just cut out the middlemen."

"OK, then, con men."

"Fine. It wasn't like we didn't have style or skill. It takes brains to figure out what people want to hear to make the decision you make for them."

I pushed away, bracing my hands against his chest. It was still so strange not to feel a heartbeat beneath my hands. But I supposed that Michael, with his beating human heart, had lied to me just as seriously as Finn. Then again, I still carried quite the grudge against Michael. "Am I supposed to find this charming?"

He shifted me over his thighs, but I think it had to do with embarrassment over a growing problem in his lap rather than anything I said.

"Well, that's how we lived, even after my dad died. You get to the point where you don't think of people as, well, people. You don't think of the guy you're selling 'mineral rights' to as a father whose life savings would be better spent sending his kids to college. You don't think of the woman investing in your swampland as a widow who's only buying in because she's lonely and she likes the conversations. You're focused on chasing that big retirement score. And beyond the cost to your soul, there are real consequences. It's not like the movies. You don't get to walk away in slow motion with a big bag of cash. People get pissed off when they realize they've been tricked. And we fooled the wrong people . . . a lot of the wrong people. But it only caught up to us when we tangled with vampires, who did *not* appreciate buying a semitruck full of skin cream we promised would protect them from sun exposure so they could go out during the day."

"So . . . sunblock," I said, as he turned me so I was straddling him. I scooted back on his thighs, so I wouldn't come into contact with the "problem." I was relishing the chance to be the one thinking clearly between the two of us for a change, and I wouldn't be able to do that if I was rubbing up against him like that.

Finn cleared his throat as the "problem" became a full-fledged situation. He seemed to be having trouble finding words, which I was enjoying immensely. "Actually, it was mayonnaise."

OK, maybe I would rub against him just a little bit.

And yes, a tiny part of me felt a little guilty for using sexual attraction and just a little bit of guilt to manipulate information out of him, especially when I didn't trust him with so much as a cheek kiss at the moment.

But this whole "turning the tables" thing was turning out to be considerably more entertaining than finding out I was the dupe.

"Why didn't you just sell them sunblock?" I asked, walking my fingers up his chest. He rolled his hips, ever so slightly, and then stopped, blowing out a breath as he curled his hands around my ass.

"It was the seventies." He practically whimpered, clearing his throat again before adding, "People didn't care so much about sun damage back then. Nothing available would have offered the vampires enough protection to go out during the day. We thought maybe if they went out in the sun with the mayo on their skin, the problem would resolve itself. But the vampires didn't trust us. When they tested the cream and figured out it didn't work, they took it personally, said they wanted to give us all the time in the world to pay them back for the offense—triple our fee plus a twenty percent 'penalty' fee. Ironically enough, our next job was enough to pay them back, so we didn't need eternity. But who were we to argue with eternal youth and superpowers?"

"And the shifters, was that another con?"

"No, I just couldn't deliver something I promised them, not because I didn't have it, but some other guy swiped it out from under me when I went to pick it up."

"The nerve of that guy," I said.

Finn didn't rise to my snarky bait, trailing his fingers along my throat, up toward my mouth. His thumb swept over the ridge of my bottom lip, sending a shiver of excitement down my spine to throb between my thighs. Maybe I was a little more into this than I thought I was. "Yeah, well, the shifters are not going to be very impressed with my delivery rate at this point."

"Could mean a really bad Yelp review," I told him.

"No sympathy from you at all, huh?"

I pointed to my more-than-a-little-judge-y expression. "That was the extent of my sympathy."

"You are a hard, hard woman," he told me, shaking his head. I glanced at the hard bulge between his thighs and quirked my lips. He laughed. "I just laid it all out there for you, exposed my tender underbelly, and nothing. What happened to the sweet girl who didn't want me to kill a possum right after we crashed?"

"You just admitted that you lie for a living. You were going to use me like a puppet to pay off your debt. Why would I feel sorry for you?"

"I have no reason left to lie," he said, leaning up as if to kiss me.

I pushed him back down, all the way, until he was lying flat on the ground. He let out a frustrated groan.

"In the history of plausible reasons, you have managed to give the least plausible. Congratulations. I will make you a little plaque from wood and pebbles later."

He frowned at me. I smiled down at him sweetly. He frowned harder. I jerked my shoulders. I was not sorry. In fact, I was feeling very . . . powerful at the moment. In control, with this big, somewhat treacherous man beneath me looking helpless as he gave in to me.

"And in all that emotional exposure, you really don't see what we have in common?" he said.

"Considering that I'm still trying to figure out whether the badger game involves an actual badger, no. No, no, I do not."

"Because we're cut from the same cloth, you and I, the products of parents who programmed us to be their little robots, carrying on just the same as Mom and Dad. I went along with it, because I didn't know any better. And the payoff for me was pretty damn good—money, the easy life, a little fun, even though I knew what it cost. Hell, I carried it on after the old man died. For you, there was no payoff, except years of propping your mom up. So you broke away. You did what I couldn't. I mean, sure, you ended up with some"—he paused, and I raised my eyebrows—"interesting side effects. But you're doing the opposite of what your parents wanted for you. You're living your own life. You seem to like your job. You're your own master."

OK, that was the first time anyone had ever said anything like that to me, and it was taking a lot of resolve on my part to remember the lying and the brain-diddling.

"That makes you very interesting to me, that you could have all that strength wrapped up under a thick layer of neuroses."

I dropped my head. Yeah, that helped.

"But I think all of your phobias and statistics, that's just your way of controlling your environment. Making you feel comfortable. And I think now that you've been through this and realize how little you can actually control and that, statistically, you're probably not going to die if something goes awry, I'll bet you won't think about that kind of thing nearly as much."

"But we have almost died. On several occasions."

"But we didn't," he countered.

"But we almost did."

"But we didn't. Also, we shouldn't start this many sentences with 'but.'"

I cleared my throat. "So what are you going to do now that you can't provide the shifters with the book? Bad Yelp review notwithstanding."

"Well, they're not going to be happy, I can tell you that much. These shifters are not your typical cuddly werewolf types. They don't like humans, and they like vampires even less. Part of the reason they're so eager to get their hands on the manuscript is that they believe that it will help them ascend to a higher level of transition, actually taking on the physical form of the animals they shift to."

"She never mentioned that." I huffed, thinking of the shifter woman and her justifications for trying to steal the book. I did notice that Finn didn't mention the final chapter's "revelation." I guessed that the shifters hadn't told him about it for fear that Finn would try to renegotiate.

"What?" he asked, eyeing me in a sleepy, addled sort of fashion.

I shook my head. "Never mind. Is that attitude typical among shifters?" I asked him.

"No," he said. "This family, they're *real* special."

"And then, once you figure something out, let me guess: you'll reform, go on the straight and narrow?" I asked, not even bothering to hide my sarcasm, as he plucked gently at my hair, pulling me closer to him.

"I can't make any guarantees," he said. "I'm trying this new thing where I don't lie to you."

"That would be a pleasant change of pace," I said, as he tried to kiss me. I pulled back from him, ducking my head. His lips brushed against my ear.

"For a long time, I didn't think I was capable of wanting someone for more than a little while," he whispered. "And then I met the woman I sired, and I found I wanted that. I wanted it so much that I was willing to turn my world inside out for her."

I tried to pull back, but his grip on my hips was tight, as if he'd expected the withdrawal. Of course, he was pining for some sexy, nubile vampire goddess. I doubted very much that she'd eaten potted meat for dinner. And she probably didn't have moss in her hair.

"But the person I was with her, it wasn't me. It was a weird, neutered version of me, smoother, more formal. I was trying to be what I thought she wanted. She saw what she thought were the worst parts of me, and she wasn't even close. I didn't call her 'kitten' or 'doll,' because it didn't feel right. I lied, and I never told her I was sorry," he added. "I made excuses. I justified. I didn't tell her I was sorry."

His hands cupped my face. "I'm sorry," he whispered against my mouth. "I was wrong. And I never admit when I'm wrong. But I'm admitting it to you. I was wrong to manipulate you and lie to you. I can't make any guarantees that I'll become a better man. Because, again, I don't want to lie to you. But I won't hurt you on purpose. Not anymore. Please just stop running from me. And kicking me. And hitting me in the face with heavy objects. You are a very violent person, do you realize?"

"Wh-why would you say that?" I groaned. "You always do that, adding the wrong thing at the right time. You took a perfectly romantic moment—"

He lunged for me and claimed my mouth with lips and teeth, making me forget for a breath that I was still angry with him, that I couldn't trust him completely. He kissed me with a ferocity that made me shudder against him, arms snaking around his neck to keep from falling. Twisting his hand in my hair, he murmured against my mouth, eyes open and focused on mine. "You're also funny and smart enough to intimidate the hell out of me. And brave, so brave to be out here on your own and scared a lot of the time and constantly in danger, not for one second asking me to take care of you or protect you. Hell, most of the time, you're trying to get rid of me." He kissed me again. "Please stop doing that."

I craned my head forward, as far as his tangle with my hair allowed. "Stop giving me reasons to do that."

And instead of recoiling or wincing, he flared his pupils wide, and his hips stuttered up against me. His cool breath fluttered against my mouth as his fingers combed down my arms. "Yes, ma'am."

I did not let things go any further physically, because, frankly, we needed to keep moving. Because I was not ready for sex with him. Sex in the woods would solve none of our problems and create a lot more. Also, it was entirely possible that there was more than one group of those corn-fed shifters, and I did not want to have a confrontation with angry cobra hybrid creatures sans pants.

Hearing more of Finn's background didn't quite give me a feeling of "even ground" or intimacy. But at least I had some insight into how his head might work. And I hoped that Finn had given me all of the bad news. At this point, what else could he be hiding?

I mentally ran away from the question. Nope, nope, didn't want to know.

"Did you get a pretty good look at the shifters?" I asked him as we walked. He nodded. "Did they have supplies, tents, backpacks, that sort of thing?"

He stopped. "No, come to think of it, they didn't."

"That's good news."

"How?"

"Well, they couldn't have come far without some sort of gear, right? And if we're heading in the opposite direction, we must be getting closer to the point where they entered the woods."

He grinned at me. "Very logical."

"Unless shifters have some sort of special ability to turn into their own tents, which Friar Thomas didn't mention in his book. And now that I think about it, that's sort of a horrifying image. Clearly, I am not prepared for the reintroduction of caffeine to my system. No more soda for me."

Finn shuddered. "So what are you going to do if we find the end to these damn woods?"

"I'm going to take a bath and then a shower and then take another bath," I told him. "And then take another shower."

He stopped in his tracks at the bottom of a steep hill, making me turn.

"What? Are you OK?"

Finn held up a hand, closing his eyes. "I'm just picturing the bathing cycle. I need a minute for my blood to go back to the right places."

"Come on," I said, rolling my eyes and dragging him along with me. "I'm going to sleep on a bed, a real bed with sheets and pillows not made of pine needles. I'm going to eat my body weight in ice cream. I'm going to write a stern letter to the airline."

"I will sign that letter," he told me.

"Thank you. And I'm going to go back and finish my PhD," I said. "Screw Michael Malone."

"I don't know Michael Malone. Would I like him before I screwed him?"

"We don't even joke about that," I muttered.

"Well, what does screwing him have to do with your PhD?" he asked.

I took advantage of the incline, pretending that I just didn't have the breath to climb it and talk at the same time. Finn had told me about his con man past and his father. Then again, I told him about my mother and her plethora of neuroses. So maybe we were even . . . No, wait, he also told me about his vampire-childe-slash-almost-sweetheart who ditched him for his dishonesty. I still owed him some humiliating backstory.

I took a deep breath. "Fine."

It took the better part of the hill climb for me to finish my sad tale of academic betrayal and romantic ridicule. It would have taken less time without the panting and occasional breaks for me to catch my breath. (Stupid hill.) Finn remained quiet as I let the whole story loose, and I was proud that I could do it without getting emotional or cursing. Much.

"So Rachel moved into my building, and whenever I started feeling sorry for myself or developing that post-break-up amnesia that told me maybe Michael wasn't so bad, she would throw a pillow at my face. I tried to get insulted about it, but it was a very effective method."

Finn was silent and angry, and not just in that "annoyed by Anna" fashion. "And where is *Doctor* Malone now?" he seethed, helping me up the hill through force of will and bracing me against his arms.

"I have deliberately tried not to keep up with him, for the sake of my emotional health, but Rachel says that in addition to serving on the University of Virginia's faculty, he was freelancing for several well-known vampire-owned auction houses as their literary appraiser. Somehow I've managed to steer clear of him, despite the similar circles in which we run. And I guess I should consider myself fortunate that we haven't competed for the same jobs yet, because that could get ugly really fast. Rachel has a special jar filled with change next to her computer. It's labeled, 'Bail money for when Anna meets up with Michael Malone.' But I think it's for her, not me. Because she is going to hurt him."

Finn didn't say anything.

"And she's probably going to do it with a farm implement."

I really thought that would get a reaction, but nothing.

"No jokes?" I asked him. "No pithy comments on the roots of my enormous trust issues?"

"No," he said, shaking his head. "I'm just sorry I added to them."

"Don't do that," I told him, my mouth hovering close to his. "Don't feel bad for me. I don't want your pity. I want a couple of other things from you." I glanced downward, toward his belt. "But not your pity."

A pleased rumble vibrated from his chest to mine, making me shiver. I let my lips travel the strong curve of his jaw, down his neck, to the hollow of his throat. A shudder rippled down his body, and his arms tightened around me.

Over his shoulder, I could see something glittering in the distance. Not the moon or a flashlight but a solid, nonwavering electric light, as if from a building. A real building, with electricity and people and phone lines and nonpotted meat.

I blinked hard, confirming when I opened my eyes again that the building was still there.

I patted Finn's back. "Finn?"

"Mmm?" he murmured against my skin.

I shook his shoulder, and when that didn't stop his kisses, I tugged at his hair until he was forced to break his mouth away from my neck. "Finn!"

His eyes were unfocused, like a man waking from a super-dirty dream. "What?"

I bent my head so my mouth hovered near his ear. "That's a light."

8

Accept that there are some situations for which you will never be able to prepare.

—Where the Wild Things Bite: A Survival Guide for Camping with the Undead

W hat?" He turned toward the direction where I was pointing. And since I was clinging to him, he took me with him. I felt like a koala on a Tilt-A-Whirl.

"That's a light!" I cried. "A real nonnatural light! People, Finn! We found people!"

His smile was radiant in the moonlight. "We made it!"

I whooped, throwing my arms around his neck while he whirled me around.

"This is how Gilligan and the Skipper *never* got to feel!" I yelled, throwing my arms into the air.

We burst out laughing and engaged in a good, long hug that was almost free of sexual tension. I had never felt so relieved in my entire life. I wasn't lost anymore. I wouldn't be presumed dead. Despite everything, I was going to get the book to Jane. I was going home.

Finn dropped me gently to the ground, and we

scrambled to right our clothes. We ran through the woods, screaming and laughing. He snickered, even as my feet dragged and I tripped. Finn slung me around his shoulders, wrapping me around him like a backpack.

"No arguments. I have plenty of strength," he said, carrying me at a quick but not inhuman pace.

Bouncing against Finn's back, I blinked away happy, silly tears as the golden electric light came into focus. I couldn't believe we'd found our way out of the lakelands, the fifth circle of hillbilly hell. I tucked my head against Finn's shoulder, giving thanks to whatever deity oversaw protracted vampire camping trips.

Thank you for bringing me through the wilderness and into almost-nude contact with Finn. Though, to be honest, you could have done both a little faster.

The trees became fewer and farther between, and the ground was smoother. Soon we skidded to a stop on a gravel drive in front of an enormous Spanish-style mansion, where lights blazed in every window. The carved wooden sign on the door labeled it "The Possum's Nest Lodge of Cooter Holler, Ky." Because what else would it be called?

The Possum's Nest was fading from its former glory. The roof was tiled in dull, chipped brown slate, and the once-creamy stucco on the walls was riddled with cracks. A water fountain stood next to the oversized carved front door, empty and split down the middle. Tree limbs lay scattered around the grounds, looking eerily like spindly arms reaching from under the earth. Even stranger, there was no one in sight.

Not one car in the gravel parking lot. All of those windows—without curtains—and we couldn't see a soul. And for some reason, that filled me with a sense of foreboding, as in "standing outside of the Bates Motel" foreboding. Maybe even "checking into the Overlook" foreboding. It definitely ranked high in terms of bathtub murder potential.

"What is this place?" I whispered.

"I'm just glad you see it, too," Finn whispered back. "Because I'm pretty sure this is one of those ghost buildings that only appears when it's hungry for more souls."

"Maybe there is different, less frightening civilization nearby," I whispered, turning around to see a huge gray form looming over me.

"JEE-sus!" I yelped, throwing myself back into Finn's arms.

The gray shape turned out to be an eight-foot-tall concrete possum, painted in lifelike colors, with oversized, bulging white eyes and pink rat tail. The exaggeration made the statue look more like a large, aggressive Chihuahua, looming over us with raised Frankenstein-posed arms. And he was one of three. He had several possum buddies frozen in mid-lurch behind him.

"Why?" Finn said, shaking his head. "Why would anyone do this?"

"I think we should run," I told him. "Now."

"I would, but I'm paralyzed with fear right now."

"You eat possums!" I whispered fiercely.

"And now they're back for revenge!"

Behind us, the front door opened, and a small, thin figure stood silhouetted against the light. "Hello?"

Finn stepped closer, carefully eyeing the elderly proprietress. She looked like a tiny goblin woman, wizened and white-haired, wearing a fuzzy pink cardigan and pleated khakis and a possum pin at her shoulder. She was adorable. I was no longer sure that I trusted adorable.

The woman gave a little wave. "Hello."

I froze. I'd forgotten how to talk to people who weren't trying to swindle or kill me. How did you make small talk? What was I supposed to say? What tone of voice should I use? Also, is it considered rude to ask someone if they are planning to lure you into their potentially evil hotel and imprison you until it was time to bake you into a pie?

"We were hoping to use your phone," I said. "And all of your indoor facilities. You do have indoor plumbing, right?"

Finn shot me an incredulous glance. "I'm so sorry, ma'am. She's had a long day. Travel makes her sort of loopy."

"Oh, isn't that sweet, you're honeymooners. You'd have to be, to be all snuggled up like that," she said, nodding at the way Finn was still cradling me in his arms. We glanced down at our dirtied, ragged clothes and exchanged a concerned look. Could she not see how disheveled we were? Maybe that was why those possums were so exaggerated. Her eyes were so far gone she could only see horrifically cartoonish features. Her glasses were so thick maybe we could hand her an index card and convince her that it was an American Express.

How exactly were we supposed to play this? It seemed wrong not to tell her that we'd survived a plane crash and a survival hike from hell. But what if the shapeshifters came looking for Ernie or, worse, came looking for us? Surely they would notice police cars and ambulances and federal aviation vehicles parked in front of the Possum's Nest. We could be putting her in jeopardy if we gave her our real names. Worse, we could be putting ourselves in danger, which was against my personal policy. Also, the woman had giant concrete possums in her front yard, which didn't exactly speak well for her sanity/potential evil.

"You are married, aren't you?" the woman asked sternly. "I don't allow for couples to sleep together here unless they're married. This isn't some back-woods love shack."

"Oh, of course," I said, quickly. "Just married."

"Yaaaay, marriage," Finn added in a strained voice that made me snicker.

"It's so nice to see a young couple in love," she cooed. "Come in, come in."

"Play along," I whispered, as she opened the door for us.

"You're insane," he whispered back. But he played the part of the doting husband, carrying me through the door bridal-style. The parlor centered around a large fieldstone fireplace, flanked by old Civil War reproduction couches and dark wood furniture. The large picture window framed a brass birdcage. Inside was a taxidermied rooster. The little old woman tottered behind a large maple sideboard she was using as a registration desk and pulled open a leather portfolio. A little brass sign near the registration table stated "Mrs. Maybelline McCreary, Proprietress."

"Now, do you have a reservation?" she asked. And despite the additional light from the refurbished oil lamps, she did not seem to register our dirty, disheveled appearance. I had to wonder how well she saw or if she was just being polite.

"No, ma'am. We just happened upon the place," I said.

"Stumbled right into it," Finn added, prompting me to elbow him in the ribs, making him chuckle.

"Name?"

"David Seever. S-E-E-V-E-R," Finn piped up before I could say anything.

Mrs. McCreary flipped through her reservations book, mulling over the list of rooms as if it was going to be a struggle to fit us in, despite the fact that the inn's parking lot had been completely empty. "Breakfast is at seven and lasts until eleven. We don't accommodate vegetarians."

The disdain in her voice made me want to snicker, but I didn't think Mrs. McCreary would appreciate that.

"Actually, my wife is pretty hungry. Is there any chance she could get something from the kitchen?" Finn asked.

Mrs. McCreary looked me over, still totally oblivious to my dirtied, disheveled state, which made me doubt the effectiveness of those bottle-thick bifocals of hers. "I'll send up a cheese sandwich," she said, sniffing.

"Thank you," I said politely. "Would you mind if I used your phone?"

"It's not a long-distance call, is it? Those charges apply to your bill," she said, peering at me over the rims of her glasses. "As well as late-night room service."

"I understand," I told her solemnly.

"Phone's in the breakfast nook," she told me, nodding to a dining table surrounded by a frightening number of silk floral arrangements. And porcelain dolls. And ceramic teapots.

Despite my urge to cling to Finn's side, I turned to him and said, "I'll just pop over to call Jane. You take care of the room, *honey.*"

Finn took out his wallet, which was still damp and water-spotted. His cash was probably a loss, but the plastic would still work. He took out a black credit card, and I noted that it had been issued to a David Seever. And I chose to ignore it, because, at this point, credit card fraud was the least of my worries.

"Send her my love," Finn muttered, as I hurried toward the phone.

For a moment, I stared at the old rotary model, wondering if I had the muscle memory required to actually dial the antique. I marveled at the weight of the receiver and immediately missed my cell phone. The idea of a phone without apps was vaguely grotesque.

I dialed the number I'd memorized from Jane's business card.

"Specialty Books," a voice drawled into the phone.

"Hi, may I speak with Jane Jameson-Nightengale, please?"

"Speaking."

"Jane?" I sighed. "This is Anna Whitfield."

"Very funny, jackass," Jane barked into the phone. "You read the news coverage just like everybody else. Congratulations. I'll have you know that Anna Whitfield was a sweet, intelligent woman who deserved a better fate. She definitely deserved better than to be memorialized by morons who can't even be clever about their prank calls."

A wave of fondness washed over me. Other than Rachel, I didn't think anyone had ever spoken on my behalf like that, all fierce, righteous loyalty. Jane was good people.

"Jane, I swear, it's me. I survived the crash with another passenger. I've been wandering in the woods for the last few days. We just now managed to find an inn, which is creepy, and I would like to not stay here overnight if it's at all possible. Because I think the owner may be a part of some sort of possum-worshipping cult."

The other end of the line was silent.

I tried again. "Ask me anything, something that only the real Anna Whitfield would know."

"If this is really Anna, what book did I promise to lend her when she reached my shop?"

I thought back to our phone conversations, those lovely exchanges that had made me think maybe I'd found a kindred spirit. They seemed a lifetime ago, before the crash, before my world got turned inside out.

And I realized I would forever define my life in two sections, Before the Crash and After the Crash. This wacky misadventure had changed me in ways I didn't even understand yet. It would take time and sleep and a lot of therapy to determine how much of that change I wanted to hold on to.

"Uh, you didn't promise to lend me anything, but you said you would *show* me your first-edition copy of *Frankenstein*. Which you keep in a glass case in your house, because you don't trust the shop's security system. Also, because someone named Georgie likes to drink mugs of dessert blood while she reads, and you're convinced she would leave thumbprints all over it. I don't think I would be allowed to touch it in this scenario, but I could look at it really closely."

Again, my ear was met with dead air. Then "Anna," and Jane sighed, her voice trembling.

I grinned, though I knew she couldn't see me. "Yeah?"

"Oh, Anna! I'm so— I can't believe it! Are you OK?"

"I wouldn't say OK, but I didn't lose myself to pine-tree madness. That's saying something." Jane's laugh was shrill and a little manic, with a teary hiccup at the end. It felt very weird to be joking about our ordeal like this, when I probably deserved a nice, messy breakdown. But it felt good to make *someone* laugh about it.

Jane cleared her throat. "How did you— Are you hurt? Where— Did anyone else surv— I swear, I'll stop sputtering out questions in just a minute. It's just that I've never dealt with a person returning from the dead.

I mean, technically, I have, but they always come back as vampires or ghosts. You aren't a vampire or a ghost, right? Because that's the sort of thing you should definitely tell me. It definitely changes how I handle the situation."

"I'm human, Jane. I promise. Hungry and tired but human."

"Who do I need to call? I don't even know what to do right now. If this was a vampire situation, I would call Dick or myself, but humans probably have all sorts of rules about reporting plane-crash survivors. Maybe I should call a lawyer. Or the Park Service. Or the—"

"Jane!" I shouted through the phone, drawing a glare from Mrs. McCreary.

"Sorry," Jane said. "I'm sorry. I just felt so guilty, Anna, knowing that your plane crashed because you were coming to meet me. I felt like it was my fault that you were gone. It's just been awful. I'm probably going to overcorrect and be sort of clingy for the next few nights. I will ignore all of your boundaries, but it will be rooted in guilt and a lame attempt to make up for my home state trying to murder you. Now, back to my original questions: Are you OK? How did you survive? Do I need to call a doctor for you?"

"I'm not hurt. I'm just tired and starving and need to bathe forever. How I survived is a story for a long evening, spent devouring fruity vodka drinks and ice cream."

Jane laughed. "Well, I promise to have plenty of both on hand for you when we get you to the Hollow. And how about the other passenger? Is he or she OK?"

I craned my neck to look at Finn, who was still chatting amiably with Mrs. McCreary. He'd said that he and Jane didn't get along well. Should I tell her that he was my camping companion or just let that problem sort itself out when Jane arrived? At this point, Jane was glad that I was alive. I didn't want to change that right away. "The other passenger is fine. You might want to bring up a supply of blood for him."

"Oh, so one of my constituents, then. Can you give me some information about him?"

I shook my head. Nope, they were going to have to handle that themselves. "He should probably introduce himself," I said.

"Are you sure you're OK? He's not standing there with his fangs to your throat or something, is he?"

"Yes, I'm fine. But I figure the two of you should work out any vampire-y issues yourselves. I am unqualified."

"That seems fair. I hate to be crude at a tender, bonding moment like this, but did you manage to hold on to the book? I only ask because I promised a friend he could show it to his family."

"I did. In fact, I would discourage you from calling the authorities, considering some of the events that led to the crash. If someone else hears that we're alive and gets here before you do, I'm not sure what would happen."

"You are amazing. So where are you?"

"An extremely off-putting hotel called the Possum's Nest." I picked up a phone book and added, "It is located in a town called Cooter Holler. What are the odds of those two words being combined into a town name?"

"It's Kentucky, so a better-than-average chance."

I could hear papers rustling in the background and keys jingling. Jane's voice was muffled, so I assumed the phone was smashed against her face while she scrambled around. "We will be there as quickly as possible. Cooter Holler is on the far side of Murphy, about an hour's drive from the Hollow. We could get there quicker, but Peter has the Council helicopter."

"Bring fresh clothes," I told her. "Two sets for two tall adults. We've been wearing the same stuff for days. Remember that we're both lanky people."

"Sure, no problem. See you soon. Wait, who is it—" Jane said, just as I hung up.

Yawning widely, I looked at the map of western Kentucky on the back of the phone book. I found Half-Moon Hollow and was shocked to see that it was the biggest city on this side of the state. How small were the other towns? I traced my finger across the green space labeled Lakelands Nature Preserve to find Cooter Holler. It took me a while, because Cooter Holler was a tiny speck almost hidden under a spot of bacon grease. We were right on the edge of the nature preserve.

I smiled, hugging the phone book to my chest. We'd made it.

I tried to dial Rachel's number, a number I knew by heart, but when I punched the last number, the line went dead. I dialed again, with the same results—

a dead line. Disgruntled, I hung up the receiver and returned to the front desk.

Finn was diligently filling out a very extensive guest registry card. He was firmly entrenched in his charming social mode, the same roguish persona he'd presented to me when we'd met on the plane. And Mrs. McCreary was lapping it up, leaning on the counter, smiling absently while she hung on every word. If Finn had a British accent, the old lady might have torn his clothes off right then and there.

"Auntie Jane says hello," I told him, smiling sweetly as I looped my arm through his.

"Oh, good," he said in a dry, unenthusiastic tone. He kissed my temple like a good little husband and signed the registration card with a flourish.

The dreamy expression evaporated from Mrs. Mc-Creary's face as I stepped into her line of sight. Apparently, my appearance had ruined her mental image of Finn's wedding. To her.

"Mrs. McCreary, I tried to make a second call, but the phone line went dead."

With a sour expression, Mrs. McCreary said, "Our phone system doesn't allow more than one long-distance call within a thirty-minute period from the guest extensions, to keep costs down."

"You're still using actual metal keys, but you have a phone system that polices your long-distance calls?"

Mrs. McCreary sniffed. "If you want unlimited phone minutes, go to a Verizon store."

My mouth dropped open to respond, but Finn defused the situation by slipping his arm around me and dangling the metal key in front of me. "We're in the Wildcat Room. Every room is themed around one of Mrs. McCreary's favorite woodland animals. Squirrels, deer, raccoons. But we get the Wildcat."

Mrs. McCreary turned her gaze on Finn and smiled sweetly. "The Wildcat Room is our very best. I installed the liner paper in the drawers myself."

"We certainly appreciate your attention to detail," Finn said in that improbably sincere way that turned a girl's knees to water.

She tittered. I'd never actually heard someone titter before, but she did it in a girlish fashion only seen in creepy anime.

Somehow I managed to get her attention without snapping my fingers in her face. "Mrs. McCreary, we may have some visitors coming along in the next few hours."

Mrs. McCreary's mouth twisted into a distasteful moue. "Late check-ins are extra."

She slid the receipt for the credit card transaction across the desk. My eyes went wide when I saw the total and the six additional charge lines for towels, sheets, late check-in, and other "luxuries." I hoped Finn had an accountant who would be able to get the expense refunded on his taxes. If Finn paid taxes. That seemed unlikely.

"What isn't extra at the Possum's Nest?" I asked her.

Mrs. McCreary's pinched expression relaxed as she gave Finn another sugary smile. "But I'll allow it just this once."

I wasn't sure I appreciated the way Mrs. McCreary

was ogling my fake vampire husband. If my morning coffee smelled of burnt almonds, I would not drink it.

"You enjoy your evening," Mrs. McCreary simpered as I placed my foot on the creaky bottom step.

"Oh, I'm sure we will," I purred back at her, because she deserved to think I was planning on taking Finn upstairs for some glorious honeymoon sex.

"Jane is on her way?" he asked quietly. I nodded.

"I'm going to try to sweet-talk Mrs. McCreary into turning off the phone-monitoring system so I can make some calls. See if I can get some intervention with our shifter friends from an outside party."

I stared at him. My suspicious hindbrain wanted to leap right to the conclusion that he was going to call the shifters, to tell them where we were so they could come grab the book before Jane got there. But when it counted, in the woods, he'd kept me hidden when the shifters were nearby. He'd gotten me through a plane crash, dehydration, and multiple levels of insanity to what was a safe place, creepy possum statues aside. I wanted to believe that he wouldn't do anything to hurt me now.

"Well, I don't want to see you flirt with a little old lady, so I'm going to go up to the room and start my bath-shower-bath cycle. I hope the water heater is sturdy, because that cycle may last forever."

He laughed and patted my shoulder while I turned toward the rough-hewn wooden staircase. I checked to make sure Mrs. McCreary's back was turned to me, watching Finn's ass as he sauntered toward the lobby's phone stand.

The stairs felt wrong under my feet, like I'd forgotten

how to manage ground that was even and structured and wouldn't collapse under me. I kept expecting to trip over a rock hidden under the carpet. I practically floated toward the door marked "Wildcat Room." And I was half afraid that I would wake up under a pine tree, with only the memories of air-conditioning or indoor plumbing to comfort me.

The Wildcat Room was not, in fact, decorated with University of Kentucky memorabilia. Genuine taxidermied wildcats prowled the walls, the dresser, even the headboard. I would have to move a stuffed wildcat from the top of the toilet tank just so I wouldn't feel its glassy eyes following me while I was undressing for the shower . . . while drinking multiple glasses of water.

My Yelp review of this place would probably include: "Good news, there's a king-size bed. Bad news, I'm pretty sure we're going to be murdered in it."

With a smack at the door, Mrs. McCreary delivered the promised sandwich, which turned out to be a single slice of bread folded over a piece of processed cheese. I devoured the scanty portion in three bites, marveling at the softness of the bread, the smooth, alien flavor of Velveeta.

While I knew that I needed a bigger meal, the thought of eating more made me a little ill. I figured surviving for days on so little food had shrunken my stomach down to a half-sandwich size. My plan to eat a porterhouse the size of my head would probably have to wait for a while.

With the sandwich lodged in my belly like an inadequate, overprocessed rock, I hid my battered purse, book and all, in the space under the bottom dresser drawer. I ran to the bathroom as if the tub was full of diamonds. I was shocked that my clothes didn't stand up on their own when I tossed them onto the floor. They did, however, leave a shower of dirt and debris on the tile, which wouldn't improve my standing with Mrs. McCreary. I couldn't find it in myself to care that I didn't have anything clean to change into when I got out of the shower. If it meant not putting on the same jeans I'd been wearing since the plane crash, I was willing to greet Jane naked.

OK, I would wrap myself in one of Mrs. McCreary's bedsheets.

The shower spray felt so good against my skin. What joy, what bliss—clean, warm, non-fishy-smelling water. I swallowed several mouthfuls, not even caring that it was warm. I poured half of the little complimentary bottle of Prell into my hands and lathered my hair viciously. I didn't want to wash it out. I just wanted to keep that lovely clean smell as close as possible. I unwrapped the soap bar and scrubbed at my skin with the washcloth. I winced over every bug bite, every bruise. I'd never been so beaten up. But it felt good in a weird way, like I was stronger somehow for earning those marks on my skin.

And despite my ragged state, I couldn't help but feel a sort of satisfaction, a smug sense of accomplishment. I'd made it. I felt like Odysseus, finally sleeping under his own roof again; like Dorothy, waking up from her dream. Or Sarah, having beaten Jareth's labyrinth and flipping him the bird while he juggled his Freudian glass balls. I'd won. I'd overcome insane odds and several near misses, but I'd lived through it all. I'd survived my own worst-case scenario. And while I never (ever) planned on doing anything this insane again, I knew that no matter what life threw at me, I would be OK.

Years of therapy and several different levels of medication, and it took a forcible camping trip for me to achieve some semblance of emotional recovery. My therapist would either be very proud or decide to retire . . . before I fired her. I was still sticking pretty hard to that point. So far, being stuck out in the woods for four days had done more for me than five years in her chair.

Over the rush of the water, I heard the door to the room open and close. I closed my eyes under the spray and prayed that it was just Finn, returning from what I could only assume was disposing of Ernie's body in a sneaky vampire fashion. If I had to, I'd survive another confrontation. I was just really tired. I needed a nap before my next battle.

I heard the soft *thwump* of fabric hitting the floor. At this point, I really did hope that it was Finn, because otherwise, this next episode of violence was getting pantsless really quickly. I tipped my face into the shower spray. I heard the shower curtain draw back. I felt cool hands slide along my ribs and settle on my hips, the contrast between the hands and the water sending a tremor along my spine.

Cool lips brushed along the nape of my neck, tracing the vertebrae with blunt teeth. I expected to be tense, being this vulnerable in front of Finn, now that I knew everything, but he'd seen me in far more naked situations than this in the last few days. At least, I was nearly clean.

I turned around, nudging his shoulder with my forehead. "Mr. and Mrs. David Seever?" I bit my lip to keep from laughing, but it didn't keep my shoulders from quaking under Finn's lips. "D. Seever? Deceiver?"

"What? No one else has caught on in years of using that name."

I burst out laughing, and he slid his hands around my ribs, spanning his fingers under my breasts. "Don't be mad that I'm better at word games than ninety percent of the population," I told him.

"You're too clever for your own good," Finn murmured against my shoulder. He pulled me close, tucking my back against his chest, and I could already feel the solid weight of him against my hip. He rained kisses along my shoulders as I turned toward him.

Smiling, I poured the shampoo over his head and worked it into his hair. He leaned into my caress like a cat, closing his eyes as I massaged his scalp. I grabbed a cloth and worked soap into it, scrubbing over his cheeks, down his neck, down his chest. I watched as rivers of gritty water ran off our bodies and collected in the tub. It felt like two new people were being born under the water, free from the grime and general weirdness of the last few days. Prell was a freaking miracle cure for pine-tree madness.

It was heaven to stand under the water and let the soap bubbles cascade over both of us, beating the tension from our muscles. Finn pulled me close, angling his mouth over mine as he combed his fingers through my hair. He backed me against the wall, running his nose along the length of my cheek.

Wordlessly, I stroked my hands along his arms, down his chest. A sudden sense of alarm took the words from my mouth. I didn't know how much more time together we had. I didn't know when Jane would be here. I found myself panicked by the idea of losing him to real life. Because I didn't know if what I felt for him, if whatever he felt for me, would survive other people. When Jane arrived, with what sounded like the full support of the Council, would he go his way while I went mine? Would we even exchange phone numbers? I couldn't imagine what we would talk about. *"Hey, remember that time you got hired to diddle my brain and then we got into a plane crash?"*

Maybe it was better if we didn't have contact in the real world. Maybe this was some sort of trauma bonding better left behind in the woods. Maybe this was better as good-bye.

Finn ran his tongue along my throat, worrying at the hollow with his teeth. He dragged his hands over my breasts, cupping them, thumbing at my nipples until they ached.

That would be a no to the "better off never seeing each other again" question.

He hitched his hands over my hips, dragging my aching flesh over his hard length. He pinned me against the wall, wrapping my legs around his waist. He teased me, rubbing the blunt head against my opening, before rolling his hips and sliding into me. I sighed at the sensation of being filled, being stretched so pleasantly that it made my teeth clench.

For a second, I worried about a condom, which was definitely not in my purse, as I'd had no need of them for a while. But then I realized how useless a condom would be in this situation. I knew I couldn't get pregnant by him, and he didn't carry diseases. It was the first time I'd felt a man naked inside me, and it was an odd intimacy, allowing him what I'd allowed no one else. There was nothing between us, and I could feel every inch of him.

"So warm," he mumbled against my forehead. He snapped his hips, driving me back against the tile. I grunted, arching my shoulders to avoid the cold contact, which only drove me further onto his length. He gave a sharp cry. "Again!"

I rolled my hips, taking him to the hilt, peppering his temples, his cheek, his chin with kisses. I wrapped my arms around his shoulders, undulating against him, angling my hips to help him find that hidden spot inside me that would make me scream. His cock scraped over it, but only just, making me whine.

"Please," I moaned. "Please, please."

He nodded, repeating the stroke, making me cry out. My fingers curled into claws, scraping down his back. He hissed, his fangs stretching to full length. His pupils went wide.

Was he going to bite me? Did I want him to bite me?

I thought I kind of wanted him to bite me.

Honestly, what did I have to be afraid of, after what

I'd been through? I'd lived through too much to be afraid of a little nip on the neck. I tilted my head, exposing my neck. He stared long and hard at the pulse I was sure was throbbing there. Any second, I expected him to lunge. But instead of biting, he nuzzled my neck, traced the line of my jaw with his tongue, and caught the lobe of my ear on the tip of his fang.

"Want to hear you scream," he ground out against my ear. "Want to hear you scream my name."

"Finn," I groaned. And I didn't even care if Mrs. Mc-Creary heard us. It would serve her right. In fact—

"FINN!" I yelled.

He chuckled, flicking his tongue across my lips, kissing along my neck, curving my back so he could drag his fangs over the top of my breast. I gasped at the sharp sting, moaning as he took one nipple and then the other into his mouth. I bucked my hips against him, taking him deeper, drawing pleasure in knowing I was taking all of him.

I heard the water shut off, too concentrated on the delicious friction between us to register Finn fiddling with the knobs. He carried me out of the shower while I worked to slide up and down his length, grinding against him with every step. He dropped us to the bedspread, never breaking the connection between us.

He rolled his hips, the momentum driving me up the length of the bed, until my crown hit the headboard. I arched, meeting his thrusts, dragging my nails down his back, until I could sink them into his ass. I looped my ankle around his, turning us until I was seated on top of him. He grinned, curling his hands around my waist to slowly grind up against me. He spanned his hand over my ass cheek, as if he couldn't get close enough.

My wet hair tumbled forward, forming a chilly curtain around us both.

That tight coil of pleasure inside me snapped, and my whole body bowed, head thrown back, hair whipping against my spine. I shrieked, vaguely registering cool hands anchoring my thighs around his as he continued to rock me against him. His movements became frenzied, moving through my tight, sensitive body at a dizzying pace.

Finn buried his face between my breasts, and I felt him shudder underneath me. He panted, crying out against my flesh, holding me so close that I swear I thought I heard my ribs buckle. He rubbed his cheek against my skin, inhaling deeply, cupping my head in his hands.

I collapsed against him, unable to move, unable to care that I couldn't move. I just lay there, my face wedged against his chest as I gasped for breath. I couldn't gather the mental energy required to operate my limbs. My hair fanned against Finn's face, but he didn't seem to mind, running his hands absently down my back.

"Are you all right?"

I made a snorting noise that was downright rude. My previous lovers, and there were very few, were all perfectly nice, safe men, and they'd never earned the right to ask whether I was OK after sex. Because, in the end, it had felt like making love to paper—blank, flat, passionless. Frankly, I would take messy and rough any day of the week. At least I knew Finn was there. I would feel him for days, every time I walked, and somehow I liked the idea. I wouldn't be able to write this off as a fever dream.

Wincing, I pulled away from him, even when he made a weak protesting mewl. He flopped back against the bed and threw his arm across his face. And he was panting, which, considering that he didn't need to breathe, I was going to take as a compliment.

"I think I'm going to need another shower," I said with a yawn. "As soon as my legs work again."

"Just sleep," he told me. "You earned it."

"No," I told him. "I can't sleep *now*."

"The trust you have in me, it's overwhelming."

"It's not because I don't trust you." I pulled the sheet over both of us. "I just want to take advantage of this bed while we can." I curled into his arms, enjoying the way his hands stroked down my back.

"Get some sleep, Anna. You're going to need it."

I laughed. "Is that a comment on the last few days or an offer for a second round?"

He pulled me closer, turning my face upward and kissing me softly. "A little bit of both."

I nodded sleepily. "OK, then. Just let me rest my eyes a little."

But before I could drift off, I heard the squeal of tires in the gravel parking lot. My eyes popped open like a child's on Christmas morning. I hopped to my feet, rushing to the window. I could see a black SUV roll to a stop, and a brown-haired woman in her thirties bolted out of the passenger-side door and up to the front door.

"She's here!" I exclaimed. Finn closed his eyes and thunked his head on the headboard.

I pulled the plastic bag from the dresser and charged out the door. Finally, I could hand this thing off to Jane and never have to think about it again.

"Uh, Anna?" Finn called as I sprang into the hallway. I dashed back into the room, slamming the door behind me. "You're naked."

I sighed, picking my crusty jeans up from the floor. "Fine, I won't wear a sheet downstairs to meet her."

"I didn't know that was an option. Uh, is that an option?" he asked, as I jerked the bottom dresser drawer off of its tracks and pulled my purse out, letting it slap against the doorframe as I ran out of the room. I winced, cradling the weight of the book against my chest.

I called over my shoulder. "It was a few minutes ago!"

Despite the relative grossness of putting my dirty clothes back on, I jogged down the inn's staircase with great alacrity. A tall brunette I recognized from an Internet search for Jane Jameson-Nightengale, proprietress of Specialty Books, stood near the front desk, smacking the "Ring for service" bell repeatedly. Behind her stood a tall man with dirty-blond hair, wearing a T-shirt that said, "You have already over-estimated my interest in this conversation," and a concerned expression.

"Hello? Why even have a bell if you're not going to answer it!" the woman growled. "This is insane! Hello?"

"Stretch, maybe your abuse of the bell is why the owners of this establishment are hiding in their rooms, refusing to come out," the man suggested gently.

"What's your point, Dick?"

"Jane Jameson-Nightengale?" I called softly. Because you do not want to startle vampires when they're agitated in customer-service situations.

The woman turned, saw me, and moved across the room in a flash. She threw her arms around my shoulders. "I never thought I'd be so happy to see a complete stranger!" she cried. "I was worried and scared and *all* of the bad emotions."

"It's good to see you, too." I laughed, patting her back even as she squeezed me so hard I had difficulty breathing. It was the most enthusiastic hug I'd ever received from a person, living or undead.

"Is this becoming awkward?" she asked, still hugging me.

I shrugged. "A little, but you've been through a trauma."

"Smartass, you're like one of the family already." She snickered and drew back, fluffing my damp hair over my shoulders. "I have a present for you."

The blond man handed her a purple gift bag marked "Specialty Books." I peeked inside and found a pair of yoga pants, underwear, a sports bra, and a T-shirt that read "Librarians do it by the book." Jane scrunched her nose. "Dick picked out the T-shirt. Sorry."

I beamed at them both. "It's clean, so you have my undying devotion. And this is the book," I told her, handing her the plastic bag. "You will find that despite the last few days, it is intact and undamaged. I appreciate your business, but I do not want to see it ever again."

Jane carefully opened the bag. The envelope containing my appraisal, provenance records, and invoice fell out of the book to the floor.

"I can't believe I had this tucked away in the shop, propping up Mr. Wainwright's old *Tales from the Crypt* comic display in the storeroom."

"Well, it did take us a number of years to finally clean out the storeroom," Dick noted, as Jane tucked the book into her shoulder bag.

"Thank you, Anna. I will be sure to leave you a really good Yelp review."

I burst out laughing, grinning at the man. "See? She gets it."

"I very rarely get it, when it comes to books, but Jane always does," he said, extending his hand to shake mine. "Dick Cheney."

"The coworker!" I exclaimed. "Hi! I've heard so much about you."

"Coworker?" The man in the inappropriate shirt pouted. "I'm hurt, Jane! I'm so much more than that!"

"Anna Whitfield, this is Dick Cheney," Jane said, in an exasperated tone that sounded well practiced. "Coworker, fellow Council member, best bro, snark twin, and purveyor of most of the inappropriate sportswear in my life."

Dick nodded. "That's more like it."

"Dick Cheney as in the vice president?" I asked, while Jane shook her head.

Dick's pout grew three sizes. Jane shook her head and mouthed the words, *Sore subject*.

"I'm pleased to meet you," I told him. "And I appreciate you coming all the way out here."

"Well, Jane gets all uncomfortable when her personal business and Council issues get tangled up. She thinks having me along will make things more objective."

"Good to know." I nodded as Finn appeared at the top of the staircase.

Jane's entire demeanor changed. Her posture grew stiffer, and her face became less friendly. I stepped away from her as she turned toward the stairs.

"Finn Palmeroy, why am I not surprised to see you involved in this?" Jane muttered.

"Excuse me, I was just an innocent bystander," Finn insisted. "And I was doing my best to be a good undead citizen, helping Anna escape from the plane crash unscathed, staying with her as we trekked through the woods, instead of just running off and protecting my own interests. I took care of a vulnerable human in an emergency situation, because I knew that's what the Council would want me to do."

I wanted to make a number of smartass cracks about his concern for Council propriety and how it related to working as a double agent for the shifters, but considering all that we'd been through, I kept my mouth shut.

"OK, sure, we'll pretend for a minute that I believe that." Jane snorted. "How did you end up here with Anna?"

"We were on the same flight," he began. "And when the plane crashed—"

"I have a feeling we should be recording this statement for the inevitable criminal proceeding," Jane muttered, patting her pockets for her phone.

Dick chided her, "Just give him a chance, Jane."

"You are *always* too soft on him," Jane hissed back.

Dick shrugged. "Hear him out. Remember how often the Council accused you of the worst possible scenarios and how much you would have appreciated someone willing to listen to you."

"The difference being, *I* was innocent," Jane countered.

I raised my hand. "Sorry to interrupt you both, but Finn did help me during the crash, by throwing me out of the plane before it hit the ground."

"We did discuss your use of the word 'throw,' right?" Finn asked.

"Sorry, he aided me in removing myself from the plane," I amended. "Does that sound better?"

"Meh." Finn shrugged. "Look, it's a long story, which we can go over later. The point is that Anna has delivered the book to you under great personal duress, so she should be paid, in full and on time. And you should recommend her to your friends as an absolute professional."

"That was oddly formal and appropriate," Jane conceded.

"I just want to make sure Anna's interests are protected."

"I do, too," Jane said. "I wouldn't want her to be drawn in by someone who didn't have her best interests at heart."

"You barely know me, and you know nothing about Anna, so how would you know what's best for her?" Finn shot back.

I stepped back with Dick to watch the words being volleyed back and forth. "I don't think my presence is necessary for this conversation," I told Dick.

"Jane has . . . trust issues with Finn. While he's never done anything to her directly, he has skirted the boundaries of what's acceptable for us. And last year didn't help."

"Last year?"

"Long story," Dick said, frowning.

"I'm so lost."

Dick nodded. "It's a common feeling when you're hangin' out with the vampires in this group. There's a lot of background information. Gigi made up an indexed reference guide for my Nola. I'll get ya a copy."

Over the increased volume from Jane and Finn, I asked, "And Gigi is . . ."

"You'll understand when you read the guide," he assured me.

As the bickering raged on, Dick and I made ourselves as comfortable as we could on the spindly Victorian furniture. Finn attempted to give a highly edited version of the events of the crash and the ensuing woods trek, while Jane accused him of everything but murdering the pilot right in front of me and brainwashing me into believing he'd helped me.

Nope, she went ahead and did that, too.

Across the parlor, a heavy oak door swung open. Mrs. McCreary appeared, wearing a pink flannel bathrobe and old-fashioned sponge rollers in her thin gray-ing hair.

"Excuse me!" she shouted, giving me the evil eye, despite the fact that I was sitting quietly on the couch. "What do you think you're doing? I run a respectable establishment here! Not some party-all-night flophouse!"

Mrs. McCreary seemed to have a lot of ideas about what her establishment was and was not. Jane and Finn immediately looked cowed and went quiet, though Finn gave Mrs. McCreary a sheepish grin and said, "I'm sorry, Mrs. McCreary."

"Oh, I'm sure it's not your fault, sweetheart," she cooed before jerking a thumb toward me. "These must be the friends that *this one* was talking about."

I frowned. "This one?"

Dick turned to me, eyebrows raised. "Have you been up to no good, Waldo? You seem like such a nice girl."

"Please don't assign her 'Waldo' as a nickname, Dick. That's just mean," Jane told him.

"Come on, we lost her for days on end. No one could find her. It's hilarious!"

"I *am* a nice girl," I muttered.

"Mrs. McCreary," Jane said, turning her back on Finn to give the cranky old woman her full attention. "I'm sorry about the noise. We were just having a discussion, and it got loud."

"Yes, loud enough that I might just have to call the sheriff!" Mrs. McCreary exclaimed. "I don't stand for that sort of behavior here!"

As Jane took a menacing step toward the old lady,

Dick stood. I stayed on the couch, content to be out of McCreary's swiping range. I was sure that the vampires didn't mean to crowd around the old lady, arguing loudly to intimidate her, which was good, because Mrs. McCreary didn't seem intimidated in the least, threatening again to call the sheriff, the local emergency management team, *and* the Council office just for daring to shout in her sacrosanct parlor.

"We *are* the Council office!" Jane exclaimed.

"Well, unless you're a paying guest, I'm going to have to ask you to leave," Mrs. McCreary sniped.

"That's no problem," Jane insisted. "Ms. Whitfield was going to leave with us anyway."

"That girl has to leave, but you, of course, are welcome to stay, young man," Mrs. McCreary told Finn.

I supposed "that girl" was better than "that one." Frankly, Mrs. McCreary was starting to remind me a little too much of my mother with her disapproving glares and high-handedness. I would not be leaving a positive review of her establishment on my comment card.

I glanced behind Jane, the last place I'd seen Finn standing, but he wasn't there. My eyes swept toward the front door to the inn, which was standing open.

"Um, where did Finn go?" I asked, looking around for my wayward vampire.

"He was here just a second ago," Jane said, spinning and scanning the living room, as if we'd just misplaced a six-foot-three-inch vampire behind the couch.

A sinking feeling gripped my chest, dragging me down to a truth I'd already accepted but didn't want to believe.

"Oh, no." I sighed. "No, no, no."

And then I let loose a stream of profanities so obscene it would have made the Phone Sex Operators of America go into permanent retirement.

By the time I'd come up for air, Jane's eyes were the size of dessert plates, and Dick had taken a large step back from me.

"So many f-words," Dick marveled.

Jane cleared her throat. "Um, Anna, not that I didn't find that entertaining and super frightening, but . . . why?"

I sighed. "Jane, check your bag."

"What?"

"Check your bag," I told her again.

"There's no way he got into my purse," she said. "I'm shocked he managed to get out of the room without us noticing." She reached into her shoulder bag, and seconds later, the only book clutched in her hand was a Gideon Bible, presumably from the nightstand in our room. She raised her fist at the ceiling. "Palmeroy!"

I sank back down to the uncomfortable, fragile sofa. "Sonofabitch."

9

There is no worst-case scenario to plan for when camping with the undead. Because no matter how bad you think it is, it can get much worse.

—Where the Wild Things Bite: A Survival Guide for Camping with the Undead

Finn was gone. Again.

I'd fallen for it. Again.

Was there some sort of an award for insistently refusing to learn from mistakes?

Jane cursed violently and ran out the door at vampire speed. Dick, however, sank slowly onto the couch next to me.

"Anna, hon, are you OK?" he asked. "You're awfully pale."

My hands had gone cold and shaky, as if I couldn't get them to obey the commands my brain was sending out. After all that—the insane woodland camping trip from hell—Finn had taken the book. He'd just taken it and run, using his evil carnie-folk sleight-of-hand tricks. No good-bye. No apology for screwing me over *again*.

And what really sucked was that at some level, I'd been expecting it. Somewhere inside, I'd been waiting for the other shoe to drop, because I couldn't believe that he'd ever really want me. I'd held back from him because at any moment, I'd expected to turn around and find he was gone.

Maybe Finn had sensed that. Maybe if I'd trusted him, he might have—

Wait.

No.

This was on him. This was not my fault. This was not Michael all over again. This was Finn's choice, to take the book, not mine. If I didn't trust him, it was because he'd given me ample reason not to trust him. I hadn't handed the book to Finn blindly; he'd stolen it.

After he'd practically forced Jane to admit receipt in front of several witnesses . . . in an apparent effort to protect the remaining shreds of my professional reputation.

OK, maybe I should have seen this coming.

Sonofabitch, it still hurt.

Finn leaving had caused an actual physical ache in my chest, like I was being crushed by some merciless, oversized hand. Just last week, this pain would have stopped my whole day, sent me running for the nearest emergency room and an EKG (followed by repeat, ritualistic hand-sanitizer use), but now I was just too angry and hurt to worry about whether I was having a heart attack.

I needed a battle-ax. Now. Like a really, really big

battle-ax. Maybe I would develop the upper-body strength to lift it by the time I found Finn. And I would find him. I would make him pay.

Right, good plan.

Dick took my cold hands between his and rubbed them carefully. His own skin was room temperature, so he didn't provide much heat, but it was comforting that he was even trying. Dick tipped my head toward his and winced at something he saw in my eyes.

"I think you might be going into shock, sweet cheeks. How about some water or a cup of coffee or something? Some caffeine might perk you up."

I shook my head. "I—"

"I knew you were trouble from the moment you walked through my door." Mrs. McCreary sniffed, having recovered quickly from her enthrallment with Finn. "Well, who's going to settle up the final room bill? This one ran up all kinds of extra charges, room service and what have you."

Room service. She had the nerve to call that nasty cheese sandwich room service.

Shrugging off Dick's friendly grip, I rose on steady legs and crossed the parlor, eyes fixed on Mrs. Mc-Creary's wizened face. She was smart enough to shut her mouth and duck behind the front desk, which offered some protection. She was also fortunate that a small white square caught my eye before I could do something regrettable.

On the front desk, on stationery labeled "Possum's Nest Lodge," were two carefully written words. "I'M SORRY."

Well, I guessed Finn had left with a few words after all. Righteous, indignant anger burned through me like a lit fuse, searing a path from my heart to my gut. Finn could keep his freaking sorrys. I didn't want them.

Growling, I grabbed a long brass letter opener and stabbed it through Finn's note.

"That's two hundred dollars' damage on top of the room fee!" Mrs. McCreary yelled. My head whipped toward her, and she recoiled, terrified by the feral expression on my face. Dick was at my side in a flash, digging the letter opener from the wood and gently prying my fingers from the handle.

"OK, OK, we're going to stick with decaf for you, sweet cheeks," Dick said, his tone intentionally soothing. "Mrs. McCreary, the Council will pay whatever you want to charge us if you will just shut your mouth right now and go on to bed."

"Well, I never!" she exclaimed.

"I figure that's part of the problem," Dick told her. "Now, send us an invoice in the morning. Go on."

Mrs. McCreary tightened the sash on her robe and swept out of the room with her nose in the air. Dick shuddered slightly. "That could have gone easier, but I feel that honesty is the best policy in dealing with cranky old ladies, don't you?"

"Uh, no," I told him, thinking of my mother again. "I have never found that to be true."

The door swung open to reveal a highly indignant Jane. "He's gone. I couldn't even get his scent trail."

"He had just taken a shower," I said absently, pondering the large puncture I'd made through the inn stationery. Without meaning to, I'd perfectly centered my strike through the "O" in Finn's "SORRY." Yay for me.

Jane seemed to note my damp hair, made the connection, and clucked her tongue. "Oh, honey."

I seemed to recall from one of Jane's e-mails that she'd mentioned she was a mind-reader. Oh, that was so embarrassing.

"Don't worry, I don't peek into people's brains at random. It's rude."

My face flushed.

Jane shrugged. "I only heard that because your brain is sort of screaming right now. But if you'd reduce the number of flashbacks to Naked Finn, I would really appreciate it."

"I didn't even realize I was doing that," I said, cringing.

"Most people end up thinking about the one thing they don't want to think about when they know I can see their thoughts."

"I'm so sorry, Jane. I thought once I put the book in your hands, it would be safe, I should have known better. And I was an *idiot,* trying to protect him when I called you. Finn was planted on the plane by some shifter family that found out I was researching Friar Thomas's book. Finn owed the family money or favors, a lot of either. They wanted the book for themselves, and they were willing to crash the plane, and me along with it, to get it. Finn had a change of heart and helped me at the last minute before the crash. He's been helping me all along, but I guess he was only trying to ease his conscience before he delivered the book to his 'employers.' I should have just FedExed the damn thing to you. It would have been safer than leaving it in my hands."

Jane shook her head, closing her hands around my shoulders. "No, I'm sorry, Anna. Frankly, I should have known better when I saw that Finn was involved. I should have been more on guard. You were just trying to be responsible, and it turned into a disaster of 'Jane' proportions."

"I'm unclear on what you mean by that," I said, raising an eyebrow.

"Someday the ladies of our circle will sit down, get you drunk, and share our humiliating 'getting turned into vampires' stories," she told me, her voice solemn. "Besides, it's not me I'm worried about, it's Jed."

"Jed?"

"He's a shifter. I promised to give the book to his family once I knew whether it was legit or not." Jane ran her hands through her thick dark hair, as if that would rake all the problems in life free from her head.

"Well, there's a problem there," I said. "I mentioned an issue with the final chapter on the phone. Friar Thomas wrote about this herbal concoction that could basically 'undo' all of the genes that give shifters their abilities. Make enough of it at that concentration, and you have yourself a heck of a supernatural threat. You may not want to give that book to anybody."

"I think I'm going to have to say some f-words myself," Jane groaned, scrubbing her hands over her face. "OK, we'll deal with the book issue when we get to it. For now, let's get you back to the Council offices," she said, a kind expression on her face, though she was still clearly disappointed. "We'll get you home, and we'll assign a protection unit to your apartment building for the next few months, in case Finn or his employers try anything."

"No, I want to see this through," I told Jane. "I feel responsible for getting that book into your hands. And I'd like to say a 'proper good-bye' to Finn. How can I help?"

"If that proper good-bye involves that battle-ax you were thinking about earlier, I fully support this plan."

"Stop that!"

"I can't help it, you're a particularly vivid broadcaster. Now, do you know anything about the family Finn was working for?" she asked.

"On the plane, Ernie the pilot called them the Kelleys. I'm pretty sure I met one of them. She was big. I mean linebacker big. So if that runs in the family, you're going to want to be careful," I told them. "Also, she's probably not going to be very happy with me, because I covered her in wasps."

"Ernie the pilot?" Dick asked.

"Wasps?" Jane added.

"I think Finn was careful not to tell me anything useful about them because this was his end game."

"Don't feel bad," she told me. "Vampires can be devious to get what they want, and Finn is more devious than most."

"That doesn't make me feel better," I told her. "What are you going to do to Finn once you find him?"

"I will give him a severe scolding," she deadpanned.

"Why don't I believe you?"

"Because you can interpret my tone of voice." Jane patted my shoulder gently. "Are you OK staying with us for a few more days?"

I nodded.

Dick put his hand on my shoulder. "You're going to have to give your official statement. Now, if Finn helped you, we need to know. I also need you to be completely honest about what led to the crash and how his actions affected what happened with the shifters. We need to know what we're dealing with, OK?"

I nodded. "It will probably help me to talk about it anyway."

"Well, I'm going to call in some favors." Jane sighed, dialing her cell phone. "And it's going to cost me a fortune in beef jerky."

I looked to Dick as Jane spoke softly to someone on the other end of her phone line. "Am I supposed to understand what that means?"

"Jane's calling our werewolf friends. They'll be able to track Finn's scent a lot easier than we can."

"Werewolves *are* a thing?"

Dick ruffled my hair in an amused, big-brother fashion. "Yeah, werewolves are a thing."

"That's nice to know for sure. What about zombies? Zombies aren't a thing, right?"

"Trust me, sweet cheeks, you don't want to know."

Jane proved to be a very understanding employer, insisting on hosting me in her home while I slept off the aftereffects of my "adventure." I was fully prepared to get on a Greyhound to Atlanta after giving my (incredibly descriptive) official statement, but instead, she'd taken me to River Oaks, the palatial pre–Civil War house she shared with her husband, Gabriel, and put me up in one of the more human-friendly guest rooms just before dawn.

Riding in a car again was a weird experience, and the motion actually made me a little sick. The lights of town seemed too bright, too colorful. Every noise, including the music on the radio, seemed too loud. It was going to take me a while to get used to being a somewhat normal, city-dwelling person.

I hadn't even realized how tired I was until I woke twelve hours later, my hair matted to my face and near-permanent pillow creases imprinted on my cheek. I'd passed out on top of the covers in my Council-issued yoga pants and T-shirt. At some point, Jane must have checked on me and thrown a quilt over me.

I rolled over in bed to see that Jane had installed a mini-fridge next to my nightstand. It was stocked with protein drinks and juice and several different types of yogurt. She'd seemed pretty worried about putting the weight I'd lost over the last few days back on my frame, but the Council doctor who'd examined me had forbidden me to eat anything more challenging than steamed veggies until the weekend, so my rendezvous with a ridiculously large steak would have to wait.

I sat up, wincing at the insane soreness in my muscles. I guess walking every waking minute combined with sleeping on the cold ground was finally catching up to me. I didn't have much to accomplish tonight, other than realizing my plans for bloody, stabby revenge on Finn.

I'd called Rachel from Jane's cell phone on the drive to the Hollow. I was struck speechless by the sound of my best friend's voice, roughened by sleep and grief. "Hello?" she'd croaked. And when I didn't answer, she repeated it. "I said, *hello!*"

"Rachel, it's me."

"You sick freaks think this is funny? How about I troll the obituaries looking for a nice painful death story in your family and call you to mock your pain. Assholes!"

"Wait, don't hang up!" I cried. "Rachel Edmona Grady, I swear by Jai Courtney's naked abs that I am alive and well and in a place called Cooter Holler, Kentucky."

There was a long pause on the other end of the line.

"Anna?"

"I promise you, it's me."

"Anna, if this isn't you, I'm going to kill you!"

"Rach, that doesn't make any sense, killing me because you're so glad I'm alive." My eyes welled up with tears. I felt sorry for joking around with Jane about pine-tree madness. Suddenly, everything I'd been through seemed so much more serious, hearing how it had affected my closest friend.

"Was it swearing on delicious Australian abdominals or the embarrassing middle name I swore never to use in vain that convinced you?" I asked, my voice quavering.

"The abs, honestly. You know how important Jai Courtney's torso is to me."

I snickered, the heavy weight of my guilt wriggling loose from my chest. "I'm sorry. The last couple of days must have really sucked for you."

"I'm just so glad you're OK! I saw the plane's disappearance on the news, and I didn't want to believe it. People kept calling and asking about you and the business and whether the projects on your calendar were going to be completed—which made me realize a good portion of our client list is made up of total jerks. Your mom has been over here, trying to get into your apartment and go through your paperwork. I had to show my power of attorney to the cops to keep her out. I always thought maybe you were sort of exaggerating about her, but she is *mean*, Anna. And crazy. That sweet little lady on the phone who's so short of breath that she can't manage much more than a whisper when she calls every week? She tried to body check me to bust through the door to your apartment. I have a bruise on my shoulder the size of a grapefruit."

I chuckled, shaking my head. "It's OK. I don't think anyone is ever really prepared for meeting my mother in person. And I appreciate you keeping her out, despite the obvious risk to your emotional and joint health."

"You are going to call her, right? To tell her that you're OK?"

I weighed the pros and cons of that in my head. Yes, my mother was in emotional distress, but if she thought I was dead, she wouldn't call me nearly as often. "Eh."

"You have to tell her that you're alive, Anna."

"Do I?"

"I will not fake a funeral for you."

"Oh, sure, if you're going to set limits on our friendship *now*."

"That's right. We finally found it. A faked funeral is my hard limit."

But despite some very earnest promises to Rachel, I had not spoken to my mother. I knew one of Jane's Council employees had called to let her know she had to cancel the big, bodyless funeral she had planned. And to my mind, that was almost the same thing.

True to every expectation I had of my mother, that employee filed for hazardous-duty pay almost immediately. I knew I would have to talk to her eventually. I needed to learn how to communicate with her in a way that didn't result in me folding like a cheap lawn chair. Even if I didn't end up having a normal relationship with her, I had to give her a chance to have a relationship with me in which I responded like an independent person with her own will.

In other words, I needed to learn to be a damn adult.

I looked out the window to find weak moonlight filtering through the glass, shining down on the gardens behind River Oaks. Some careful hand had planted a variety of night-blooming flowers there. And with Jane sitting on a bench, her husband's head pillowed on her thigh while she read from a book, it was a perfectly lovely, albeit nocturnal, scene of domestic bliss.

An unexpected pressure squeezed at my chest, knowing that this was something I would never have. The vampire I'd believed could be mine had walked away. Whatever it was that we'd shared out in the woods was just that, in the woods. It didn't survive the transition into the real world. He was a con artist, and I was a book nerd who was still working through the remnants of agoraphobia. Maybe he hadn't meant to hurt me in that way, but he had. He'd given me a taste of something special and then taken it away without a thought.

What was I going to do now? Try speed dating? Date nice, safe accountants I met through Internet matchmaking sites? Go to the movies and dinner and pretend it was exciting and fulfilling, when I knew what it was like to strip down to nothing under the full moon and attack a man like an animal? The very thought was depressing. I'd tasted freedom and adventure and horror. You couldn't really go back to speed dating after that.

I'd outgrown my own damn life. And I had no idea what to do about it.

I shoved a brush through my tangled hair, slipped into a slouchy lavender sweater Jane had left thrown over the vanity chair, and padded down the stairs. In the kitchen, I found a glass of orange juice on the counter, condensation beading thick on the glass. I drained it in three long gulps and poured another from the pitcher in the fridge.

The garden was even more beautiful up close, the light of the moon casting a bluish glow over the trumpet-shaped flowers that bore its name. Small yellow daylilies stood in banks along the path to Jane's bench, their faint yellow aroma blending with the heady scent of jasmine.

"Whoever did this sure knew what they were doing," I muttered into my juice glass.

"I'll tell Iris that you said so," Jane called, tapping out a message on her cell phone and setting it on top of a book on her garden table. I noted the title, *Mansfield Park,* in faded gold lettering on the dyed canvas cover. It was definitely mid-nineteenth century, maybe one of the first mass-produced editions, but worth little beyond potential sentimental value. I smiled, even as the book-related gears seemed to whir in my head. It felt good to touch base with my bibliographical instincts, to know that they hadn't been replaced by sunrise timetables and possum cookery.

"Iris?" I asked.

Jane's husband, Gabriel, sat up, giving me a polite smile.

"My landscaper and one of my best friends in the vampire community. She insists on taking care of the gardens for me, otherwise I'll just kill everything off," Jane said. "As it is, she's taken several of my desk plants into foster care for their own protection. How are you feeling?" she asked. "We've been keeping tabs on the Finn situation but didn't want to wake you up until it was necessary. You needed the sleep."

"Exhausted but OK," I confessed. "And starving. I

drank the juice in the fridge, but it's like my jaws are aching to chew on something solid."

"Well, you did sleep through the last twelve hours," Jane told me. "Tess, one of my nonvampire friends, sent over some tummy-friendly heat-and-eat meals. Heavy on the carbs and protein to put some of the weight you've lost back on your bones."

"I'll go heat one of them up now," Gabriel said. "How does bacon-infused macaroni and cheese sound to you, Anna?"

"Like I will cry if it's not in my stomach very, very soon," I told him. "But not a big portion, because the orange juice will probably fight for dominance in my belly, and that could get ugly."

Gabriel glanced at Jane. "I can see now why you two get along so well."

"Wear the gas mask!" Jane reminded him. Gabriel nodded, waving without looking back at her.

She sighed the contented sigh of a person fully satisfied by her life (unlife?), watching her husband walk back into the home they shared together.

She turned her head toward me. "What?"

"Nothing," I said, shrugging, wincing at the soreness in my shoulder. "I don't want to put you out. I already feel like I'm taking advantage being paid for this job."

But Jane would hear none of my protests. "Hey, you showed determination and resourcefulness in the face of some pretty serious complications. I think I should give you a bonus."

"That can't possibly be true," I said, laughing as the back door opened. I had never seen such a classically handsome man in all my life—sandy hair, tawny eyes, a wide, generous mouth made for sin. And he seemed to be built in the manner of a Greek statue, with a barrel chest, a narrow waist, and long legs clad in weathered jeans. And I couldn't help but notice he had a healthy tan, so clearly not a vampire.

Dick and Gabriel ambled out of the house after him. Gabriel was wearing a gas mask around his neck to deliver my steaming plate of macaroni and cheese, something that seemed to tickle both of his companions. I guessed I could understand why, considering I could smell the cheesy, bacony goodness from yards away. Gabriel was polite about it, though, even setting a napkin across my lap before handing me the plate.

"Thank you," I whispered, watching the fragrant steam rise from my plate.

"The happy expression on her face is worth suffering the smell," Dick said.

"Well, before you tear into one of Tess's legendary mac-and-cheese experiences, I should probably introduce myself," the human said, his deep Delta accent thick as molasses and twice as sweet. "Hi, I'm Jed Trudeau, not a vampire, not a member of the Council, more of a good friend than a bro, and my girlfriend destroys most of the shirts Dick gives me."

"My granddaughter doesn't have much of a sense of humor about the shirts," Dick said, shaking his head.

"Sorry, what?" And before I could question exactly what Dick meant about his granddaughter, I recalled the name Jane had mentioned at the inn. "Wait, are you Jed the shapeshifter?" I asked him. He nodded. "I'm so sorry I lost the book."

"Not your fault," he assured me. "You did more than anyone could ask of you. And from what Jane said, you damn near died in the attempt."

"I appreciate that."

The gentlemen took their seats around us, while I tried to prevent myself from inhaling the pasta so quickly I'd hurt myself.

"So we've had a pack of werewolves tracking Finn from the inn through the woods for most of the day," Jane said. "They also happened to pick up on the shifter pack's scents. The good news is that the scents went in two different directions. We're hoping that means he hasn't met up with them again. The better news is that they followed Finn's scent here to the Hollow before they lost it. They're searching that same area now. I'm waiting for their text so we can meet up with them."

Just a few seconds after she said that, Jane's phone beeped.

"And we need to meet them behind the Cellar. Now. Jed, we'll need your big, manly truck."

"Of course you will," Jed scoffed.

"I think that hurts my feelings," Gabriel muttered.

"Definitely hurts mine," Dick told him.

I took one more huge bite of the macaroni and hopped to my feet, following the group to the F-350 parked in Jane's driveway. Even with my long legs, the huge tires put the truck at such a height that Gabriel had to boost me up. Jed peeled out of the driveway, throwing me against the window. Dick helped me buckle my seatbelt while I flopped around in my seat. Jane gave Jed directions to the Cellar, which was relatively close to her house.

Dick grinned at me, with the same devil-may-care charm as Finn's but without the underlying threat to my panties. "You're going to love this," he said. "You don't have a problem with unnecessary nudity, do you?"

My head whipped toward him. "What?"

I suddenly felt very protective of my panties.

We drove past a cement-block building with a neon sign that blinked "The Cellar." Jed spun around the mostly empty parking lot and parked behind the bar. And behind that bar? Trees. Lots of them.

"Aw, man." I groaned. "More woods? I just got out of the woods."

"Don't worry, sweet cheeks," Dick told me. "We'll have you back in the house before midnight."

Several large wolves in varying shades of brown and gray seemed to melt out of the tree line, standing in a semicircle in the glow of Jed's headlights. Jane climbed out of the truck and approached a large gray female, who seemed to unfold into a human shape in a flash of golden light. There stood the most beautiful woman I'd ever seen: beautiful peachy skin, a perfectly symmetrical face, long waves of auburn hair, and wide green eyes with an almost feline shape. And she was naked. Not just a little naked but super naked.

"You were not kidding about the nudity," I whispered to Dick as we slid out of the truck.

"No, I was not."

"Anna, these are some family friends, the McClains, and our good friend Jolene Lavelle. Jolene, this is Anna." Jane waved for me to come closer.

I stayed where I was, which made Jed snicker behind his hand.

Gabriel pushed me gently toward Jane and Jolene. The gorgeous woman's full, rosy lips parted, and out came the most aggressively nasal backwoods twang this side of *Deliverance*. "Hi there! Nice to meet ya!"

She extended her hand, but I couldn't make eye contact, trying to look anywhere but at the woman's naked body. Still not looking at her, I put my hand forward, hoping I wouldn't make contact with anything personal. She took it in her strong grip and shook it hard. "Jane's been such a mess these last few days. I'm glad you're OK. And don't worry, hon. We'll track this guy down quicker than you can spit."

Behind Jolene, the other wolves made an odd noise, a combination of whickering and huffing that would have made me very nervous if I were Finn.

"That would be great," I said, still not making eye contact. "I don't spit a lot, but I can appreciate the sentiment."

"Am I makin' you uncomfortable?"

"Decidedly."

She snickered. "OK. And that's about to get worse, because I'm going to sniff you."

"I'm sorry, what?" I was shocked enough to look down and saw that everything else about Jolene was perfectly symmetrical, too—as if my self-esteem hadn't already taken a beating tonight.

"Um, Jolene and her cousins need to refresh their scent sample to track Finn. And, uh, you kind of reek of him," Dick said in what I imagined was supposed to be a delicate tone.

I winced, thinking back to our activities just before Jane showed up. I might as well have wallowed around in a big vat of cologne labeled "Finn."

"And that's why you needed me to stick around?" I asked. Jane nodded. "Well, that's humiliating."

"It happens to the best of us, hon," Jolene assured me. "Now, just stand still, and don't worry. We don't bite."

With a wink, Jolene transformed from two feet to four in a flash of light. I found comfort in the fact that I could finally lower my eyes. Jolene's cold, wet wolf nose nudged at my hand, inhaling deeply. She walked in a narrow circle around me, sniffing and snorting. She whirled around, thumping her heavy tail against my thigh. The Jolene wolf barked sharply at the other wolves, and they swarmed around me, sniffing at my hands and legs. It was hard not to panic, being surrounded by that many huge predators, no matter how friendly and puppy-like they seemed.

Jolene sat on her haunches and waited while Jane hooked a pink leather collar around her neck. The vampire reached for a little black plastic box attached to the collar and switched on a green light.

"OK, Jolene, the GPS unit is on. When you're ready, unleash wolfy hell."

Jolene barked, a sharp, staccato sound. The other wolves straightened suddenly and turned to her, like soldiers falling to attention.

"Dick and I are going to follow them on foot," Jane told me. She tossed a small black handheld device to Jed. "This is all set up. Follow as closely as you can in the truck. And if you get any hints that the situation has gone south, you get Anna back to the Hollow and into the Council offices as quickly as possible."

Jed nodded. "Got it. Come on, Anna."

The Jolene wolf yipped and launched herself into the trees, a furry missile on a mission. The other wolves moved as one flowing organism, following her in perfect sync. I climbed back into Jed's huge black pickup truck. From behind the seat, Jed flipped forward two shoulder harness straps that clipped around the regular lap belt. Jed climbed into his own seat, plugging the small black device into the dashboard. When he turned the ignition, the video screen above the radio controls lit up, showing a map covered in green.

"We're about to do some really ugly driving, aren't we, Jed?"

Jed gave me a proud little boy's smile as he strapped on his own harness. "Yes, we are."

I expected a thrill of fear to sweep through my belly as I ran the potential outcomes of this situation. A crash, carsickness, getting lost in the woods with another man I didn't know. But honestly, those seemed like minor inconveniences compared with what I'd already been through. My plane had crashed. I'd been way more than lost. Finn had betrayed me. I'd been through the worst-case scenarios, and I was fine. Exhausted and itching for violence but fine. And I would continue to be fine, no matter what happened, because I'd left that germ-wiping, stat-quoting, phobic girl on the plane.

"We're following the signal from Jolene's collar," he said. "The trees are a little sparser here, so we have a pretty good chance of being able to squeeze through. And if we can't, we'll get to flatter, clearer ground until we can."

"So when we catch up to Finn, what happens?" I asked as Jed revved the engine and pitched us forward through the tree line. "I was sort of afraid to ask before."

"That's up to Jane," he said. "And you."

I grabbed the canvas handle on the ceiling to steady myself as the truck sped over uneven ground, my stomach rolling as the truck pitched and tilted. I immediately regretted everything I'd eaten since finding the inn. But I figured werewolf-following was a non-pit-stop activity. To take my mind off my inner turmoil, I asked Jed, "So you're a shapeshifter. What's that like?"

"Never met one before, huh?"

"Well, once, but she wasn't really up for conversation. She was more of a 'punch Anna in the face first, engage in polite conversation maybe later' type," I told him. "According to Friar Thomas, some shifters can only change at night. Is that the case with your family?"

"We thought so for a while, but it turns out we can shift whenever we feel like it." Jed paused and put the truck into a lower gear to roll over a fallen log. "My family thought we were cursed for generations. We thought—and it sounds so stupid now—but we thought that we could only shift when the moonlight hit our skin."

"But there's nothing about that in any of the lore," I told him.

"Yeah, well, we ran afoul of a witch a couple of generations back, and she was awfully good at the power of suggestion," he said. "We think she was able to sense the change coming and took advantage of our not knowin' about it."

"Friar Thomas would say that the magical vapors in that generation's blood had mixed in just the right combination to bring out your ability," I told him. When Jed frowned, I added, "Friar Thomas wasn't familiar with the concept of DNA."

Jed made an indignant noise in his throat. "We were just scared and worried about passing the shiftin' along to the next generation. The Trudeau clan is the largest group of shifters in the Southeastern states, and we didn't know what we were or why suddenly certain members of the family could turn into scary monsters in the middle of the night. That's how closed off we are from the rest of the supernatural world. My Nola, she helped us understand it a little better, but when Jane said she'd found a book that might be able to help us get better control of the shifts, maybe even find other packs of shifters? Well, I may have gotten my family's hopes up a little bit. I shouldn't have said anything to them."

"I'm sorry, Jed. I can't apologize enough."

He waved my concerns away with a casual toss of his hand. "Please, Anna, of everybody involved in this situation, you're the one who fought like hell to do your job. Did you foul up along the way? Sure. Did you trust the wrong man? OK. Did you sleep with that man, against your better judgment? I'm guessin' yes."

"Hey, Jed, stop trying to make me feel better."

"My point—and I'm not good at making them, so just bear with me—was that you survived a plane crash and a trek through some pretty ugly country, with no supplies or gear, all to get a job done? That's pretty badass."

I rolled my eyes. I didn't feel badass. I felt like an idiot. And I wanted to tell Jed that I'd only survived because Finn had helped me along the way. But then, he hadn't been with me while I walked through that daylit, wasp-infested wilderness. He hadn't been with me when I'd faced off with She-Hulk the Shapeshifter. I had made it through some of the hardest parts of my journey alone. Maybe I was a tiny bit badass.

"Thank you, Jed."

"You're welcome."

I stared out the window, watching the trees fly by as Jed worked the stick shift like a teenager controlling his favorite video game. We covered miles and miles in what seemed like a ridiculously short amount of time. How much easier would it have been for me and Finn if we'd had this truck? We would have made it out of the woods in a matter of hours instead of days. And we would have slept in one hundred percent fewer caves, I was guessing. Then again, we would have spent way less time skinny-dipping, and there would have been a drastic reduction in cave-snuggling.

I watched as the little red dot on the video screen suddenly veered right and then stopped. Jed slowed the truck to a smooth stop and watched the screen. When it became apparent that the dot was not moving, he switched off the ignition and pressed a finger to his lips. I nodded and unfastened my harness. Jed unhooked the small GPS device and climbed out of the truck. I landed on quiet feet, careful not to step on any branches while I followed Jed away from the truck. He watched the screen, following the coordinates from Jolene's collar, which still hadn't changed. I supposed this meant that Jolene had found Finn.

Was Jolene's pack waiting in the woods, ready to spring on Finn and whoever he was meeting? I didn't know how to feel about that, partially because I didn't want Finn to be hurt by werewolf fangs and partially because I wanted to do the hurting myself.

A message popped up on the video screen from Jane. *Get here NOW.* Jed grabbed my elbow, running through the woods toward the dot. I was pleased to find that with water in my system and tightly tied boots on my feet, I could keep up with him. Of course, there were limits to my newfound stamina, and fortunately, I hit that limit right around the time we found Jane and the wolves standing in a huddled group.

In the distance, I could see headlights shining through the trees, and I could hear voices and laughter. It sounded like a kegger in the middle of the forest. I sincerely hoped that we hadn't just stumbled onto some hapless hunting party, because they were about to get the Pabst Blue Ribbon scared out of them.

Jolene transformed to human while her cousins stayed on four paws. I kept my gaze above Jolene's shoulders.

"You're sure?" Jane asked quietly.

Jolene nodded. "Unless our new friend here has been rollin' around with a bunch of drunk hunters."

I hissed indignantly, swinging my gaze to Jolene and catching a full-on visual of her breasts. "Watch it."

Jolene gave me what I can only call a wolfish grin.

"So, Jane, you want to do a quiet, subtle 'vampire appears like a puff of smoke' thing or a more dramatic, full-on werewolf storming of the beach?"

Jane grinned at me. "Oh, I think I have an idea."

Jane and I ever so casually walked toward the lights, knowing that Jed and the werewolves were hiding in the trees. As we got closer, I could see several SUVs parked in a semicircle with their headlights on high. Their lights shone on a group of a dozen or so people all huddled around a familiar figure, who was holding the book aloft, loudly declaring that it was "the real deal" and he could tell because of the silk stitching on the binding and the lead-based ink used by the author.

Only it wasn't the familiar figure I was expecting.

"Michael?"

There stood Michael Malone, Ph-freaking-D. Handsome, golden Michael, with the same sparkling blue eyes and stupidly adorable butt dimple in his chin, among a group of hulking blond giants. And despite my most fervent wishes, he had not gone bald or toothless or been injured in a tragic acid explosion.

Worse yet, he was holding *A Contemplation on Shifters* in his hands, showing it off to the crowd, opening it wide enough to endanger the delicate material of the binding—with his *dirty bare hands*, exposing the fragile pages to the damaging oils of his skin. Anyone who cared about books, or at least claimed to be a scholar, would know better than to handle a priceless work without any attempts to protect it. Why didn't Michael go ahead and use the table of contents as a napkin while he was at it?

"Kind of ruined the element of surprise there," Jane muttered out of the side of her mouth.

"Really, of all the clandestine, illegal artifact transactions you could have showed up for, it had to be this one?" I demanded, as the blond shifters whirled toward us.

The seconds that ticked by, the seconds it took for him to remember my face, were so infuriating that a haze of red mist crept into the edges of my vision. There was a serious danger of a vein in my forehead exploding, but that didn't seem nearly as important as trying to find some way to jam Michael's head up his own ass.

"Uh . . . Anna, how nice to see you!" he said.

"Oh, do not pretend like you don't remember me, you lying, plagiarizing, knuckle-dragging Ken doll!"

In the distance, I heard a familiar snicker. I peered into the blinding brightness of the headlights. Finn appeared to be strapped facedown to the hood of a truck with bungee cords, like a freshly shot deer, with a bandanna knotted around his mouth.

OK, maybe the Kelleys were growing on me a little bit.

"Finn, I wish I could say I was surprised by this," Jane called.

Finn jerked his shoulders, looking exasperated by the whole thing.

"I'll deal with you later," I told Finn as he manipulated the gag out of his mouth. "Seriously, Michael, what are you doing here? Are you telling me that you're using the doctorate you *stole* from me to horn in on my very limited, specialized field, and now you're trying to swipe artifacts from me, too? Do you have a shred of originality anywhere in your body?"

"Look, I know you had a rough time with the way things . . . ended between us, but I can't believe you would track me down like this, while I'm working. It's just so unprofessional."

Jane grabbed my arm before I could spring forward at him. She stepped between me and the rough-hewn blonds who were slowly edging toward us. They scanned us from head to toe, as if they were gauging the threat we posed. Their eyes shifted immediately from me to Jane, because—despite the murder eyes I was giving my former paramour—I guessed I ranked somewhere near "cranky Pomeranian" in terms of my estimated potential for violence.

And then a tall woman, her arm in a sling, pushed through the shifters, glaring at me. And while I was thrilled that she wasn't dead, my old friend She-Hulk did not look happy to see me. Or possibly the swelling around the eyes just made it look like she was glowering. Also, her face was riddled with hornet stings, which just made the glowering scarier.

"You," she hissed. "You're mine."

"That's fair," I conceded. "I am responsible for your face looking like that."

She-Hulk's male cousins snickered, and her glowering increased tenfold.

Jane gave me extreme side-eye. "You just make friends wherever you go, don't you?"

I dutifully avoided eye contact.

"Who the hell are you, lady?" the biggest of the blonds demanded. He looked like a hungover Viking, with a big barrel chest, a full, bushy golden beard, and heavy bags under his Delft-blue eyes. Given the way the other shifters shrank from him, I guessed he was in charge.

"I am Jane Jameson-Nightengale, the rightful owner of that extremely fragile book that—Michael, is it?" Michael offered Jane his familiar winsome smile, but Jane was having none of it. "That Michael is handling so carelessly."

"Right?" I exclaimed, making Jane shake her head sympathetically.

"I appreciate that you put a lot of planning and effort into hijacking a plane, attempting a midair James Bond–style theft, and trying to murder my employee, I really do. I mean, the deposits alone must have been insane. But that book is my property. I have plans for it, and I will be taking it back," Jane told them, holding out an imperious hand, as if it were a foregone conclusion that they would just hand over her lost property.

I got a distinctly uneasy feeling about the way they laughed at that . . . and the way they were closing in around us . . . and the way Michael was backing out of the circle, clutching the book to his chest. Again, with his bare hands. I was having a hard time letting that go.

"Is that right?" The Viking sneered. "How exactly do you think you're going to do that? There's two of you and a lot more of us."

Jane pursed her lips, an expression of distinct annoyance marring her even features. "Look, I didn't want to play this card, but maybe you should think twice before you steal from a representative of the World Council for the Equal Treatment of the Undead."

Each and every one of the shifters froze, and their heads simultaneously whipped toward the Viking. Who looked like he wanted to throw up. "What?"

Finn cackled. "You didn't know Jane works for the Council?"

"You didn't say anything about it! It's bad enough, you makin' us follow you to this hick town for the drop-off. And you're just now telling us that we're stealing from the Council?" the Viking shouted back. He snarled at me. "And you! You never said anything about working for a Council representative!"

"I don't work for you!" I cried. "It wasn't my job to tell you who you were stealing from! And Finn didn't know about Jane until after the plane crashed. Thanks for that, by the way."

"I said I was sorry!" Finn called back.

"We—we put my name up on the Council Web site!" Jane exclaimed. "What is the point of having a Web site if all the other monsters don't bother to read it? Honestly!"

"She even set up a Twitter account," I told the shifters, patting her shoulder sympathetically.

"Well, Gigi set it up," Jane grumbled. "But I approve the tweets!"

The Viking shook his head. "Twitter wha?"

"It's all about making the Council more accessible," Jane said. Behind her, I could see Finn wriggling out of his restraints, shrugging off the bungee cords. "A major public relations undertaking I've spent months arguing for with the international board. There's so much about the Council that the general public doesn't know, and that leads to distrust. For instance, we require that each local Council office do a charity toy drive for needy children every Christmas. New vampires are now required to take orientation classes *and* complete at least ten hours of community service in their first year post-turning. And did you know that as a Council member, I have this little personal alarm?" She raised her hand, showing them what looked like a keyless-entry fob for a car. "When I press this button, it summons a furry, angry cavalry."

In a perfectly timed dramatic entrance, the were-wolves exploded from the trees, accompanied by Dick Cheney, two big vampires dressed in black SWAT gear, and a bipedal great white shark. In response, the Kelley shapeshifters transformed into two-legged armadillos, giant sloths, the creature from the *Alien* movies, and several trolls. Once again, I had to wonder whether I had actually died in the plane crash and this was a prolonged hallucination brought on by a lack of oxygen.

Arms swinging, Jane jumped into the fray. She hopped onto the back of a giant Cthulhu-type monster I believed to be the drunk Viking, locking her legs around his neck. Finn made a beeline for me, but a huge bipedal crocodile monster jumped in between us. The wave of werewolves bowled over the shifters, because, after all, the latter weren't actually transforming into the scary monsters. They only had the appearance of those monsters, a panic response in the face of so many predators with real fangs and claws. Still, I had to respect the fact that they stayed in these foreign forms even when they didn't do them any good.

All except She-Hulk, who was charging at me like a linebacker.

"You're mine, you knock-kneed, wasp-flinging bitch!" she howled.

I yelped, dodging out of the way when she lunged. At the last second, I dove to the ground and rolled out of the way. She wheeled around and ran at me again. I stood just in time to catch the strap of her sling, pivoting on the ball of my foot as I threw my weight back. The dramatic shift in weight slung her off course and sent her sprawling into the grass face-first.

"Look, I get that you were just trying to help your family, which is why *I* didn't take it personally when you tried to beat the hell out of me," I told her as she writhed on the ground, clutching her shoulder.

"You say that, and you still wouldn't give us the damn book!" she growled.

"Because it wasn't mine to give!" I cried. "It's Jane's! But maybe if you would stop trying to steal it, she would share some of the information with you!"

"Wha—what?"

"Do you even know what's in the book, information-wise?" I asked.

She shook her head. "No, there have been rumors about it for hundreds of years. But no one knows for sure what's in it. We just know that if it's real, we want it. The shifters in my family, we've done well for ourselves, money-wise, but we struggle with our shifts. Sometimes we get . . . stuck . . . in our forms. My cousin Briar has been a panda-butterfly hybrid for a year now. It's embarrassing. The poor kid was just screwing around, trying to keep his little sister enter-tained. And now he can't go to school. He's only six-teen. He doesn't even want to come out of his room. We thought that if we had the book, we might be able to find something that could help make him normal again. Well, as normal as a sixteen-year-old willing to turn himself into a butterfly-panda could be."

"And I'm sure if you asked Jane, she would want to help you. You just have to *ask*."

She-Hulk blinked at me, dumbfounded.

"Please tell me this isn't the first time this occurred to you."

She-Hulk frowned. "Well, everybody in the shifter

community is so secretive, and we're not real popular with the vampires. We never thought Jameson would consider such a thing."

"Oh, my God." I sighed. "Just talk to her."

Just then, a thick grayish shape stumbled into my peripheral vision. Ernie the pilot looked the worse for wear. While he'd changed out of his stained pilot's uniform, his lips were red and cracked, and he had a nasty swath of blistering red welts sweeping across his face.

It seemed that I had better forest-coping skills than I thought, at least by comparison. I would be proud of that later. Finn must have ditched the Croc Man, because he was at my side, trying and failing to shove me behind him. She-Hulk had run in the direction of her cousins.

"You two," Ernie growled, pointing a sharp stick the length of my leg at us. "You two assholes are more trouble than you're worth. I swear to God, if it wasn't for that stupid book, I would have just left your dumb asses to die in the woods."

"What are you even doing here?" I asked. "After you failed to kill us, I would have thought you'd run like hell so the shifters wouldn't ask for a refund."

"No, I asked to be here, just so I could have the privilege of staking this guy," Ernie grunted, waving his death stick at Finn. "I even told the Kelleys they wouldn't have to pay me."

"How nice for you," I said drily.

"You think this has been fun for me? I'm from Brooklyn. I don't *camp*. Not even when I was in basic."

Finn moved slowly between the two of us and the

point of the makeshift spear, which I considered a bad move because of the whole "wooden object through the heart" thing.

"You mean when you were in basic training?" I asked. "Meaning you *were* in the military?"

Ernie scowled, but he nodded.

"I got that right!" I exclaimed, pumping my fists in triumph, much to Finn's chagrin. Ernie looked equally annoyed, so I crossed my arms over my chest. "I make my own fun."

"And you," Ernie snarled at Finn. "It's your fault I'm even out here. If you'd just done what the Kelleys hired you to do, we'd have been in and out, no problem. But you had to pull your stupid noble vampire bullshit to impress a hot piece of ass."

"Hey!" I exclaimed, pausing to think about that for a moment. "That . . . is more complimentary than I expected it to be."

"I tell you that you're gorgeous, and you don't believe me. He calls you a hot piece of ass, and you turn into a blushing schoolgirl," Finn muttered.

As we talked, Ernie's body language changed from hateful and focused to just exasperated. His arms relaxed, and the target he seemed to be drawing with the spear point slacked. I glanced at Finn, who gave the tiniest of nods.

Picking up on his goal, I shrugged. "He has no reason to lie."

"I have no reason to lie!" Finn exclaimed.

"And yet you still do it, pretty regularly." I snorted, crossing my arms over my chest.

Finn threw his hands up in the air. "I *said* I was *sorry*. I've done everything I can to make sure you're not touched by this. I did everything I could to keep you from getting hurt. I kept the shifters from finding you in the woods. I made sure Jane got her hands on the book before I stole it. I led the shifters to Jane's backyard, so she'd be able to find us! I know I've screwed up, but I was trying to shield you."

I strayed closer to Ernie, giving Finn reason to get closer to Ernie, all while the frustrated pilot dropped his arms to his sides and rolled his eyes. "And yet, somehow, 'I'm sorry' doesn't quite cover me getting thrown out of a plane and stranded in *Deliverance* country for days! I guess I'm just an unforgiving bitch."

"Would you both just *shut up*," Ernie groaned, flopping his head back like he was overseeing an argument between two teenagers.

That was his mistake.

Finn was so quick I didn't even see him move. He lunged at Ernie, knocking the stick aside. Ernie swung out, punching at Finn but missing. Finn jerked him forward, his fangs in full play, and pulled Ernie's head to the side. He reared his head back to strike, and I yelled, "Finn, don't!"

Finn stopped, mid-bite. But before I could provide my in-depth list of reasons I didn't want to see him commit murder, even if the victim had crashed our plane, I saw Michael backing toward a BMW parked on the flatter, clearer side of the clearing. And he was sliding Friar Thomas's book into his pretentious leather messenger bag.

"Nope!" I cried, running after him. "Nope, nope, nope, nope!"

"Anna, where are you going? Don't go after him!" Finn cried, dropping Ernie to the ground.

"Nope!" I yelled again, as my legs pumped.

I didn't know what I was going to do when I caught up to Michael. I just knew that I couldn't let him get away with taking the book *and* acting like he hadn't stolen my work. The more rational parts of my brain were still unsure of how this was going to work out even as I reached Michael's car, lowered my shoulder, and tackled him around the waist, sending his messenger bag tumbling across the grass. Slamming him to the ground had far more to do with the fact that his left knee was bent than any force on my part, but still, he was down. And to my surprise, I wasn't panicked or scared. I was angry. So very angry that—in my adrenaline-hazed brain—Michael didn't pose much of a threat in comparison with vampires, killer pilots, and cantankerous innkeepers.

"What the hell is wrong with you?" Michael cried, wheezing as I sat on his chest.

"You are all that is wrong with academia!" I growled, rearing up so I was out of swinging range when he tried to punch me in the face. "You're arrogant and lazy and careless, and you don't even care about what you can learn, only what you can get. How did you even get involved in this?"

Michael rolled, throwing me onto my side. "When people want an expert on supernatural texts, an expert who's *qualified*, they call me."

"And how exactly did you get those 'qualifications'? You've based your entire career on credit you took for *my* research," I scoffed.

"You never would have gone anywhere with it, and you know it!" he shot back. "You were too neurotic, too timid to teach a damn class, much less lecture at the higher levels. You didn't have it in you to make a name for yourself in the field! You didn't have to, you could just ride Daddy's coattails to some nice, cushy community-college job until your crazy mother decided it was time for you to take up nursing duties for her and you died a dried-up old maid. I did you a favor, presenting your research, sharing your information with the world. You never would have done anything with it. You were too scared."

As hot as the words burned, I knew that Michael, to some extent, was right. The old Anna, the Anna who hadn't quite come out from under her mother's thumb, wouldn't have been able to function as a faculty member at a top-tier university. I wouldn't have been bold enough to get my work published in the more respected journals. I wouldn't have risen as high in the academic echelons as my father hoped. And it was probably better that way. I felt far more fulfilled by the work I did for my clients than I would have teaching or lecturing.

A little wound in my heart, a tear I hadn't even realized was still open and festering, closed with a rush of exhilaration and acceptance. The pain I'd felt from disappointing my father, from failing to reach what was supposed to be my potential, faded away. I owed Michael a debt for helping me find some peace after all these years. But I would never tell him that . . . because he was still a remorseless, plagiarizing, knuckle-dragging Ken doll.

Instead, I smiled nastily, leaning close enough that he shied away from me. "And how does it feel? Knowing your whole life is based on a lie? I mean, how did you even publish anything after your doctoral thesis without my research to prop you up?" He flinched, and my eyes went wide. "You didn't, did you?"

"Shut up," he growled.

"You couldn't get anything published, because you had nothing to back it up!" I cackled. "I bet the 'publish or perish' die-hards at the university loved that! Poor little Michael, suffering from academic erectile dysfunction. Is that why you got into 'freelancing'? Because you didn't get tenure? How much longer before you figure out you can't fend for yourself out here in the real world?"

At this point, I sounded more than a little hysterical, howling with laughter at Michael's expense. Red-faced and livid, he roared, flipping us over and trying to pin me. But my right arm slipped out of his grip, and I snaked it up between us to poke him in the eye with my thumb. He yelped, letting go of me while we rolled. I skidded to a halt at his side, then threw my leg up. I brought my heel crashing down on his crotch with a satisfying *thud*.

"Now you're who they'll call if they need an expert with a doctorate and no functioning testicles."

Keening, Michael shriveled into the fetal position, clutching at his injured junk.

"And by the way, that's not silk stitching on the cover, it's cured catgut," I said, scooping up his messenger bag from the ground and carefully extracting *A Contemplation on Shifters,* using one of his intellectual poseur scarves inside as a protective barrier between the book and my dirty hands. "And the author, Friar Thomas, used iron-based ink, not lead. And both of these characteristics and the aging can be pretty easily faked, so it's hard to determine the age of a work unless you also look into the author's history and tendencies. If you'd done the tiniest bit of research before declaring the book 'the real deal,' you'd know that." I paused to shove him over with the toe of my boot. "Prick."

"Your trash talk is not like other people's trash talk." Finn was standing by Michael's Beamer, completely free of his bungee restraints.

"How did you get loose?" I asked, swinging at him. He ducked out of the way but kept me from falling into the car when my fist didn't connect.

"I have superhuman strength. You think I can be contained with a couple of bungee cords?"

Michael stumbled to his feet. "You're crazy," he spat, his face nearly purple with rage. "I'm going to tell everybody worth anything that you've gone completely crazy. That you assaulted me and you used some sort of vampire gang to steal an antique from my paying clients."

"I couldn't care less," I told him, waggling the book in my silk-covered hand. "I'll mail you the scarf."

"Or I could deliver it personally," Finn offered. His full-fanged, hateful smile made Michael recoil.

"Stay away from me!" Michael squealed, in a high falsetto that may or may not have been connected with my footwork.

"Let him go, Finn. I doubt very much he's going to try to get tangled up in Council business or any direct contact with the supernatural world again," I said, smirking at my former boyfriend, who had turned the color of overripe Brie. "He obviously doesn't have the finesse required for it."

Suddenly, Michael's knees gave out from under him, and he flopped down onto the ground face-first. He groaned.

"Finn, I already kicked him in the balls. I don't need you to hurt him further."

"That wasn't me," he scoffed, as Michael pushed to his feet.

When he opened his car door, he misjudged the distance between his head and the window, smacking himself in the face.

"*That* was me," Finn admitted, the gray draining from his eyes as Michael tumbled into his car and peeled out across the grass. I watched his taillights disappear in the direction of a gravel road, smiling to myself. It probably said something terrible about me that taunting Michael and kicking him in the junk had given me such a sense of closure. But I felt better than I had in years, freer, lighter, as if I'd been wearing a lead suit since my grad-school days and had finally managed to shrug out of it.

When I turned to Finn, he was looking at me, his face expectant. "So . . . this turned out better than I expected."

"So . . . you should probably go," I told him, imitating his glib tone. "Jane is not going to be happy with you for switching the Bible out with the book. In fact, she said she was unhappy with you for switching the Bible out with the book."

"I meant what I said earlier. I am sorry that I took the book from Jane. I know that hurt you, and I told you that wouldn't happen. My only defense is that I had to get the Kelleys the book to get them off my back. And you and Jane and the rest of the brute squad showed up right on time to get it back. It all worked out. Also, not to claim complete credit, but I did make sure you were able to turn the book over to Jane!" he exclaimed. "You completed your job. You got the book to Jane. It wasn't your fault that Jane didn't hold on to it."

"You know, somehow that doesn't make me feel any better," I said, crossing my arms over my chest.

"What's it going to take to get you to trust me?"

"I don't know," I told him. "When I realized you'd disappeared from the inn, that you'd taken the book after all we'd been through to get it to Jane, *and* left me alone holding the bag, it really hurt me. And not just in a 'wounded pride' sort of way. I thought I was building toward something with you, and you used me, and—what the hell is Jane doing?"

The brawl between the various monsters raged on. The shifters were slowly losing their advantage. Sure, they had speed and strength, but they couldn't keep up with highly trained werewolves and cranky vampires.

Jane had a Cthulhu facedown on the ground, with his forelegs pinned behind his back, as she yelled, "Just call your family down so we can take you into custody and get out of these godforsaken woods!"

"No!" the creature yelled back. "You vampires are so arrogant, you think you own everything! Well, that book belongs to the shifters! And we won't stop."

"Why are shapeshifters so stubborn?" Jane growled, as she slipped some plastic zip-tie handcuffs around the Cthulhu's webbed paws. "And by the way, that book *does* belong to me. So your point is moot!"

"Jane, I've got the book!" I yelled. "You can stop fighting now!"

"Oh, great!" Jane beamed at me, her fangs shining bright in the headlights. "You see, Mr. Kelley. I have the book back. I have no reason to keep your family alive anymore. But if you stop resisting arrest, I will be far less annoyed with you, which will greatly decrease the chance of me killing you."

The Cthulhu, who I assumed was the Viking leader, groaned and dropped his face to the ground.

"Fine, fine," he growled. "Kelleys! Stand down! Stop fighting before somebody gets hurt."

There was a collective groan from the nonvampires, who transformed back into their blond human shapes. Except for the giant great white shark, who was running a victory lap around the clearing. In a move that did not look at all like pouting, the shifters dropped to the ground, on their butts, and allowed the vampires to handcuff them. Jane allowed the lead shifter to sit up in a more comfortable position.

A black SUV rolled into the clearing. I turned to Jane, handing her the book. "Who's that?"

"I've called an undead emergency response team here, and they'll take the book to the Council archives," Jane said. "Frankly, I had them on standby the moment I realized Finn was involved. I knew we'd have to take *someone* into custody at some point."

Finn touched a hand to his heart and feigned injury. "I had all the best intentions. Why do you think I had the Kelleys meet me here? I was cooperating. Honestly, your lack of trust hurts me."

She glowered at him. "Not yet, it doesn't. Also, how did you get off the hood of the truck? I was more comfortable when you were trussed to the hood of the truck."

Finn pouted, in a way that was more obvious than the shifters. Men in black SWAT gear poured out of the SUV. Finn held his hands out to Jane, palms up. "OK, Jane, I surrender."

My jaw dropped. "What?"

Jane lifted her eyebrow. "Are you serious?"

"Yes. I will cooperate and answer any questions you have."

"Right . . . up to the moment you disappear from the back of the transport truck with my wallet and the keys to my office."

"Use two sets of cuffs if it makes you feel better," Finn said drily.

"Don't have to tell me twice," Jane said. "McElray!"

A stocky SWAT member whipped off his mask, letting his dark curly hair spring free around a round face. "Yes, ma'am?"

"Take Mr. Palmeroy into custody. And put this in level six containment. Protocol: John Carter."

McElray accepted the book with a grin, his white fangs glistening. "Yes, ma'am!"

With an air of great authority, McElray clapped a pair of titanium-reinforced handcuffs around Finn's wrists, in a none-too-gentle fashion, murmuring to himself about having the "coolest damn job in the whole damn world."

"Finn, what are you doing?" I demanded.

"I'm taking responsibility for my part in the plane crash, the book theft, all of it. Because that's what the kind of man who deserves you would do."

I thought about protesting. I thought about begging Jane for leniency. I thought about highlighting all the times he'd taken care of me in the woods and how I might not have even survived the crash without him. But honestly, he needed to own up to what he'd done. If I had a pattern of evading conflict and not trying anything remotely new, Finn's lifelong tendency was to use his charm to get out of consequences. He was like a giant toddler in need of a time-out. So I said nothing.

I would process the part about the kind of man who deserved me when my head wasn't reeling.

"It's going to be OK," Finn promised.

"You don't know that," I told him. "They could throw you in jail, give you the Trial."

"We'll worry about that bridge when we get to it," Finn swore.

"If it makes you feel any better, we eliminated the part with the coffin full of bees," Dick noted in a cheerful tone. "Now we just lock you in a windowless room and play nothing but polka music at top volume for a week."

I turned to him, a stunned expression on my face.

"Not helpful," he admitted, stepping back.

Finn's voice was rough as he said, "Just go home, Anna."

I turned my face away, anything to avoid seeing the sorrow in Finn's eyes. I didn't know if he felt sorry for hurting me or about going to vampire jail. But it hurt me to see it.

"Jane, could you let her know where I end up?" Finn asked without looking at her.

Jane looked none too pleased, but she eventually nodded. McElray yanked on Finn's cuffs and pulled him away from me. He dragged Finn off while he looked back at me, as if memorizing my face.

"Wait!" I called.

Finn positively beamed as I jogged over to him, a bright, sunny smile that might have had me concerned for his skin if I weren't so distracted. I pulled his shirt, yanking him closer to give him one last, lingering kiss. Not knowing when I would see him again, I poured every bit of longing and intensity into it, making sure that he felt every last cell of my lips. Because he had done all that he could to keep me safe in the woods. For every hurt he'd dealt me, he'd tried to do something to make up for it. He wasn't perfect. But nothing in my life was without some complication.

Behind him, I heard Dick coo, "Awww," until Jane

elbowed him in the stomach. "What? They're cute together."

Finn smiled, leaning his forehead against mine. "Thank you. That will get me through the next few years."

I nodded, kissing his nose. "And one more thing."

"What's that?"

I brought my knee up so quickly Finn didn't have time to brace himself for the impact. He yelped and doubled over, and for a moment, I thought he was going to throw up.

"I had that coming." He wheezed.

"Yes, you did."

"Well, I feel better," Jane said, while McElray offered Finn a comforting pat on the back, giving me a scathing look that sprang from male solidarity. "Take him to the transport truck."

"Come on, buddy," McElray told him. "I think there's an ice pack in the first-aid kit."

"You really have a thing about kicking men in their giblets, Waldo."

"Keep calling me 'Waldo' and see what happens, Dick."

He shuddered and took a step back.

I took a deep breath and walked to Jane and the head shifter, who was spelling his name for her. "C-K-Y-O-U."

Jane glared at him. "I'm sorry, I refuse to believe your full name is Eric 'Eff You' Kelley."

Eric shrugged. The other shifters snickered. I rolled my eyes. My patience with monsters and their personality issues had officially come to an end. I stood next to Jane, rolling my shoulders and squaring off against Eric.

"OK, so this whole night has been an example of how terrible supernatural creatures are with communication," I said. "All of you want the same thing, but you're so quick to make with the fighting and the weird monster transformations that you don't bother talking to each other and asking politely." I turned to the Viking. "You guys want the information in the book to make your lives as shifters easier. Yes?"

Eric glowered at me.

"And what I am hearing from you, Jane, is that you are more than willing to share the information contained in the book with the shifter community."

"Yes," Jane said. "But not just with one family. That's not fair. Though it should be noted that I don't appreciate the Kelleys trying to kill someone in my employ. I tend to take that pretty seriously."

"We'll make it up to you." Eric sighed.

"Don't worry about me," Jane told him. "Make it up to the employee you nearly killed."

He turned to me.

"I will give you an itemized invoice for my pain and suffering," I told him. "It will be several pages long."

"Fair enough," Eric grumbled.

"And you'll replace the plane for the airline," I told him.

"Fine."

"Where do you even make all of this money?" I asked.

"We're in the salvage business," he said. "There's a lot of money in garbage."

"Good to know."

Jane seemed pleased by this turn of events, her shoulders relaxing the more I spoke to Eric "Not Really His Legal Name" Kelley. She cleared her throat. "And I'll tell you what, the first portion of the book I'll give you will be the sections Anna said will help you track down the other shifter families. In fact, I have some people in our offices who helped program our human descendant genealogy program, and they'll help you find the other shifter families. If you idiots put together a panel of major shifter factions who can decide how to proceed, set rules for yourself on public behavior and interactions with other supernatural creatures—translation: create accountability for yourselves—then I will consider trusting you with the entire book," Jane said.

Eric's thick yellow brows rose. "You want us to create a shifter Council?"

Jane helped Eric to his feet. "Yes, without coming out to the humans, because we wouldn't ask you to do that until you're comfortable. And if it makes you feel any better, we've been talking to the werewolves about doing the same thing."

"Still trying to get used to the fact that werewolves are a thing." I sighed.

Dick patted my shoulder. "Let it go, sweetheart."

"Were you serious about the polka music?" I asked.

10

～

Now that you have endured your first wilderness experience with your vampire companion, your only task is to ask yourself: What challenge will I take on next?

—*Where the Wild Things Bite: A Survival Guide for Camping with the Undead*

Despite the fact that I had technically only known them for a few days, Jane's friends threw a farewell barbecue for me in Jane's backyard. Heck, some of them I was just meeting that night. But they all showed up, covered dishes in hands, at Jane's house, to hang out in her beautiful garden, to give me a send-off.

I met more new people in two hours than I'd met in a year. (Because I didn't count an outdoor shifter rumble as "socializing.") Tess, she of the macaroni-and-cheese miracle, brought her vampire boyfriend, Sam, and more important, more macaroni. Jolene the werewolf was there—with her clothes on—and I got to meet her human husband, Zeb, and their two children. Iris, the clever gardener, was there to explain her landscape design, while her husband, Cal, looked on fondly. Iris's little sister, Gigi, brought her boyfriend, Nik. I even met Dick's improbable but lovely grand-daughter, Nola, who also happened to be Jed's girl-friend.

Dick insisted that Nola, a registered nurse, give me a full medical checkup after the perils of my trip and getting into multiple scuffles with shifters and former boyfriends. Nola assured me, in her strange Boston-Irish accent, that I was perfectly fine. A little underfed but fine. She prescribed a diet of whatever the hell I wanted to eat and lots of liquids.

It took me a while to adjust to this many people in one place wanting to talk to me. They were friendly and sincere. They were also loud and boisterous and laughed a lot, and did I mention loud? They really seemed to enjoy one another. Not because they were obligated to be there but because they genuinely needed to spend time together.

I didn't think I would ever reach the sheer scope of relationships that Jane's group had, but I didn't think I would mind expanding my circle a little. Maybe I would finally join that book club Rachel had been bug-ging me about. Mass-market paperbacks only, nothing valuable.

Friar Thomas's book was safely contained in the Council's sixth level, wherever that was. Jane had agreed to photocopy everything but the last chapter and distribute the information to whichever shifter clans requested it. Being an insular species, they weren't ex-actly clamoring to join Jane's proposed shifter Council, but members of the Kelley and Trudeau clans were volunteering. And that was a start.

Jane brought me yet another bottle of water while I chatted with Zeb. She'd noticed that I'd taken to carrying a drink with me wherever I went over the last couple of days, a by-product of thinking about dehydration constantly while in the woods. She put the bottle next to me on the garden table. "So is this a humans-only conversation, or can anyone join in?"

"I was just telling Anna here that she should come back when she can spend more time at your shop," Zeb said.

"And I was telling Zeb that I wasn't sure if I wanted to hang around your shop if you have more 'treasures' like Friar Thomas's book lurking around," I said.

"Probably wise," Jane agreed.

"It was nice talking to you, Zeb," I said, as he stood up.

"Keep in touch," Zeb told me. "This group, it's kind of like the Mafia; once you're marked as ours, it's a lifetime commitment."

"But a friendly Mafia," Jane assured me. "With Secret Santa exchanges and hugs. I don't think the Mafia does Secret Santa."

"Not the East Coast branches, at least," I said, before I drained my water glass in two gulps. "Can you tell me where Finn ended up?"

"I'm not sure. We questioned him, determined that he *eventually* did the right thing, and sentenced him to community service and a fine to compensate for his part in endangering you. He also has to write a thousand-page essay on why it doesn't pay to be an unscrupulous douchebag."

"You mean a thousand words?"

"No, a thousand *pages*," she said again. "He has the time. And I think it will do him good to invest some effort into something that doesn't come easily to him."

"Still a lighter sentence than I expected," I told her.

"I may not like him. But I know you do. And I generally try not to kill people my friends find redeemable."

"I appreciate that," I told Jane. I sighed. "I'm really going to miss the people I've met here. I mean, I know I just met you and Jed and Dick. It's probably trauma bonding or something. But really, I wish I could just pack you all up and take you home with me."

"Well, I'm all for it, but the Council probably wouldn't appreciate it after taking the time to saddle—I mean, appoint me to this job," she said, rolling her eyes. "You know, when I was human, my circle was pretty limited, and that's if you consider the one human friend I'd known since elementary school a 'circle.' But after I was turned, it was like my whole world opened up, and I just collected people along the way. I'm much happier now."

"That point sounds awfully pointy, Jane."

Jane put her arm around me, a gesture that only last week would have made me tense up if it came from anyone but Rachel. "I know what it's like to limit yourself because you're afraid of being rejected or hurt. And thinking that way can only hurt you in other ways—other less healthy, more sad ways."

"I will try to keep that in mind," I promised. "Besides, after the week I've had, going to the grocery store for myself, meeting new people, joining a gym— they all seem a lot less scary."

"You don't have to rush off, you know. You're welcome to stick around for a few more weeks. The public relations division of the Council is still spinning your 'miracle survival' with the assistance of an upstanding undead citizen pretty hard. You might want to wait until the reporters lose interest before you head home."

"Well, I would, but news of my not being dead has gotten around to my clients, and they are asking Rachel why I'm not meeting their deadlines," I said. "And I have consultations scheduled with about twenty new clients in the next month. Somehow word got around in the supernatural community that Michael's appraisals may not be up to snuff, because his PhD is under review. It turns out he might not have written the original research he used for his dissertation. You don't know who might have placed an anonymous call to the administration tipping them off, do you?"

"The Council donates a lot of money to a lot of colleges," Jane said, smirking. "It's not my fault if that carries some weight. I'm just glad I can swing that weight around for good instead of evil."

"Well, thank you. I appreciate it. Someone from the *American Historical Review* called me for an article she's writing about 'Shameless Academic Fraud,' and from what she says, Michael's already lost his tenure-track position and most of his freelance contracts. All of the journals that published his articles over the years are reviewing every word he's ever written, preparing official apologies, just in case." I told her. "Do you really not know where that swingy weight might have landed Finn?"

"I'm not going to try to talk you out of having contact with him, even though I think it's a terrible, *terrible* idea. Because I know that will only drive you toward him. I'm seriously considering telling you that he's the most datable, wonderful person ever to grace the planet."

Ignoring the obvious segue, I said, "It's really beautiful here."

"Thank you. And you're always welcome here if you want to come visit." She hugged me tight. "We book nerds need to stick together."

I enjoyed the hug for a moment. "Maybe you should come visit me next time."

She nodded, her chin bumping against my shoulder. "Yeah, probably."

A few days later, I was boarding a plane at the tiny, one-gate Half-Moon Hollow Municipal Airport to prove that air travel hadn't beaten me. My trip through security was remarkably fast, seeing as I had no luggage and my new purse contained only a Council-issued phone, a replacement photo ID, my check from Specialty Books, and several hundred dollars in cash.

I was not at all worried about boarding this plane. For one thing, Ernie the pilot had been taken into Council custody until they could figure out what to do with him. While Ernie had committed several crimes in the employ of the Kelleys, no one had been (permanently) injured. And the Kelleys weren't being charged with anything, beyond service on the shifter Council—the not fun, not powerful, spend-a-lot-of-hours-doing-thankless-tasks kind of service. But Ernie did have some extremely sketchy ideas on acceptable ways to make extra cash, not to mention violent tendencies. Jane thought maybe they could make Ernie do something similar, using his piloting skills to do community service hours for one of the vampire Council's new charitable efforts, just so they could keep an eye on him.

But it did make me feel better that there were already other passengers aboard and a flight attendant who didn't look at all shifty. And there were two pilots. I knew what was possible and that I could get through it. I wasn't afraid anymore.

I settled into my seat, still careful to take the one I'd been assigned, because of *manners*, thank you. I leaned forward, imagining the vacation I would give myself after I got caught up with my work. No texts, no phones, no e-mails for a week, just silence and a bed and a refrigerator full of food I didn't have to scavenge.

Before my backwoods adventure, that would have sounded like heaven. But suddenly, a week of solitude seemed sort of lonely. Maybe it would be better to travel somewhere? Maybe somewhere tropical? Then again, I'd had enough heat and humidity to last me for a while. Canada? England? Alaska, maybe? The sun would set earlier in that time zone, wouldn't it? Because Finn—

I shook my head. I didn't have to worry about the sun anymore.

A happy thrill zipped up my spine. I'd had a passport for years, but I'd never used it, fearing the chaos of long-distance travel. And now I was thinking about a last-minute trip to Anchorage? The world was opening up in a way that was terrifying and exciting all at the same time.

The only drawback was that I would be doing it alone. I wasn't worried about the safety aspects of it, but it would be lonely. Maybe Rachel would be willing to tag along? If we visited a few bookshops along the way, we might even be able to write it off as a work trip.

My replacement phone beeped, reminding me that I needed to put it in airplane mode. I pulled it from my purse and checked the screen. Jane had texted me.

Make it through security OK? --Jane, she'd written.

I wrote back, **Yep, Burt says to tell you hi.**

I could practically hear her snickering through the screen. **Small town. ☺**

What are you even doing awake right now? Isn't this super early in the vamp morning?

Not going to rest easy until I know you're home safe.

Sweet but unnecessary, I wrote.

She sent me a picture of a huge stack of papers on her desk. **Tell that to the incident reports I gotta fill out after your "hike."**

Fair enough. But as a warning, I'm thinking of doing some more traveling.

If it's not in my region, not my paperwork. Where are you thinking?

Canada? Alaska, maybe? Somewhere cooler, I typed.

Andrea knows some people in Alaska. I'll check with her.

Thanks. I'll text when I land.

Do that. Talk soon.

I smiled when I switched my phone off. It would be nice to have a friend like Jane, someone who loved books as much as I did and seemed to understand my neuroses. And she had such a nice large group of friends, who all seemed to care about the people she cared about. What would it be like to have that sort of network of people who knew you so well? Maybe I would take her up on her offer to come visit sometime.

I felt the seat sink under the weight of another passenger sitting beside me. I didn't look up. I was amazed that I didn't need to scan whoever it was, assess the threat. But honestly, after fighting off a crazy pilot, badly behaved wildlife, and shapeshifters, what was a small-town airline passenger going to do to me?

"Fear of flying?"

My eyes popped open. I knew that voice, capable of packing so much smug sarcasm into just a few syllables. I looked up and smirked when I saw Finn sitting in the seat next to me, wearing some very large sunglasses and a baseball cap slung low over his face. "Fear of awkward conversations before crashing," I told him, echoing my first words to him.

I reached over to the window shade and pulled it down. I gently took off his sunglasses and leaned in to kiss him. It went on and on, until someone in the row behind us made an uncomfortable *ahem* noise. I pulled back, licking away what tasted like sunscreen on my lips.

"How?" I asked.

"Very high SPF and a lot of caffeine," he told me. "Please don't walk away from me. I can't promise that I'll suddenly become a model citizen, but I can promise that I won't lie to you. I won't ever hurt you intentionally. Just give us a chance to figure out what we are when we're not on a survival death march through the Kentucky marshlands?"

I kissed him again, people in row eleven be damned.

"You haven't said anything," he noted. "What are you thinking?"

"I'm thinking of our next adventure," I told him. "I'm thinking travel but in style this time. Room service. Beds with actual mattresses and sheets. No marsupials allowed."

"I know this great hotel in St. Thomas."

"I was thinking of somewhere cooler," I told him. "Somewhere with fewer daylight hours. Andrea knows some people in Alaska. I was thinking that sounded interesting."

"That *does* sound interesting," he agreed, twining our hands together as the flight attendant started the safety instructions. "But I have one request first."

"What's that?"

"We stop at the first library we find and have sex in it."

I burst out laughing and buried my face in his shoulder. "You're not going to let that go, are you?"

"Never. And I'm never letting you go, either," he told

me, pressing his mouth against my temple. "Are you sure you don't want to stay home for a little bit before striking out again?"

I grinned and shrugged. "What's the worst that could happen?"

Keep reading for a peek at the next hilarious
Half-Moon Hollow romance from

MOLLY HARPER

The Accidental Sire

Coming soon from Pocket Books!

1

There is no such thing as a dignified accidental vampire transformation.

—*The Accidental Sire: What to Do When*
You're Forced into Vampiric Parenthood

I was dead. And then I wasn't.

I liked dead better.

I catapulted from absolute dark, inky silence to being completely and regrettably aware. I blinked into the soft light of the cool, windowless room where I'd slept. And while it was perfectly nice, it was not my dorm room. Where was I? Why did my head hurt so bad? Like I could feel every vein in my head and they were all *angry*.

I rolled over on the strange bed with its crisp white sheets and hospital rails. Had I been in an accident? Was I in the hospital? I didn't recognize the room, but it certainly wasn't a dorm room. I would know if my dorm housed a medical wing, wouldn't I?

I bolted up and *immediately* regretted it. My head felt like it was being clamped between Tom Hardy's muscular thighs . . .

"*Argh*, I should be so lucky," I mumbled, flopping back onto the bed. I was wearing my favorite purple *Adventure Time* pajamas. Someone had taken the time to braid my hair into pigtails.

Other than the headache, I felt OK. I wasn't nauseous. In fact, I was hungry . . . well, no, I was thirsty. My tongue was dry and gritty, begging for something, anything to drink. I would wrestle Morgan to the ground for one of her disgustingly healthy "green machine" smoothies. And I was of the opinion that kale was God's way of making CrossFitters suffer karmic payback for all those humblebrag selfies.

My gums felt raw, like I'd lost teeth. Smacking my dry lips together, I ran my tongue over my teeth. They were all there, which was a relief. It was hard to get dates with meth mouth.

I could see too much. I could tell that I wasn't wearing my contact lenses, but I could see every inch of this sterile, cold room. I could see every wrinkle in the thin cotton blanket. I could count every hole in the ceiling tiles. Also, everything smelled like industrial-strength cleaner. I closed my eyes and pressed my head into the blessedly scent-free pillow.

I remembered the party. Ophelia Lambert, a nice vampire girl from my world literature class I'd been spending time with, had arranged a human-vampire mixer in the student lounge on the sixth floor. It was, hands down, the best party I'd ever been to. Ophelia had spared no expense turning our silly student lounge into a swanky nightclub, complete with fancy-looking mocktails that dutifully complied with the campus's no-alcohol policy. And I'd been dancing with a sweet guy that Ophelia introduced me to . . . Ben. Ben Overby, a boy she knew from her hometown. I remembered dancing with him and his cute little jerks and kicks. I remembered that he kept his hands on my hips, but in a respectful, non-gropey way.

Ben had been sweet, sincere in a way that I hadn't seen in ninety-nine percent of the boys I'd met so far this year. I felt like I could trust him when he smiled. I didn't spend the whole dance trying to look for hidden double entendres when he spoke. He asked for my number as I walked him to the lobby and I programmed it into his contact list as "The Most Interesting Girl You Will Ever Meet."

I heard a strange thrumming noise through the hospital room door. *Thump-a-thump-a-thump.* I rolled my eyes. Some douche-bro must have turned his car's bass as high as it would go to get that kind of reverb all the way into the building.

In slightly less head-cringey developments, I heard a single set of footsteps making their way closer to me. I heard the click of the door being pushed open. I could smell flowers, waxy and sweet, as a weak top-note over a much stronger scent of soap and . . . moss? My eyes opened, but I didn't move a muscle.

Ben, the boy I'd danced with the night before, was standing beside my bed, setting a pretty little bouquet of gerbera daisies on the nightstand. He was so much cuter than I remembered. It was like I was seeing his face for the first time. Everything was so clear: the smooth, tan skin of his oval face, the straight lines of his nose, the hints of gold and auburn in his hair, the distinct wrinkle forming between his—frankly, luminous—jade-green eyes.

"I know you're still, uh . . . sleeping. Jane says you won't wake up for a couple of days," he said softly. "But I hated the idea of you being in here in this cold white room with no color. And it will be something nice for you to see when you first wake up. I didn't know what kind of flowers you liked, but Keagan said you like yellow."

"They're perfect, thanks," I told him.

"What the!" Ben yelped, head whipping toward me as he stumbled back in alarm. He tripped over his own feet and landed hard against the white tile of the floor. "Ow!"

Ben winced as he cradled his arm against his chest. He'd scraped his knuckles when he landed and the tiny wounds were weeping little ruby droplets of blood. I could see each of them in sharp detail, like he was bleeding in high-definition.

Thump-a-thump-a-thump.

I opened my mouth to speak, but it immediately started to water. The whole room was filling with a scent that was better than fresh coffee or melting caramel or double chocolate cheesecake brownies. I threw my legs out of the bed and stepped closer to Ben, inhaling that wonderful, *beautiful* scent as deeply as I could, as if I could drink it. That *thump-a-thump-a-thump* noise came back, faster now, and the sound was pleasing to some weird instinct deep within my brain.

That same raw sensation had me stretching my jaw as my teeth seemed to shift outward. My lip scraped across something sharp and the taste of my own blood filled my mouth. I pressed my fingertip against the long, sharp canine poking out over my bottom lip and winced.

Oh, no.

Suddenly memories of what happened the night before came flooding into my brain.

I'd enjoyed dancing with Ben so much, I hadn't wanted to walk away from him. Something about him made me feel like he saw *me*, not body parts that happened to have a personality attached, or a chance to brag to his friends. But me, as a person. And for a female undergrad at a state college, that was a pretty rare thing.

After the party, I'd walked Ben downstairs to the lobby and we'd sat on a little bench outside the dorm, far from the smokers, enjoying the cool evening air. To my surprise, some vampires in the courtyard in front of New Dawn Hall were playing Ultimate Frisbee. I kind of thought the undead were beyond playing Ultimate.

We talked about our favorite movies, our favorite bands. We talked about our fandoms. (I was a Ravenclaw and he was a Hufflepuff, which almost ended the conversation right there.) We talked about our favorite obscure gummy candy. (I didn't even realize there was such a thing as gummy bacon strips.)

It was almost two when he finally had to go, but he'd grinned kind of sheepishly and said, "So, I was thinking that we'd skip the whole 'will he call or won't he' drama by my just asking you out now. And I'm not going to play around with some silly coffee date, either. I'm going straight to dinner. Maybe even a place with actual metal silverware."

"A true gentleman draws the line at plastic sporks," I told him, my lips quirking as I fought a smile. It was a charming, if wordy, way to ask me out, and I could appreciate that. "And, if you were to ask me out, there's a pretty good chance I would say yes, just to take the pressure off you."

The smile that broke over his face was blinding. "That's good to know."

I waited, in silence, while he stared at me.

"Oh, you want me to ask now?" he said. I pursed my lips and waggled my hand back and forth as he leaned closer. "Man, you're pushy."

I burst out laughing, even as his arms slipped around my waist. This was what girls my age were supposed to do. Flirt with nice boys and stay out late, not worry about bills and my hours getting cut. "I thought Hufflepuffs were supposed to be all forthright. This whole conversation reeks of Slytherin sass."

"Oh, wow," he said, his lips barely brushing against my own. "You are a nerd."

"Still better than being a Hufflepuff," I murmured against his mouth.

"You're gonna have to let that go," he said, his mouth closing over mine. As far as first kisses went, it was . . . pretty amazing. Sweet and slow and warm, with just a hint of tongue. I felt it all the way down to my toes, which were currently curling in my cute little black boots. We only broke apart when kids leaving the party came filtering out of the lobby and catcalled us.

"It's not likely," I said, when he pulled away.

"So . . . dinner," he said. "In a place without sporks. When would be a good time for you?"

"Saturday would be good," I told him.

"Six?" he asked. I nodded and he gave me another quick peck on the lips. "Awesome, I will call you. And if I don't call, you text me, call me a dumbass, and I will send apology cookies."

"Cookies?" I asked as he backed away.

"Flowers have been overdone," he called back.

I giggled—honest-to-God giggled—but I managed not to do the awkward little wave my arm ached to give.

Suddenly, I heard a quick bark of warning, but before I could even respond, I felt a crushing blow against my chest. I was knocked off my feet and thrown into the wall behind me. I felt my head collide with the stone with a sick *crack* before I collapsed to the ground like a broken doll.

Ben screamed my name but I couldn't even lift my head. His voice grew closer, but I couldn't make out what he was saying. I had never known pain like this in my life. My chest felt hot and wet, on the inside *and* outside. I couldn't feel anything below my waist. I couldn't breathe. I couldn't move enough air through my throat to produce words. People gathered around me, staring down at my twisted body with expressions of horror on their faces.

Ben lifted something off my chest. It appeared to be a forty-five-pound dumbbell weight. The vampires were playing Ultimate Frisbee with a forty-five-pound weight. And they'd *missed*.

My brain was going dark, as if I was slipping away into some corner deep inside my head, where it didn't hurt so much. I could feel the grass under my back getting slick and hot while I got colder.

Ben was screaming for help, for someone to call 911. I managed to lift my arms enough to feel that my ribs were definitely going the wrong direction. Tina, our dorm director, suddenly appeared over me, her frizzy brown hair forming a cloud around her head. Through the haze of pain and blood pounding in my ears, I heard her squeaky voice say, "This is bad. I can see her ribs poking out through her shirt. This is really bad."

That was exactly what I needed to hear.

I opened my mouth to point out how unhelpful this was, but blood was bubbling up between my lips, making it hard to push air through to form sounds.

Please, help me. Please.

I didn't want to die. I was too young. I hadn't seen anything of the world. I'd barely left Kentucky. I'd barely lived.

"You're going to be OK," Ben told me sternly, like he could command me to get up and shake it off. He cupped my chin in his hand and moved my head gently so I was forced to meet his eyes. "Meagan, just keep breathing. Stay awake."

I was trying. Couldn't he see how hard I was trying? The tiny flow of oxygen I was drawing in through my nose seemed like a championship effort.

"Meagan," Tina said, wiping at my mouth and smearing her hands with bright red. "I'm not a doctor, but you have a lot of injuries and they are pretty bad. The chances of you surviving this . . . I don't know if the ambulance will get to you in time. You signed your consent form before you moved in, but I have to ask you again: Do you want to be turned?"

I nodded my head, or at least, I thought I did. I couldn't really feel much anymore.

Anything to make the pain go away. Anything to avoid dying. Please.

"Can I get a vampire volunteer?" Tina yelled. "I need a vampire to act as an emergency sire! Get over here and present your Council card!"

My eyes fluttered shut and I heard Ben cry for me to stay awake, to keep my eyes open. Everything felt heavy and cold, dragging me down into the darkness. Someone lifted my arms and slashed at my wrists, pain that barely registered against the agony in my chest. I was cold and tired and I hurt so much. It seemed so much easier to just go to sleep, to let go and drift off, even as something cool and coppery dripped into my mouth.

The last thing I remembered was Ben yelling, "Meagan!"

The memory faded and here was Ben again, standing in my hospital room, bleeding, and my fangs were out. Because I was a vampire. This was bad. This was so very bad.

"How are you already awake?" Ben asked, pushing to his feet and stumbling toward me as I backed away.

Thump-a-thump-a-thump.

"I don't know," I said, shaking my head, clamping my lips around my teeth. "But I think you need to get away from me. Ben, you're bleeding."

"What?" He glanced down at his hand. "Oh."

I slapped my hands over my fangs, but he didn't move away like I expected. In fact, he stepped closer, edging me back until the backs of my legs bumped against the bed. That burning thirst crackled through my throat, making the act of swallowing painful.

Thump-a-thump-a-thump.

"But you're OK?" he asked, the corners of his mouth lifting into a hopeful smile.

"Ben, you need to get away from me," I told him, even as my nose followed that delicious scent and urged me forward. My lips parted and I could literally feel my mouth water at the scent of him. I was lucky I wasn't drooling down my chin.

"You're so beautiful. I mean, you were gorgeous before, but now? You should see yourself." He reached his uninjured hand up to my cheek and stroked his thumb down the curve of my face. I leaned into the caress like a cat, nuzzling my nose against his wrist. He smelled so good and my throat was so dry. And every cell in my body had my neck straining forward, lips curled back from my fangs.

Thump-a-thump-a-thump.

I couldn't. I couldn't hurt Ben.

But I was so thirsty, so thirsty and empty and in need of Ben's blood. And that speeding heartbeat seemed like it was taunting me, ringing in my ears, reminding me of what I desperately needed.

"Ben . . ." I lunged forward, sinking those sharp teeth into his wrist. He yelled out in surprise, his arms contracting around me and scrabbling harmlessly at my back.

The most luscious, delectable flavor I'd ever tasted

flooded my mouth. It was better than ice cream and brownies combined, warm and sweet and electric. I swallowed, and the ache that had tickled my throat since the moment I woke up faded away in an instant. I swallowed again, whimpering with pleasure, even as Ben's fingers dug into my back.

I took a few more swallows. Now that the worst of my thirst seemed to have burned away, I loosened my grip on Ben's arm. He relaxed against me, breathing harshly into my neck as if he'd just run a marathon.

"Be careful," he wheezed through gritted teeth. "Don't take too much."

Ben. My brain seemed able to focus now, on something other than my thirst, and I could pick up Ben's good, clean, mossy scent beyond the smell of his blood. Ben, the boy who had kissed me and teased me and asked me on an actual date instead of texting me for a hookup.

Thump . . . thump . . .

His heart rate was slowing, ever so slightly. If I kept drinking, his heart wouldn't have enough blood to pump through his body, and his blood pressure would drop. I would kill him.

Groaning, I forced myself to pull my fangs from his skin. It took all of my strength to push him away. He stared at me, his eyes wide and pupils blown, as he gulped in greedy lungfuls of air. Wiping my mouth with the back of my hand, I eyed Ben carefully. He seemed fine—out of breath and a little pale, but fine. And I could hear his heart rate returning to normal.

"I'm so sorry," I told him. "I don't know what I'm doing!"

"No," he said, shaking his head, cradling his bitten arm against his chest. "It's just a bite, right?"

"I suck," I groaned, flopping onto my hospital bed.

"Well, yeah," he said with a laugh. "But that's to be expected."

I snorted. "That's not funny, Ben."

He shrugged. "It's a little funny. And hey, you stopped, right? That's crazy advanced for a newborn, stopping yourself mid-feeding without hurting anybody."

"Yay for me," I muttered.

Thump . . . thump . . .

"I'm just glad you stopped drinking my blood. Otherwise, worst first date ever," Ben intoned.

I sat up, tilting my head. "If this is your idea of a date, I do not want to know the rest of your romantic history."

"It is a sordid and blood-soaked romp," he deadpanned.

"No, it's not," I told him.

He grinned. "No, it's not. But it *is* incredibly weird and a teeny bit sordid."

"But you're OK?" I asked him, standing again.

Thump . . . thump . . .

He blew a raspberry. "Fine. Give me a cookie and juice and I'll be at a hundred percent."

"Really? You got blood donation jokes right now?"

Thump . . .

Ben snickered and parted his lips to say something else, but suddenly his face went slack. The rosy glow faded from his cheeks and they went ashen and pale. His eyes rolled up and he dropped to the floor, like a marionette whose strings had been cut. He flopped into a boneless heap, his head smacking dully against the tile.

"Ben!" I shrieked, launching myself across the room to kneel over him. He wasn't breathing. His heart rate had slowed to nothing. Why hadn't I noticed? I hadn't taken that much blood. Why had he collapsed?

"Help!" I screamed. "Help me! Please!"

I tilted his head back and tried to breathe some life back into him. But his chest rose once, and nothing. Trying to remember *something* from the first-aid class I'd taken in high school, I crossed my hands over his heart and pushed down to start CPR. I felt something crack dully under my hands and I shrieked.

I'd broken his ribs. I forgot about my strength and I'd broken his bones in my panic. "Help!" I screamed, before trying to breathe into his mouth again.

I glanced around the room—there had to be something in here to help me. There was no phone. There were no medical kits. But near the door, next to the light switch, there was a bright red button labeled "V11."

It looked like a nurse call button in a hospital room. V11 was the World Council for the Equal Treatment of the Undead's hotline for humans with vampire problems.

And I was up to my ass in vampire problems.

Scrambling to my knees, I slapped my hand against the call button and crab-walked back to Ben. An alarm roared to life, echoing down the hall. I left a bloody handprint on the plaster near the call button.

Ben still wasn't breathing and his skin was getting paler and grayer by the minute. I couldn't hear a heartbeat. His eyes were unfocused, staring off at the ceiling.

"I'm so sorry," I whispered, cradling his body in my lap. "I don't know what's happening."

Twin drops of water fell onto Ben's gray cheek, tinged with a hint of pink. Because vampire tears have the tiniest bit of blood in them. And I was a vampire.

This was bullshit.

Before I could release more of those tears, the alarm bell stopped and the door burst open. I closed my eyes, expecting some sort of vampire SWAT team to come spilling into the room and stake me. Because they were going to kill me. The Council did not tolerate vampires who attacked innocent humans, no matter how newly risen. They were going to come in here and stake me. I could only hope they made it quick.

But the expected staking did not come. I cracked one eye open and saw a pretty brunette vampire in a purple Specialty Books T-shirt standing in the doorway. The ID badge around her neck read "Jane Jameson-Nightengale." Her jaw was slack and she was shaking her head as she stared at me.

"Help me," I whimpered.

She seemed to snap out of her stupor and glanced down at the dead boy in my arms, then blanched. "Holy hell, what did you do to Ben?"